Following My Toes

a novel

by

Laurel Osterkamp

PMI Books

Boulder, Colorado

ISBN-13: 978-1-933826-27-1
ISBN-10: 1-933826-27-4

Front cover photo © Richard Fleischman
Fleischmanphoto.com

Compass photo © Joerg Hausmann, Image from BigStockPhoto.com

Published by
PMI Books
an imprint of
Preventive Measures, Inc.
254 Spruce St.
Boulder, CO 80302

Printed in the United States of America

For information regarding special discounts
for bulk purchases, visit our website at:

pmibooks.com 

Following My Toes

1

Let's face it—we all can be self-involved at times, though none of us want to believe it of ourselves. I certainly didn't. Then when I was abducted I was forced to reevaluate my behavior. Actually, being abducted forced me to do a lot of unpleasant things, but more on that later.

We were sitting, tied up at the dining room table, if you could call it that. It was actually a cheap card table with a plastic gingham tablecloth draped over it. His photo albums were spread out in front of us, and the smell of sautéed onions and tomatoes permeated the stale cool air.

"You betrayed me," he yelled, directing his rage equally towards the three of us. "So now we're going to do things my way!" I hate to admit it, but he was reminding me of myself. "You all are going to take turns. When it's not your turn, you will watch. Then you will know how it feels."

"How what feels?" she asked.

"How it feels to be betrayed." I answered for him. He turned to me.

"Oh, so you understand. Wonderful. You get to go first."

Somehow that didn't sound like quite the reward it was meant to be. And this is what I got for following my instincts? Looking back on it now, it's hard to decipher my bad decisions from my good ones. Perhaps I need to tell the entire story in order to achieve true perspective.

❊   ❊   ❊

First, let me explain one thing; I am a normal person. Actually, I am so normal that I border on boring. My name is Faith Emerson, I am 27 years old, I teach high school English, and I've lived in Minnesota for my entire life. However, I do have one "quirk," as you may call it—I have always felt I'm psychic. Most of my friends and family laugh at me for this, and lately I can't blame them. I didn't predict being abducted after all.

Granted, my psychic abilities have never been incredibly potent, but it used to be I'd always know when something bad was about to happen because my skin would hurt. In turn, when something good was about to happen, my toes would itch.

That said; the best place to begin my story is in Duluth, Minnesota, approximately two years ago. The remarkable chain of unpleasantness—which ultimately led to my abduction, began with what else – a guy. I met Peter at this coffee shop by the shore of Lake Superior where he worked. I grew up just north of Duluth, if you can believe anyone actually lives north of Duluth. After college I got an apartment of my own and a job teaching English at one of the high schools in the area. It was a plum time, and meeting Peter made the plum all the more sweet.

He was kind of aimless, which I loved. I've always been a rule follower, but Peter wasn't even aware of what the rules are. He said that he wanted to be a writer, so he worked in a coffee shop because it gave him time to pursue what he truly cared about. Also, all the people he met while working there gave him inspiration for his novel.

Anyway, when I first laid eyes on Peter it was a Saturday, and I had just bought a new book. I had planned to treat myself to a leisurely hour or two, reading while sipping a mocha. But I couldn't concentrate on anything but him.

I was consumed with his bright blue eyes and dark blond hair, hidden in part by a fedora. I would later learn Peter idolized Frank Sinatra and chose to dress like him. So he draped his long, thin body in old suits he found at the Goodwill, complete with vintage ties and bright red socks, usually with holes in them.

But I knew none of this on that first day in the coffee shop when I sat there for quite a while, wanting to speak to him but not having the nerve. I did go up to the counter at one point, but I got all flustered when he looked at me with his intense gaze, and asked me what I needed. I wanted to say, "You! I need you!" But I chickened out, and ordered a brownie instead.

I went back for three more Saturdays, always unable to do anything but stare. I couldn't help behaving like I was in junior high, rather than the college graduate, woman of the world I was supposed to be. I had been in relationships before, but never with a guy like Peter. The guys I had been with were as predictable as my life up to that point. They were stable, nice, Wally Cleaver type of guys. Peter was like a cute but eccentric Eddie Haskell.

Finally, on my fourth visit there, Peter recognized me, and grinned. "Back again huh? How's that book you're reading?"

I had just missed the Saturday morning rush. Dishes were piled along the wooden bar, and the baked goods stand was nearly barren. He obviously should have been cleaning or restocking, but he chose instead to talk to me. I looked down at my book, which was Jane Austen's "Persuasion." I had read it many times before, being a huge Austen fan. But somehow I couldn't think of a thing to say about it. "Well," I stammered. "It's good."

Peter smiled. "Jane Austen. Hmm. You must be one of those literary types."

"You say that like it's a bad thing." I replied. "I've just always liked to read."

He tilted his head, and gave me a look that transformed the shape of his long, angular face. "You like to read, huh?"

"Sure." I said.

"Well, I hope I don't seem too forward, but perhaps, if you're not in a hurry, you wouldn't mind reading this." He reached into his backpack from behind the corner, and brought out a thick manuscript with the words: "The Infant Phenomenon, by Peter Belfer."

I looked up at him and my toes started to itch.

"I'm writing a book," he said. "So obviously, I have nothing against you literary types. Do you mind reading it?"

"I'd love to."

"Great," he said. "Go have a seat. I'll bring you out your skim, no-whip mocha as soon as it's ready."

I smiled and walked towards a seat by the picture window, with a view of Lake Superior sparkling in the late morning sunlight. It was early April, and the dark blue waves were hitting the shore with unusual ferocity. But I barely noticed. He remembered what I drink! That was surely a sign. I sat down and began to read.

Now, you would think I would have been all self-conscious reading his book in front of him, but I wasn't. I was instantly so engrossed with what I was reading that I barely even noticed when Peter brought me my mocha. His novel was about how the little incidents from childhood determine who we become as adults, with every other chapter written from an infant's perspective. Then it would switch, and we would hear from the infant as an adult. I know it sounds kind of typical soul-searching coffee shop guy, but it actually wasn't. It was inspired.

I told Peter that. He chuckled and looked down at his shoes. At the time I took the chuckle as being modest. Now when I look back, I wonder if it wasn't superiority.

"I'm glad you like it," he said. "It's obviously not finished though. Do you have any suggestions?"

"Suggestions. Gosh, I don't know. I'm an English teacher, so the only kind of suggestions I'm used to making have to do with grammar."

He tilted his head, and gazed like he was considering asking me a question, and then thought better of it. It was a look I would soon get used to.

"How does it compare to Jane Austen?"

I laughed. "It's nothing like Jane Austen."

"Does that mean it is not as good?"

"Well, I don't know about that. However, she is one of the most brilliant female novelists of all time. What am I saying? She's simply a brilliant novelist; her gender is irrelevant. So for me to say that you are as good as her would be a huge compliment. But that's beside the point, because it's impossible really, to compare you to her. There is obviously such a difference in style, and of course, in syntax. It's almost like you're speaking in a completely different language, and considering the way the English language has evolved, or devolved, depending on how you look at it, I don't think saying that is a stretch."

I couldn't help babbling. I felt hot all over, and he hadn't even touched me. Yet.

Peter smiled. "Perhaps we could discuss this more, later? My boss is giving me some evil looks, so I should probably get back to work."

"Oh! Right, sure. I understand. I should go too. I actually have a very busy day." Big lie—but I was trying to play it cool.

"Are you busy tonight?" he asked me.

My heart skipped a beat. I had been sure he was trying to get rid of me. Ideally I should not have accepted an invitation out for that night. Perhaps if I had played a little harder to get, our relationship wouldn't have ended in the way it did. But I hadn't had a date in what seemed like forever, and I was in shock, so I jumped at the chance.

"Um, actually, no, I'm not busy."

"You want to get something to eat? I know a great Korean place."

"Sure. That would be fun. I love Korean food."

"Wonderful. Hey, by the way, I'm Peter."

"Nice to meet you Peter. I'm Faith."

"Faith, huh? As in you gotta have it?"

"Something like that." Even though it was kind of dumb, we both smiled.

"Well anyway," he said. "About tonight. How about I meet you there? I would pick you up, but I don't have a car."

"Oh. Well, do you want me to pick you up?"

"If you don't mind?"

"I don't mind."

And that was how it began. A significant beginning, in that I found myself saying "I don't mind" quite often over the course of our relationship. But I told myself I never did mind all the impositions during our two years together. Having to pay all the time when we went out was no big deal because money isn't important. He was a struggling artist, and I had my steady teacher's salary to rely upon. When Peter would cancel a date at the last minute because he suddenly got the urge to write, I figured I was sacrificing for a higher cause. At the same time, when he would show up unannounced at my door in the middle of the night because he, as he put it, was feeling "romantic," I was eager enough for the affection to not worry about getting up at 5:30 a.m. for work the next morning.

However, the next day when I was exhausted I might feel a tiny bit of resentment. Or, when Peter got kicked out of his apartment and lived with me rent-free for three months, I confess I felt mildly annoyed, especially when he ate all my food and never did any house work. He wouldn't even change the roll of toilet paper. "You use more of it than I do," he would say when I brought the subject up.

Why didn't I break up with him? Sometimes I wonder that myself. But you see, being a high school teacher in Duluth is not an optimum position to be in if you're single. Most of my fellow staff members were female, save for a few married gym and shop teachers. And in the winter it's too cold and dark to want to go out, so I didn't meet many people. I was afraid of ending up bitter and alone, and besides, Peter did have his good points.

There were times when he gave a lot. He wrote me poetry all the time, poems about me (like how beautiful I am, or how much he loved me.) We would go for romantic walks along the beach of Lake Superior, which if you've never seen it, looks just like the ocean. We had long talks about important things. Peter didn't care about sports or other guy things; he was more into his feelings. And, he was hot. Being with him was an adventure I couldn't turn down. But in the end, he could.

"We need to talk," he said to me.

"That sounds ominous." I replied. "Is something wrong?" I had asked mostly out of courtesy, because as soon as he had said it, I realized there was.

"Well, I was wondering, where do you see our relationship

going?"

Panic shot through me like a strong urge to pee. We were sitting in my apartment late on a Sunday afternoon. Peter hadn't come over all weekend, begging off because he wanted to write. However, Sunday morning he called, saying he would be over around one. We went to get something to eat, and over pancakes and coffee he had been chatty about odd things. The whole day felt like a General Mills Coffee commercial gone wrong.

"Um, I don't know. I don't think about it that much because I'm happy with our relationship as it is," I said with a smile. That seemed to be the safest answer.

"You don't think about us?" he said in an incriminating tone.

"I.... well, obviously I think about us some. But I don't feel like..."

He cut me off. "So when you think about us, what do you think? Where do you want us to be, in say, five years?"

"What is this," I said, "a job interview? I don't have a five-year plan for us Peter, if that's what you're getting at. I enjoy being with you, isn't that enough?"

He paused and tilted his head in that questioning and familiar way, then reached down and tugged at the loose strings surrounding the hole in his red sock. I wanted to know what he was actually thinking but could not read his mind. He said, "For you, no, it's not enough. You deserve better."

"What do you mean, I deserve better? Better than what?"

"Better than me. Better than what I can give you."

I flashed back to the one time I rode a roller-coaster, remembering the creaking sound of the wheels as the car strained uphill, and the awful pause at the top right before the terrifying plunge. I felt the same sensation now as I had at the time, desperate to grip onto something and powerless to stop what was coming.

"I don't know about that," I said. "I'm not so great. Did I ever tell you about the time I stole my sister's Barbie dolls and cut off all their hair? Maybe I don't deserve crap." I gave him a weak smile and a forced laugh. He wasn't buying it.

"Faith. Come on. I'm serious."

My breath caught in my throat, my palms were wet, and my voice betrayed me, trembling as I spoke. "What are you saying, Peter? Is this you saying you want to break up?"

"Yeah. I guess it is."

"Why? And don't tell me it's because I'm too good for you. Give me the real reason."

"That is the real reason."

"Please!" I cried, half in anger and half in hopelessness.

Peter got up and wandered towards my bookshelf, as if he was genuinely interested in perusing its contents one more time. He kept his back to me as he spoke. "No. Right now you may not mind so much, that I am always broke, that I don't have a "real" job; that I care more about writing than anything else, including you. But what about five years from now? You're the sort of person who will want to get married some day and start a family. I can't promise you that that will ever happen with me."

"I'm not asking you to promise me that."

He still wasn't looking at me, but now his gaze had shifted to out my window with its view of fast-food restaurants a block away. "Not yet. But someday you will."

"Peter, why don't you let me worry about me?"

He turned and faced me. "Because this isn't just about you, Faith. It's not always all about you. Jesus, sometimes you can be so selfish."

That word—"selfish"—it set me off like I was a human cannon ball. I jumped from the couch and confronted him in a standing position. "Me, selfish? I'm selfish? I'm selfish when I pay for us to go out all the time with my generous teacher's salary. Or when I let you live here rent free, while you eat all of my food, which you never even offered to pay for. I'm selfish when I drive you around town so that you don't have to take the bus to do your errands. I'm selfish when I give up time with my friends because you would rather have us hang out with your pretentious writing group friends. Or how about when..."

He cut me off again. "You're right. I am the selfish one. You certainly do deserve better, and you obviously feel that way too. So we should break up."

Then I knew. In a sick moment of clarity I realized there was just no room for doubt. It took me a moment, but finally I said, "You set me up. You made that comment because you knew how I would respond."

"Faith, let's not do this. I don't want this to get ugly. After all we've shared, we should try and end this on a good note. That way, perhaps we can still be friends."

"Why?" I said, ignoring the 'friends' things. I mean, come on! "I don't get it."

"I told you," replied Peter. "We want different things."

"Peter, if you're going to do this, at least be honest. Tell me the real reason. Is it me? Was it something I did, or didn't do? What?"

"It's nothing like that. You've been great."

"Did you meet someone else?"

He looked down, away from me. My skin was burning and my heart was pounding. But I am proud to say I remained calm.

"Who?" I said in a voice from deep within me. I sounded more like Darth Vader than myself, and it scared us both. Peter looked up, startled.

"What does it matter?"

"Do I know her?" I asked.

Peter looked me directly in the eye, and simply said, "No." And I believed him.

"Do you love her?"

To that he replied, "Yes. I'm sorry, Faith." I didn't believe him on that one, at least not the part about his being sorry. But there was nothing left to say. Okay, there was nothing interesting left to say. Not that I didn't try. My dignity soon escaped me, and I kept Peter there for over an hour, begging him to stay, then screaming at him to go. It was not pretty. But in the end he left, and I was devastated.

❄ ❄ ❄

Afterwards I realized I had more experience with heartbreak than I thought. For instance, I wasn't making up that story about cutting the hair off of my sister Margaret's Barbie dolls. They had been brand new, birthday presents, barely even played with. I was curious what they would look like with short hair, and jealous she had recently been the recipient of all the attention. So I stole them from her closet, and gave them both a horrible butch haircut.

Margaret cried and cried, devastated I could have done such a thing. The only thing I regretted was my parents' decree that my allowance for the next three months would go towards buying her new dolls. Looking back, I am surprised at my ability to be so careless and cruel. But at the time, I was mostly surprised with my power to make another person cry. Now I wonder, what separates me from a cheating boyfriend, or even from an abusive stalker? We all make mistakes, and I'm certainly no exception. Perhaps in the end it all comes down to our comfort level with power.

I suppose that's my problem. The only power I've ever been comfortable with is one nobody even believes I have.

fter Peter left I did not want to sleep. Actually, it wasn't sleep
I was afraid of; it was waking up. I hate that moment when
you wake up the morning after something terrible has happened. At first you don't remember; for about a second your life feels
normal. And then it hits you. Oh yeah, my world is in shambles and I
will never be the same. It's like experiencing the awful event again for
the first time. As it happened, however, waking up and remembering
the night before was not as traumatic as I had feared it to be. On the
other hand, sleep had been a nightmare. Literally.

I dreamt that I had been with Lacey, my best friend since 5th
grade. We were at a high school dance, not the high school that we
went to, but the high school where I taught. Except, in this dream,
we were both students, conversing with the kids from my classes.

Lacey and I were standing together when the cutest senior boy,
Matt Kendel, approached us. I was excited because I was sure he was
going to ask me to dance. (Okay, two things: a: Matt was eighteen
at the time of my dream, so it is not quite as gross as it seems, and
b: I am sure that in my dream Matt was meant to be symbolic of
something, like an emotion or a fear. Really!)

So Matt came up to us, and instead of asking me to dance, he
slunk up right in front of me, really slow. Then he took my face in both
his hands, and he kissed me as if he were going to devour my mouth.
But when he pulled away, he had turned into Peter. Peter took one
look at me, said, "You are so selfish," and walked away. Then I looked

out on the dance floor, and I saw Lacey was now dancing/making out with Matt Kendel.

Suddenly I wasn't a student anymore. I was a chaperone, and I knew their behavior was inappropriate, so I went to break it up. But when I tried, Lacey turned to me and said, "You don't understand. You never have. Nobody is as blind as you, Faith." Then everyone on the dance floor turned and started laughing at me.

So I woke up disoriented, but I had not forgotten what happened with Peter. I also had that "Eww, I dreamt I kissed a student" feeling, but in light of recent, more important events, I pushed that to the back of my mind. Instead I got up. My head was throbbing and my eyelids fought to stay open. It was like I was hung over—I must have been dehydrated from crying so much.

Once at school I gave my students busy work to do, and avoided conversation and eye contact with anyone who approached me. It wasn't until lunch that I had time to call Lacey, and only then I remembered her role in my dream. But I didn't mention it to her, I just told her something bad had happened, and we agreed to meet at her place that evening.

This felt natural. Growing up Lacey and I had shared everything—clothes, crushes, class notes, and all our secrets. She was more of a sister to me than my real sister Margaret was. But lately things between us hadn't been quite normal.

It began with a telephone conversation we had one night. I called her because she hadn't called me for several days. Fifteen minutes into the call she dropped the bomb.

"Oh, you should probably know, my dad was diagnosed with liver cancer. The doctors say he only has a few months to live."

She described his condition as if she were describing an uninteresting book she had read—she sounded detached even as she admitted to being devastated. I didn't know what to say, or how to crack her demeanor. And I never figured it out, not that I didn't try. Four and a half months later I stood next to her at her father's funeral on a cold March morning. The tears were streaming down my face, but Lacey's eyes were dry.

"Faith!" she whispered fiercely, "Don't be so dramatic. You didn't even know him that well."

That was the only thing she said to me all day, and she apologized later. I told her an apology wasn't necessary, and explained I had been crying out of sadness for her. I didn't tell her my tears had also been out of frustration. For the first time in our friendship I didn't know how to help her. And that separated us.

She was in a slump for a while, but then started to find ways to make herself feel better. She redecorated her apartment, using this feng shui book a friend of hers from work had given her. She got into yoga and Buddhist philosophy, and started talking about fate and the paths we take. According to her, everything that happens, happens for a reason, and we have to trust ourselves and the universe.

It all would have been great if she weren't also taking a lot of anti-depressants without going to therapy as well. In my humble opinion, she needed to talk to someone. But I knew she would lose her temper if I told her that, and I was too much of a wimp to risk it.

Anyway, the afternoon after Peter had broken up with me, I admit I was focused not on her, but on myself. Yet, once I remembered that dream, I also couldn't stop thinking about her role in it. What did she have to do with the whole thing, why was she even there? (I might mention at this point, I sometimes feel my psychic powers through my dreams.)

When I got over to Lacey's, she had just finished cooking dinner, some rice with chicken and vegetables.

"Would you like some?" she asked. I looked at what she had made, and it didn't look like there was enough for two.

"Is there enough? I don't want to steal your food."

"Don't worry about it," she said. "I'm not actually all that hungry."

"Then why did you make it?" I asked.

"I don't know, I thought I was hungrier than I am. These anti-depressants do weird things to my appetite."

I looked over at her, and noticed how thin she had become. Lacey always had a tendency to be small and round, but in an attractive, voluptuous way. I was always jealous of her looks, especially in high school, where I remained flat-chested through the 10th grade. I was sort of scrawny, with red hair and skin that freckles rather than tans. Although I've now grown into my looks, memories of the nickname "Pippi Longstocking" still haunt me. Meanwhile, Lacey's lovely olive skin and dark hair weren't even what most people noticed about her. She had been the first girl in our sixth grade class to need a bra. However, after high school she became jealous of my ability to stay thin without a huge amount of effort. My figure was by no means boyish, but at 5'6" I was a size 8, and she didn't think that I worked hard enough for it.

But then, Lacey always had a weird relationship with food. We would be out, or at her place, and she would start talking about how hungry she was. So we would go get something to eat. Almost inevitably, she would take a few bites, and claim to be full, while I'd feel like a pig for wanting to finish my meal. But that night at her place it was a non-issue. There is no better diet plan than a breakup; my heartache had caused my appetite to disappear. The chicken and rice remained on the stove, congealing at room temperature, looking more plastic and less appetizing as the evening progressed.

I sat down in her living room, which I have to admit, immediately invited me in. She had decorated the room in varying shades of blue, and anywhere you sat you could easily see the front door. There were plants everywhere, and shelves with books on subjects like the enneagram and new-age feminism, along with lots of framed photographs of her college friends and family vacations. There were two photos with me: one of the two us posing before a high school Christmas formal, and the other taken by Peter about a year ago. It had been a perfect lazy Sunday in July; our arms were around each other as we smiled into the camera, while the lake shimmered in the distance. None of the pictures were of her dad though; she put those pictures away.

Lacey poured us some wine and handed me a glass. I noticed she poured a fairly large glass for herself, and I stopped thinking about my own tragedy for a second. Aren't you supposed to stay away from alcohol when you're on medication?

"So tell me what happened." Lacey said.

I took a sip of my wine. I wanted to be able to tell this story without crying, if at all possible. "It's Peter. Last night. He said we...want different things...he said that...he met...someone else." Too late—The tears were already streaming down my face. Lacey put down her wine, and came and sat next to me on the couch. She took my wine from me, and placed it on her coffee table. Then she hugged me close, for a really long time, while I cried on her shoulder. But when we pulled away I was reminded again of my dream, in that her face was not the face I was expecting to see. I mean, obviously it was her, Lacey, but at the same time it wasn't. For a moment it was like we were in that movie, "Invasion of the Body Snatchers." I was looking at someone who appeared to be Lacey, but it was as if her soul had been replaced by a pod. Or whatever.

" Oh Faith. I am so sorry. Did you see it coming at all?" Lacey handed me her Kleenex box, a dark blue floral design, perfectly matched to her living room.

I took a tissue and blew my nose. "Not really. I mean, yesterday my skin hurt all day, so I knew something bad was coming." I caught Lacey rolling her eyes at that comment, but I pretended I didn't notice, and went on. "And I suppose I should have known, especially when he didn't come over on Friday or Saturday night. But he said he wanted to write, and he's said that before, and meant it. And it's not like things had been bad between us. They had actually been pretty good. Like, last week we went to this tiny little Mexican restaurant, and he ordered us a pitcher of margaritas, which he even paid for. And we sat there and drank and ate and talked for hours.

"It was like when we first started going out. He told me what he believes is the meaning of life, and I felt like he was telling me something important, something that he wouldn't tell just anyone. And then after that we went back to my place, and had truly good sex. I mean, truly good. And more than once, which is altogether impressive, considering how much he had to drink." Lacey's face turned white and she clenched her fist. I perceived this as a sign of sympathy.

I continued on. "And the next day he stayed for a while. I cooked breakfast and we read the paper. I never imagined it was the last good time we would have together." I resumed my crying.

"What does he think is the meaning of life?" Lacey asked.

Her words caused me to double take. I took a huge sniff, grabbed another tissue, and wiped my eyes. "What?"

"You said he told you what the meaning of life is. What is it?"

"He told me what he thinks the meaning of life is. I don't know if he's right."

Lacey grabbed the two used tissues I had placed on her coffee table. I meant to throw them out later, but she got up and put them in the wastebasket in the corner of the room.

"Okay. But what is it? What did he say?" Lacey seemed kind of exasperated, which I thought was unfair. True, my crisis was not on the same level as what she had recently endured, but then again, it isn't every day a boyfriend of two years dumps you either.

"He told me the meaning of life is to take in the images around us as cosmic signs, and to turn them into ideas that we put out into the world. Then they'll keep recreating themselves, but they'll also be changing. Sort of like recycling. I don't know, I was kind of tipsy by the time we were onto that subject. Why is it important?"

"What do you mean?" said Lacey.

"I mean, why do you care what Peter's philosophy of life is? What does it have to do with anything?"

"It has to do with a lot of things." Lacey paced as she launched into her explanation, attempting to tidy her living room, which was already spotlessly clean. "It speaks volumes about who he is, what he thinks, and whether or not the two of you are actually compatible."

"Why wouldn't we be compatible?" I nearly yelled. "We were together for two years. I would think if we weren't, we'd have discovered it by now!"

Lacey took a gulp of wine, and sat back down, directly across from me. "People change, Faith. They grow apart. It just happens. And it's not anyone's fault."

I wanted to throw up the dinner I hadn't eaten. This was not the conversation we were supposed to be having. A year ago we would have talked for hours, eating chocolate and drinking wine, while she fed me tissues and cursed all men. But that was not going to happen tonight. So I asked her. "Who are you talking about growing apart? Me and Peter, or me and you?"

Lacey looked at me with tears in her eyes. Softly, she said, "Oh, Faith. What Peter said, about the meaning of life—It's something I told him, something I read recently. I'm sorry. It's just that, well, we've all changed. I didn't want it to happen, but once it did, it felt right. I couldn't help it, and neither could he. We, you know, we connected."

My legs and arms had turned to stone. I sat there for what felt like a very long time, saying nothing. In reality, it was probably only a few seconds, a minute at the most. But time stood still. As Lacey waited for me to respond I was aware only of my own forced breathing. Finally I asked, "How exactly did you connect? I mean, to what extent did you...connect? Tell me. I need to know."

"Faith, we never meant to hurt you."

"How long have you been sleeping together?" I demanded an answer, but she just took a deep labored breath, as if she was the injured party.

"Faith, I needed someone, and Peter was there. And he, well, he needs someone who is going to be more accepting of his lifestyle, of his choices. His working in a coffee shop, living on a shoe string, that never would have been enough for you. But I don't care about that stuff anymore. I've realized what's actually important. Don't you see, everything happens for a reason. This will all work out."

"How, exactly, is this going to work out, Lacey? Because I don't see it."

"You simply have to trust that it will."

"Don't even talk to me about 'trust'. I trusted both of you, more than anyone! Peter didn't even have the decency to tell me the truth when he was breaking up with me. And you! You act like you're still my best friend, you let me cry on your shoulder, when all the time, you're deceiving me!"

"Jesus, Faith, you can be so melodramatic. Did you ever stop to think this isn't entirely about you?"

There it was again. Had the two of them talked about me, agreeing I'm self-centered? It certainly seemed like it. But I wasn't, was I? Suddenly I wasn't so sure. If they both believed it, maybe it was true.

I started to cry again. This time Lacey didn't come over to comfort me; instead she sat there, drinking her wine. So without saying anymore, I got up, crossed the room, and closed the door both to her house and to our friendship.

They say when one door closes, another opens. Little did I know I was about to open several new doors—which would lead me toward danger, adventure, self-discovery, and possibly even love.

3

After Lacey and Peter dumped me I wasn't myself for a while. Instead of being pleasant and stable, I spent my time:

- Consumed with grief and anger
- Fantasizing painful death scenarios for both Lacey and Peter.
- Not going out (except to work)
- Not returning phone calls.

Instead I stayed home, rereading the entire *Sweet Valley High* novel series and following a strict diet of ramen noodles, gummy bears and Tang (things that reminded of me childhood – thus giving me a false sense of security).

My parents worried about me. I didn't see them all that often because they live about 45 minutes north of Duluth, just past Two Harbors, in the bed and breakfast they own and run.

Two Harbors is this little tourist town right on the North Shore of Lake Superior. It's a huge summer destination. You could actually blind-fold a New Englander and take him to the North Shore, and once you take the blind-fold off he'd still think he was in Maine. At least that's what I've heard; I've never actually been to Maine. But I understand the rocky beaches and crystal blue waves of the North Shore and the Atlantic are almost identical, the only difference is we don't have lobster. (Well, not the only difference. And I suspect once you did take off the blind-fold, the New Englander would be kinda pissed.)

The bed and breakfast my parents own is friendly and quaint. Their slogan is "a home away from home"—unoriginal, but true. And it's not like I had a weird childhood, growing up with strangers always staying with us. My mom made sure we had family dinners, just the four of us, at least once a week. That is a tradition she still likes to maintain.

However, after Peter and Lacey broke my heart I lost interest in almost everything, including making the drive up for our Tuesday night meals. You would think I'd have been tougher, especially considering all the northern Minnesota winters I've tolerated. After several weeks of hibernation my mother insisted I come, she would not take no for an answer. I decided it would be good for me to get out of my apartment, so I agreed.

"How are you doing? You're looking awfully thin," said my mother. She, my father, and I sat at the dinner table, unsure of what we should be talking about. "Are you eating?"

"I'm eating," I said. And to prove my point I took a big bite of the spaghetti and meatballs my mother prepared. She knew it was my favorite and was hoping to entice back my appetite. Lately I hadn't seen the point in eating. It wasn't going to make me feel better, nothing would. At the same time, I didn't want to upset my mom, so I valiantly continued with the meal. Besides, it did taste kind of good.

"How's school?" my father asked, in an effort to keep the conversation safe. He's never one to talk about relationships or personal problems.

"It's fine. The school year is almost over. That's a good thing."

"Do you know what you're going to be doing this summer?" My father scooted in close to the table in order to serve himself a second helping, as he was already done with his first.

"No, not yet," I mumbled, because I knew what was coming next. I avoided eye contact with him by keeping my head down and using my fork to push around the food on my plate.

"Well, you know you're always more than welcome to lend a hand up here." There it was. I'd heard this spiel every spring since I was fourteen. "We have a particularly busy summer planned, with several wedding parties, and the stuffing convention at the end of July."

Every summer a group of hunters/taxidermists come to the bed and breakfast to talk about the unique problems and issues of stuffing the animals they shoot and kill. It started out small, but has grown so big that now there isn't enough space to accommodate everyone, so people stay at neighboring hotels or they camp.

It drives my younger sister Margaret crazy. When the convention first started she was too young to understand what it was, let alone pronounce the word "taxidermy" – hence our calling it a stuffing convention. Now, years later, she is an environmentalist, and thinks both hunting and stuffing are wrong. But the label and the tradition have somehow stuck, despite Margaret's feelings. I'm not so worried about the moral issues, but I sure remember being creeped out by it, especially as a kid. The guys would leave out all of their projects: dead animals in some sort of attack pose. I used to have nightmares of the animals coming to life and biting off my arms and legs, leaving me as nothing but a torso with a head.

"I don't know, Dad. I'm not sure what I want to do this summer."

"Then come work here," he said, as he chewed open-mouthed his most recent bite of food. My appetite was starting to disappear again. "We'll pay you. There's no way you're going to ever pay off your student loans with what you make as a teacher."

I sighed. "I know. But I may not want to work this summer. I feel like I need a break."

Dad dropped his fork in exasperation and leaned forward to lecture me. The light bounced off his bald spot and his shirt strained against those extra pounds middle age had given him.

"I'm sure that we all would like to live a life of leisure, Faith. But you have certain responsibilities as an adult. How are you going to meet them if you're goofing off?"

My dad's rhetoric hadn't changed much in the last ten years. I had heard this speech many times since turning 17 and leaving for college. Somehow his words still had an effect on me.

My mother broke in. "Honey, maybe what you need isn't so much a break, as a change of pace. I'm worried if you stay down in Duluth with no plan or routine for the entire summer, you'll grow even more depressed than you already are. You need something to get your mind off things."

"I know what you're saying, Mom. I'm just not sure what it is I want to do." It wasn't like I hadn't enjoyed working for my parents in past summers, and they were quite generous when it came to salary. Maybe that was it. I never felt right about letting them pay me at all, especially when they had already given me so much. But if I was going to work, I wanted to get paid. Better to go work for total strangers where guilt is not an issue. However, I couldn't say that to my mom. "Can I think about it? Let you know later?"

My father swallowed too quickly and let out a cough. "Faith, we need to know what your plans are, because if you aren't going to be working for us, we'll need to hire someone. Now I know the last couple of months have been hard on you, but you can't use that as an excuse for acting like a wet rag. Enough is enough."

How exactly do wet rags act? My father loves that term, and since he always uses it to imply something bad, being compared to one must be unfavorable. However, in my opinion, a wet rag is far more efficient than a dry one. And what's the point of being a rag if you're not going to be useful?

"What about Margaret? Why can't she work for you?" I said, trying to pass the buck.

My parents both laughed, as if my words were as witty and acerbic as the Seinfeld reruns they watch every night at 5:30, right before dinner. "You know Margaret," my mother said. "She claims she's way too busy."

This let her off the hook? I suffered an emotional crisis and felt the need for some down time, and my parents basically told me to stop whining and go to work. Margaret claimed to be busy (which she never really was), and my parents laughed it off, finding it cute and endearing. Oh, to be the younger child.

"Where is she, anyway? I thought she was only going to be a

few minutes late." Apparently Margaret had called, claiming some last minute crisis had come up, where she had to lend her car so her best friend could pick up her aunt at the bus station, or something like that. With Margaret you never knew. But then, as if on cue, she walked right in.

"Hi! I'm sorry I'm late," she said breathlessly, as she went to give both my mom and my dad a hug. "Wow, that smells really good. Is there a version of it for me?"

"Of course," replied my mom. "There's some with eggplant on the stove." Margaret is a vegetarian. She went to grab some food, and then sat down at her place at the table. "Hey Faith," she said, finally acknowledging me. "How's it going?"

"Fine," I said. "You know, you could always get a ride up here with me. That way you wouldn't be late. And it would be more environmentally conscious, because we would be burning less fossil fuel."

"That would be great," she said in reply, ignoring my ironic tone. "But Tuesday nights I volunteer to pick up garbage at Split Rock State Park. I always go there straight after here. So it wouldn't work, unless you would want to volunteer with me."

"Oh Faith, maybe you should." That was my mom. "Maybe you'd meet some interesting people, make some new friends."

"I don't think so, Mom. I would be getting home awfully late. I like to be home and in bed by ten."

"Yeah Mom, don't forget. Faith needs her beauty sleep."

"I have to be up at 5:30, Margaret. We don't all have jobs where we get to work at three in the afternoon." Margaret worked for Green Peace, going door to door canvassing for money. She must have been good at it, because she was always winning these awards for the most donations in any given month. The job had light hours, and she had a lot of time on her hands. So she volunteered at State Parks and the Duluth Aquarium, and she had adopted this holier-than-thou attitude about the whole thing. She has never gotten past her post-adolescent idealistic phase.

"Faith, I was only kidding. Don't be so sensitive."

"Sorry." Why was I the one apologizing? "So Margaret, Mom

and Dad tell me that you're too busy to work up here this summer. Is that true?"

Margaret grabbed one of her long dark braids and tossed it back. She had inherited my father's complexion; both her skin and hair were fairly brown. The only things that kept us looking like sisters were our similarly sized frame and facial structure.

"Yeah," she said. "If I want to keep working with Green Peace, I can't work here too. I need to keep regular hours. And..." she said, with a smile of anticipation flashed at both my mom and at my dad, "I got a promotion."

"That's great Margaret! What's the promotion?" My mother beamed.

Margaret replied. "I'm going to be a team manager. I'll organize, and perhaps even hire a group of canvassers. I'll take them out, assign them to an area, and coach them on how to be effective door to door." She turned her smile my way. "Sort of like teaching, huh Faith?"

Actually, it was nothing like teaching, seeing as how she wouldn't have hundreds of assignments to grade each week and lessons to plan, but I didn't want to sound bitter, so I smiled and nodded my head.

"That's great honey. Congratulations. Does anyone want more garlic bread, because I do." My mom got up to get the extra loaf from the oven.

"I thought this Green Peace thing was only going to be temporary until you found something in your field," said my dad.

"What do you mean Dad? What exactly is my field?" Margaret laughed as she said this. She had a knack for never taking my father's crabbiness too seriously.

"Your field is what you majored in, in college."

"Dad, I majored in liberal arts. That can be anything. Actually, I was thinking about going back, for marine biology or maybe environmental studies."

"How are you going to pay for that?"

Margaret smiled again and shrugged her shoulders. She turned back to me. "So why don't you work up here this summer, Faith? I think it would be good for you to get out of Duluth."

"Why?"

"Because. Anything would be better than moping around your apartment, doing nothing all summer but feeling sorry for yourself over the whole Peter and Lacey thing."

If I didn't know Margaret so well I would have been taken aback by her bluntness. But that's Margaret.

She continued as she ate. "Why shouldn't you work up here? What have you got to do that's better?" I couldn't answer her.

"It would be one thing," said my father, "if you had something else going on. But you don't. So come work up here. Get your mind off yourself."

My head snapped up. "What do you mean, Dad?"

My dad laughed. "Well, come on Faith. We never put it past you to be a little self important." Mom and Margaret snickered along with him, and my face fell. Mom must have noticed, because she stopped laughing.

"Oh Faith, you know we're only kidding. We're all worried about you, none of us like seeing you this unhappy."

"Okay fine, I'll work here this summer." I whined, hating the way I sounded.

"We don't want you to work here if you're going to hate every minute of it."

"Mom, I'm not going to hate every minute of it, okay?"

"No, not okay. If you're going to work here, great, but don't go into it with that attitude. Faith, only you can figure out what you want, but I'm telling you, you'll regret it if you don't make a change."

"So what's that change going to be, Faith?" My father asked. My eyes darted around the room, as if I could find the answer to his question by looking at my familiar surroundings for the millionth time. All I found was a mounted ferret with one brown eye and one blue (a project someone had left from the summer before.)

What did I want? I wanted my life back to the way it had been, when I trusted people and took love for granted. More than anything, I mourned the loss of being a person who could do that.

❄ ❄ ❄

Imagine being eleven years old, attending your first slumber party. You're excited but scared, because before you left your mom told you in her sternest of voices you had to get some sleep because you are still recovering from a cold. You're enough of a goody-goody that you take her words to heart, and balk when the other girls suggest sneaking out in the middle of the night to tee-pee Brian Montgomery's house. (Brian is not only the cutest guy in the fourth grade, but an excellent kickball player.) Everyone else thinks it's a great idea, except for this one quiet girl who lives across the street from Brian. She was sure her parents would find out and punish her.

Mandy, the snotty host of the party, says, "If you two aren't going to do this with us, then leave!"

So you do. But you can't go home because your parents and your sister have gone to your grandma's, and will be gone all night. The quiet girl's parents say you can stay over with them. Suddenly this girl you never took the time to get to know is showing you how to make s'mores over the gas fireplace. Then you give each other makeovers with her mom's discarded beauty products, and stay up late enough to watch Saturday Night Live. And although the next morning your mom is disappointed you got no sleep, it turns out to have been worth it. Because on Monday you have a new best friend.

Through the years she is the one you rely upon. You tell each other all your secrets, share your victories, and your defeats. And other than the time in the 8th grade when you both had a crush on Mark Terrance, your bond is unbreakable. (He had asked you out instead of her, and she didn't speak to you for 3 months. You only had the one date him with; afterwards you agree to never let a guy come between you again.) Besides your immediate family, your friendship is the most important relationship in your life.

That is, until you meet him. He's everything you ever fantasized about, even though you are acutely aware of his flaws. But he rubs your shoulders at the end of the day. He actually listens to the stories you tell him about your students, and adopts funny voices for them that make you laugh. He cooks you chicken parmesan from his mother's recipe, which is good even though the sauce is made with Campbell's tomato soup. All of these little moments add up to a relationship, and you realize you are happy.

You still need and value your best friend as much as ever, but feel guilty because having something she doesn't separates you. Then her father dies, and there are two more men in your life than there are in hers. So she steals one of them from you, which ought to make things even.

But it doesn't. You're left wondering how much of this is your fault, which moments you should have played differently. You feel so changed on the inside that you are surprised every time you notice your reflection and it's still the same. The worst part hasn't been losing your boyfriend or your best friend, but yourself. Being hurt this way changes everything.

❆ ❆ ❆

I told my mom and dad I would work for them, and I even tried to sound enthusiastic. The school year was going to end in a couple of weeks, and I was preparing to pack up my stuff for the summer. Then, one evening, my old college roommate Carolyn called.

"How are you holding up?" she asked. A couple of weeks before I had told her about Peter and Lacey.

"Okay," I said, which was sort of true. I had at least managed to get past my mopey stage. "I decided to work for my parents this summer."

"Why?" she asked. "A couple summers ago you swore you'd never work there again."

"I know," I sighed. "But I need something to do. I didn't plan ahead to get a job teaching summer school, and I need a change."

"Yeah, you really do. But why Two Harbors? You always complain about how dead it is."

"Well, perhaps I'm selling it short. We are hosting the stuffing convention again this year. Ninety-nine percent of the participants are male. Maybe I'll meet someone."

"Faith, you don't genuinely believe that, do you?"

"What? There are a lot of men who go to this thing. You should come, you'll see." Truth was, the sort of men Carolyn would see at this thing would most likely pass as John Goodman body doubles (sans deodorant) but for some reason I was unwilling to surrender my fantasy.

I wrapped the phone cord around my hands as we spoke, imagining Carolyn on the other end of the connection. Carolyn is one of those people who always look great, even on Sundays when she's hung-over and wears pajamas and her glasses all day.

"No thanks," she said. "No offense, but I think I can skip the stuffing convention. And you can too. There has to be a better way for you to put yourself out there than that."

"Like what? You don't realize how hard it is to meet men in Duluth because you only lived here during college."

"Then why stay in Duluth? What's keeping you there?"

"Well, my job for one thing."

"Faith, there are schools in other places. Take Minneapolis, for example. We have a ton of schools down here. I bet you could get a job down here easy."

"I don't know about that. The teacher shortage only applies to math and science. We English teachers are a dime a dozen."

"Well, it wouldn't hurt to apply to some Minneapolis schools, would it? You could stay with Charles and me for a while."

"I appreciate the offer, Carolyn, but I don't know...."

"You said yourself that you needed a change. So change! Change in a big way. What's stopping you?" All of a sudden my toes started to itch, and I knew Carolyn was right. I was amazed it hadn't occurred to me before. Why not move down to Minneapolis? But before I could answer Carolyn continued with her sales pitch.

"Faith, this is your life we're talking about, and you're not going to be young forever. If you're going to make a major change you should do it now, while things are still... uncomplicated."

"What do you mean, uncomplicated?"

Pause. "I'm trying to give you the wisdom of my experience.

That's all."

I thought for a moment. It was unlike Carolyn to even hint at being unhappy in Minneapolis with her longtime boyfriend Charles.

"At least come down here for a visit," she said. "You can look around, see if there are jobs, look at apartments, stuff like that. Then, if it feels right, decide to move. Aren't you the one who always gets a sense about these things?"

I couldn't argue with her on that point. So I agreed. Two days after school got out I drove down to Minneapolis, where for better or for worse, I would be forced to make some major changes.

Change never came easy for me. I think it has something to do with my horrible sense of direction. I am one of those people who get lost quite easily, and I have a terrible time reading maps. The same holds true when trying to steer through the phases of my life.

But if an old map was no longer getting me where I needed to go, maybe it was time to throw it away and start fresh. And if the person who I relied upon to navigate wound up steering me straight towards hell, perhaps it was time to find a person who knew the way toward some place nice. At least that's what I thought at the time.

4

I made it into the city and was fairly close to where Carolyn and Charles live when my car started to give me trouble. Then I passed a gas station, so I pulled in to see if someone could take a look.

The front read Honest Abe's Car Repair, which I figured was a good sign. I got out and went into the office area, but it was completely deserted. I stood there for a while, taking in the wall decorations, which were mostly velvet paintings of things like Elvis, dogs playing poker, or sad clowns. The biggest painting was of Abraham Lincoln, also done on velvet, hanging in the place of honor right above the cash register in a huge garish frame. It was the classic one of him, standing tall with his left hand in his chest pocket. I could almost hear the far away cry from the photos of nearly nude girls on top of cars, asserting that surely their omission went against the natural order of car mechanic decor.

My patience waned after waiting for several minutes. I rang the bell a few times, and still nothing. After another 10 minutes passed I decided to leave. Then a man in his early thirties with thick-rimmed glasses and loosely curled, dark hair that stuck out a little, emerged from the back.

Seeing him for the first time was like experiencing de ja' vu. I've read a lot about reincarnation, and supposedly when that happens it's because you have a connection with that person from a previous life. Part of my ability is a keen sense of intuition, and as soon as I laid eyes on this guy I could sense there was a connection.

"Can I help you?" he asked as he wiped his hands with a grease stained rag.

I almost said, "I think maybe you can!" But I didn't want to scare him off, so as an opener, I asked, "Are you honest Abe?"

He gave me a half smile. "The shop was named by my cousin, Andy."

"Oh. So what's your name?"

"Ethan."

"Is it you who is obsessed with velvet paintings?"

"I collect them, but I wouldn't call it an obsession."

"You know, my uncle collects them too. He has a ton, but I'm positive that he doesn't have any of past presidents. That one of Abe Lincoln is really cool."

"Thanks." He began to drum his fingers against his leg, and shifted his weight from one foot to another. "So did you need something?"

His manner wounded my ego and killed the conversation. Maybe I was being overly sensitive, but keep in mind, I was suffering from a bad mood that had been with me for approximately three months.

However, my voice was smooth as stone when I said, "Yeah, I've been standing here for over ten minutes. Didn't you hear me ring the bell?"

"Yeah, I heard," he said, "And I'm here now."

I didn't answer right away, so he took a deep breath and continued on. "What's the problem?" As he asked this he picked up a spare car part that rested on the counter, which he appeared to be far more concerned with than he was with me. I couldn't help but notice that underneath his greasy coveralls was a body that appeared to be in good shape, with well developed biceps and a tight, well, you know what I'm saying.

Not that I'm super concerned with how a person looks. I'd be sort of hypocritical if I were. I don't think of myself as ugly, but I'm certainly not knock-em-down, drop dead gorgeous either. I suppose my hair is my best feature, in that it's long, auburn, and kind of wavy. But coupled with the hair is skin that freckles rather than tans, and barely detectable eyebrows. Plus, I think my front teeth are way too big. People close to me say I'm too sensitive about it, but I say, don't expect to see me on the cover of *Cosmo* anytime soon.

So I reminded myself that looks are purely superficial.

"Well," I began, "I was driving down from Duluth, and everything was fine until I got into the city. Then my car started to make this chugging sound and jerky movement."

He yawned. "Uh, huh." He scratched his forehead, leaving a dark spot of grease right below where his brown hair hung. I had this sudden urge to reach out and wipe if off for him, with my tongue perhaps. Which is gross, I know.

"Has your car ever made that noise before?"

"It's not just the noise, it's the jerky movement. And no, it's never done that before."

He took out a pad of paper, speaking as he wrote. "Car makes chugging sound and jerky movement." He looked up at me, and I noticed how green his eyes were. "Does it make a difference that I put 'chugging sound' first, or is the jerky movement so important that it deserves top billing?"

"Very funny," I said. His sarcasm was an intensely sour palate cleanser, ruining the feast he was on the eyes. "Look, are you going to help me or not? Because there are plenty of other places where I could go if this is a problem for you."

He did not even acknowledge my question. "What kind of car is it?"

I answered in a tight voice. "A 1990 Mazda 323."

He laughed. "What's so funny?" I demanded.

"Nothing. You get what you pay for."

"Fine," I said. "If my car isn't good enough for you to service, I'll simply go somewhere else." I turned, about to leave, when his gentle teasing stopped me.

"Hey, I'm sorry. I never meant to imply that I wouldn't service your... car."

I turned to face him. "Excuse me?"

He smiled. "Do you want your car serviced or not?" He asked

me this with a smile and a tilt of his head that suggested familiarity, as if we were bonded together by some inside joke. Yet inside me I felt a wall go up.

"Can I speak to your manager, please?"

His smile did not fade. "Why, is there a problem?"

"Yes, you're the problem." I managed to retort, though I was shaking on the inside and probably a little on the outside as well.

But he wasn't fazed. Instead he took a step towards me, invading my personal space. "Why, what did I do?"

I took a step back, jutted out my chin, and answered. "You made me wait for forever, then once you finally helped me, you were condescending and lewd. I don't need this."

All of a sudden his mood changed from playful to tense. "Then leave," he barked, "I don't need this either."

His words stung. Without thinking about what I was doing or whom I was actually speaking to, I laid into him.

"Look, I don't know where your attitude comes from, but I don't appreciate it. You obviously think you're too good to carry on a conversation with me, and you have no problem being rude. I'm so sick of guys like you!"

To my horror, he laughed. "Explain it to me then," he said. "How should 'guys like me' ought to be treating you?"

I felt my face turn bright red. Then, when I was sure that things could not get any worse, my eyes welled up with tears. I turned around so he could not see me, then said, "Forget it. I'm having a bad day."

His demeanor changed suddenly, as if his "nice guy" switch had been turned on. His hand reached out, and brushed my shoulder. I turned, and saw that his expression had changed; his face had softened. "No, I'm sorry. You've been dumped lately, haven't you?"

I forced a smile. "Is it that obvious?"

He grinned and tapped my shoulder again. "Kind of – you have that energy about you, half anger, half desperation."

My mouth opened in shock. "I don't think anyone has ever been so insulting to me without trying to be."

He laughed again, not offended. "Sorry. Given my own history,

I'm probably the last one who should be making jokes. I didn't mean to act like such a jerk." Then he walked back behind the counter, turning more business like. "Actually, there's nothing wrong with a Mazda 323. I mean, if you need a new part it might be kind of hard to find, but if you want to leave your car here, I'll take a look and give you a call."

I walked over to the counter, and placed my car key down. I grabbed the notepad he had been writing on; then I wrote down Carolyn and Charles' number. "This is where you can reach me. Ask for Faith."

"Will do. Nice to meet you Faith."

"Yeah," I said, "Nice to meet you too."

❄ ❄ ❄

As I walked away from his garage, I feared that already my trip to Minneapolis was off to a bad start.

"Forget it." I told myself. "You'll pick your car up in a couple of days, then you will never have to talk to that guy again. Just get to Carolyn's. Seeing her will make you feel better." I looked at my map, and hoped I was turning onto the right street.

Carolyn lived in an apartment building on the southern side of Minneapolis, in an area called "Uptown." It had grown as trendy as an Ikea store over the years, but way more pricey. Luckily Carolyn and Charles moved into their rent-controlled building several years ago. Otherwise they could never afford this neighborhood, let alone the cheap Swedish furniture that went with it.

Their neighborhood was not far from where I was, so I walked. As I did, I noticed the charming surroundings. Most of the buildings were brick or brownstones, built in the early 1900s. However, they were well maintained and had a lot of character. Plus many of them had beautiful gardens out front, the type you would only see in a city. Unusual colors, unique lawn art, and rock formations made the most of limited yard space. Soon I found Carolyn and Charles's building, and after I rang the doorbell once, she buzzed me in. They lived on the second floor of a two-story building. Carolyn was waiting for me at the top of the stairs.

"You made it! Charles and I had a bet running. He wagered $15 that you would bail and not come. But I said I knew you better, and you would show. Thanks for proving me right."

Carolyn leaped down the stairs, grabbed my bag and with a few simple bounds, ushered me into her apartment, which was small but nice. Big windows, hardwood floors, and built-in shelving contributed to its appeal. In the center of the living room was their Ikea futon couch, which was where I would be sleeping.

"Did you have a good trip down? Do you want anything to eat or drink? I would give you a tour of the place, but all you have to do is stand in the center of the room, and you can see everything. So have a seat." Carolyn flopped down on the futon, and I took a seat across from her in the oversized pink armchair she had inherited from her grandmother while we had still been roommates. No chair before or since has ever been so comfortable. At the end of our senior year Carolyn promised if I ever got married she'd give it to me as a wedding present. That's as good a reason as any to find a husband.

"How are you?" Carolyn asked.

"Good," I said. "Your neighborhood is so cool."

"Oh yeah," Carolyn said. "When you look for your own place you should look in this area. It's great, Charles and I love it."

"When I look for my own place?"

"Faith, we both know you're staying. But we don't have to talk about it right now. There's plenty of time to iron out the details."

It was no use arguing with her, and anyway, it was so good to see her. She and I were randomly assigned each other as roommates our freshman year of college, and found we were both a little messy and easygoing in our approach to life. So we shared an apartment all the way from sophomore year through graduation. We parted ways after college when she moved down to Minneapolis to find work as an actress. She's done pretty well, not surprisingly. One great thing about Carolyn is her seemingly effortless ability to make everyone around her instantly comfortable. Being with her now made me realize just how much I missed her.

"Where's Charles?" I had scanned the apartment a couple of times, and there was no sign of him, unless he was hiding in the bathroom, or in the corner of the bedroom I couldn't see from where I was sitting.

"He had to work, but he'll be home soon. Someone who covered for him recently called and needed him to take his shift." Charles was a waiter like Carolyn, but he was also a musician. His band, Shiver Thrust, had achieved a good amount of success. They had played at some of the more well known Minneapolis clubs, like First Avenue and The Fine Line, and the album they released a few months ago was on the shelves of a lot of local music stores, where people were actually buying it. Charles and Carolyn both have a dream of being able to support themselves solely from their art, but I hear that isn't very easy to do. So they wait tables to help make ends meet.

Carolyn continued. "He told us that we don't have to wait for him if we want to go out. He can meet up with us later. What do you want to do? Are you hungry at all?"

"Sure. I mean, I could eat. Are you hungry?" I don't know why I bothered asking. Carolyn was always hungry, and unlike Lacey, she actually ate the food she ordered.

"I'm starving."

"Okay," I said. "Where should we go?"

Carolyn smiled as she got up off the futon, and grabbed her purse. "I know just the place. Come on, it will be my treat."

We walked to the center of Uptown to a building called Calhoun Square. Uptown is jam-packed with ethnic restaurants, bars with rooftop patios, chic clothing stores, and new condo developments. Inside Calhoun Square were a bunch of trendy and expensive boutiques, along with a huge Borders bookstore and a Starbucks. Now, I realize as far as cities go, Minneapolis is an anthill compared to New York, London, Chicago, or LA. But to me, it was a booming metropolis.

Keep in mind, I grew up in a town where the population is under 4,000, and Sorel boots are the footwear of choice, even at the fanciest restaurants. (Well, the one fancy restaurant, Splashing Rock Restaurant—where the elk steak is superb.) When I moved to Duluth I was overwhelmed, and Duluth is a third the size of Minneapolis alone. But if you take Minneapolis and combine it with St. Paul (which is just over the river from Minneapolis) and all of the suburbs, that's at least a million people. There are a lot of options in a town of a million, and options were one thing I needed a lot of.

"Why do you have grease on your shoulder?" Carolyn asked as we walked.

I looked down, and lo and behold, there was a brown stain on my green Gap t-shirt. Oops.

"My car broke down," I explained. "And the mechanic was kind of a jerk."

"Then why did you let him get close enough to touch your shoulder?"

"I don't know. He was a cute, touchy-feely sort of jerk."

Carolyn shook her head. "I hate these new age car mechanics. What ever happened to the good old days, when they'd simply stare at your breasts, talk to you like you're five, and rob you blind?"

Carolyn led me to this Italian restaurant called Figlios. It had huge brick ovens behind a glass wall, where the chefs in poofy white hats and aprons prepared the food. It also had a bar away from the dining area that looked out onto the street. Carolyn told me that the bar is always hopping in the evening, especially on weekends. However, since it was late afternoon on a Monday, things were rather slow.

"Two please," Carolyn told the hostess. "We'd like to sit outside if possible."

We were seated at a table where we could watch all the Uptowners walk by. This included professionals, grungy youth, same-sex couples holding hands, and all sorts of individuals with various hair colors and body piercings. Our table may as well have been for three: Carolyn, me, and my culture shock. Uninvited as she was, she was nevertheless a welcome friend, as I was too accustomed to the industrial-city-full-of-old-people feel of Duluth. Carolyn ordered us a bottle of wine and some appetizers. Soon we were sitting back, dipping bread in olive oil, and discussing life's problems in a way that's only possible if you are slightly drunk in the middle of Monday afternoon.

"So how are you and Charles? Are you two going to get married soon?"

A cloud passed over Carolyn's pretty face. For a moment I regretted asking such a blunt question. But the unspoken agreement in our friendship has always been we can say anything to each other

"I don't know," she said. "He wants to get married." Charles and Carolyn met around three years ago and have lived together for the last two. They've always seemed like an undoubtedly happy couple.

"Really? Did he like, propose?"

"No, not exactly."

"What do you mean? Either he did or he didn't. You can't sort of propose."

"If you're Charles you can." Carolyn put down her drink, and leaned forward to explain. "You see, we were at his mom's for dinner one night. She had made his favorite, meatloaf and garlic mashed potatoes. You know I hate that sort of food. But I ate it, because I didn't want to be rude. Well, afterwards we're driving home, and I said something about how I felt ill after eating that stuff. He got all offended, thinking that I was insulting his mother's cooking. I'm like 'Charles, I have nothing against your mom or her cooking. I just hate meatloaf and mashed potatoes. They're mushy, and you know how I can't stand mushy food.' We've been together for nearly three years. You would think he would get that."

I looked at Carolyn as she took a bite of pasta. "What about what you're eating now? Isn't that mushy?"

"No!! Pasta is not mushy, it's soft, but it still has texture. There's a huge difference. Mashed potatoes and meatloaf lack texture."

"Sort of like my hair."

"No, not like your hair. Your hair is great. All those natural highlights, I wish mine was like that."

Carolyn was being nice. She has great hair. It is thick, straight, and long. And in addition, it's blond, real blond, which complements her rosy-tan complexion perfectly. Combine that with her effusive smile and dark brown eyes, and she could easily be a model. But

Carolyn aspires to be a serious actress. She's actually said she wishes she wasn't so good looking, because it's hard to get directors to take her seriously. I only wish I had her problems.

"Anyway," she said. "So Charles is like, 'Carolyn, once we're married, you're going to have to learn to actually cook that food, so you may as well learn to like it now.' And I'm like, 'You're joking, right?' not even paying attention to the married thing, but only thinking about the cooking stuff. Because Charles has never expected me to cook him anything. But he gets all huffy. 'Why would I joke about getting married? We've been together for a long time. Why is getting married such a funny idea?' I'm like, 'It isn't.' And that was all we said. We got home, he turned on the television, and I went to bed. Then he didn't come to bed until several hours later. We haven't talked about it since."

"How long ago was that?"

"A couple of weeks."

"Well, maybe you should bring it up again. What's the worst that could happen? Charles is a great guy, and the two of you have such a wonderful relationship."

"You don't get it," said Carolyn. "Not everything with us is as great as it seems."

"Don't you want to get married?"

Carolyn shrugged her shoulders, and took a gulp of wine. "Sure, someday. But now? I don't know. I mean, I love Charles. But I've loved myself longer, you know?"

I laughed, and Carolyn smiled. She fingered the rim of her glass and continued. "No, but seriously. I feel like it's a choice. Like if I marry him, that's it. I will never be a serious actress, and that's all I've ever wanted, for as long as I can remember. I've already sacrificed so much, just by staying here. If I'm ever going to leave for New York or LA, I have to do it soon. Otherwise..." she didn't finish, but her thoughts remained out there, like an imminent rainstorm. I could almost smell the dankness in the air.

"You would leave Charles?" I said in almost a whisper, not wanting to sound judgmental.

"Maybe. I don't know, it's just...He'll never leave here. His band is here, and his family, who he's very close to. I can understand, but at the same time, I sort of resent him for it, even if it isn't his fault. And I don't want to resent him."

I didn't know what to say so I tried to lighten the mood. "Who says it isn't his fault? I've come to the conclusion that all relationship problems are caused by men. They don't know how to communicate, and they forget all the important stuff."

"Like what?"

"Like, it's not okay to bone your girlfriend's best friend. Stuff like that."

Carolyn forced a smile. "I thought I was your best friend."

"Well, you certainly are now. You've been promoted."

"Thanks," she said. "I'm honored."

At that moment Charles showed up. He was still in his work clothes, a white shirt and black pants, so he looked like he could have been one of the wait staff at the restaurant where we were. He almost looked too clean cut to be in a successful rock band, except for the way he wove his blond curls into dreadlocks. He sat down next to Carolyn and, putting his arm around her, gave her an adoring look. Together, they could have been Barbie and Ken, only with more depth, and no doubts about Ken's sexuality. "Hey." he said.

"Hi!" she exclaimed back, her face relaxing into a delighted smile, and with it all of her reservations seemed to have disappeared. Charles turned to me.

"So you made it."

"Yup, she did." said Carolyn. She gently poked him in the stomach, and then began to tickle him. "You owe me fifteen bucks."

Charles laughed. "How about I pick up the bill?"

❅   ❅   ❅

I am psychic in a fairly normal way. In fact my ability is the most common one to have, which is precognition. That's the ability to know about something before it happens. And, the most widespread way to experience it is through dreams. It can also happen through waking visions, auditory hallucinations, flashing thoughts, or a sense of knowing. I've only ever had the dreams and the sense of knowing, except for once when I was sure that I saw a cloud formation that looked like a heart, and later that day I had chest pains.

I used to have my premonitory dreams several times a month. Of course, they didn't all come true. But you see, precognition is the ability to sense how things could be. Nothing is fixed, my visions are meant merely to offer up something that *might* happen. So I'm never going to be one hundred percent accurate.

But once I got down to the cities my abilities all but vanished. It wasn't a matter of whether or not my premonitions were accurate; they simply didn't exist at all, save for two exceptions. I'll get to the second one later, but the first one happened during my first night at Carolyn's.

I was having a fitful night sleeping on the futon. Although they were whispering, I was sure Charles and Carolyn were fighting on the other side of their bedroom door, although I could not hear what about. I kept drifting off to sleep and waking again, but I swear their fight lasted more than a couple of hours. After three or four cycles of this, I woke up, but I was no longer in Charles and Carolyn's living room. I was on the couch in the lounge of my parents' bed and breakfast. And I felt very good, like I was about to melt into a perfect pool of birthday cake, silk pajamas, and hugs.

Then I noticed all of the stuffed dead animals that surrounded me. They were as creepy as ever, staring at me with their claws and teeth bared; they appeared truculent and ready for battle in an "I'm stuffed and dead" sort of way. But I wasn't scared, because I sensed a presence in the room, a good presence keeping me warm and safe. Then the presence got up and left me, and I thought, "I have to reach Carolyn!" Then I woke up and realized the whole thing had actually been a dream.

The next morning I got up before Charles and Carolyn, so I had made some coffee by the time Carolyn emerged from the bedroom in her white kimono, man's undershirt and boxers. Although she was clearly attempting to wear a brave face, the fight had taken its toll. Her eyes were puffy and her expression grim. I was tempted to ask what was up, but I figured she would feel self-conscious if she knew I heard them last night.

"Hey," she said, walking to meet me in the small kitchen. "Thanks for making coffee. How did you sleep?"

"I slept fine," I told her, pouring a cup and handing it to her. "And I made a decision. I want to stay in Minneapolis."

Instantly a smile broke onto Carolyn's face, and I was rewarded by my news cheering her up. "Oh, Faith! That's great. I think you're making the right the decision."

In case you're confused, my decision to move had nothing to do with my dream. I had simply come to the conclusion there was no way I could stay in Duluth. I do have a way of just knowing things, and having been in Minneapolis for less than twenty-four hours I already felt like my life was back on track.

"Me too," I told her. "But there is one thing. I still need to go up north in July to help my parents with the stuffing convention." That decision was based on my dream.

"Okay," said Carolyn. "That's no big deal."

"Yeah, but you need to come with me."

5

After breakfast I called my landlord in Duluth and the principal of my school to let them know of my decision. I also called my parents to fill them in. All in all I think they took the news fairly well, especially after I told them Carolyn and I would work for free for the entire weekend of the stuffing convention.

Of all my friends, Carolyn is the only person who actually believes in my psychic abilities. So when I told her that it was very important that we go, she bought it. I didn't mention the part in my dream when I sensed I needed to save her from dead animals; it didn't seem necessary. I only described how good I felt in the first part of the dream, and how I had an awareness of urgency to get to her. I felt sure if I could only reach her, then good things would happen to us both. She said, "If it's that important to you, I'll go." I wish everyone were as agreeable as Carolyn.

Anyway, that day she was off from work. Since I still didn't have my car, she drove me around so I could do some apartment hunting, as well as check out some potential jobs. It's all well and good to decide rather impulsively to move to a new city and start a new life, but doing so makes the need for a job and place to live immediately important.

Our first stop was a little office called "Roommate Referrals." There I paid a small fee, and filled out a questionnaire about whom I was and what my living habits and preferences were. You know, things like whether or not I'm a smoker, and if I like to stay up late and party, or if I prefer peace, quiet, and the like. I was also supposed to answer questions about whom I *wouldn't* want to live with, i.e., do I have any prejudices. I tried to be as open-minded as possible. I said that I was willing to live with the opposite sex, with any given ethnic minority, and alternative life styles weren't a problem. The only place I drew the line was with transvestites. I couldn't stand the idea of a guy roommate looking better in a skirt than I do.

Before I left, the lady entered my questionnaire into the computer, and it spit out a list of people who were both looking for roommates and would supposedly be compatible with me. She also said my number would be handed out to people until I told her I found a place and they closed my file. I vowed to call all the people on the list later that day.

Then Carolyn drove me to the Minneapolis School District main office, the bureaucratic heart and soul of the dozens of schools throughout the city. Once there, we were told that the list of current job openings was on the second floor. Carolyn reached the list first, which was hanging from the wall in a similar fashion to how a phone book in a booth is hung. She started looking for me.

"Hmm," she said, as she rifled through. "There are a lot of openings in English as a second language. Can you do that?"

"No. You need a whole separate license for that. Look under 'L' for 'Language Arts.'"

Carolyn skipped through several pages of the list. "Language Arts. Oh! Here's one. At Olson Middle School."

"Is that it? One job opening in Language Arts for the entire district?" The Minneapolis district has six large high schools, and many more middle schools. I was expecting at least a few jobs open in my area.

"Yeah, unless it would be listed as something else?"

"No," I said. "That's what it would be listed as. No, wait, did you look under the section called 'useless degrees'? Maybe there's something there?"

Carolyn smiled, refusing to feel sorry for me. "Do you want to apply for the one that's open?"

"I don't know. It's middle school. I'm not experienced in teaching that. Do you know anything about the school?"

"Well, no, but it is on the north side of town."

"Meaning what?" I enquired.

"Nothing. I'm sure it's fine."

Carolyn is a terrible liar. "What?" I demanded.

She sighed. "It's just that the northern side of Minneapolis is known for being kind of seedy. You know, like there's a problem with gangs and poverty, that sort of thing. But I'm sure it's all blown out of proportion."

"Great," I said. "So the only job open is teaching 13 year old gang members. Every educator's dream."

Carolyn said, "Then don't apply. There are all the suburban districts, and St.Paul, and private schools. You'll find something."

"No," I said. "If jobs are scarce in this district, then I bet they're scarce all over. I might as well cover my bases where I can." I marched over to a secretary. She was sitting in a cubicle covered with pictures of koala bears and Ricky Martin. Her sweatshirt, which I expect she bought before she gained those holiday pounds, read "Proud Parent of CSU Student." Maybe her son picked it for her. I'm assuming it was her son; a daughter probably would have gotten the size right.

"Excuse me, I would like to apply for a teaching position." I was oozing professionalism, but the woman did not smile.

Instead she sighed, reached under her desk, and brought up a heavy stack of papers. In a voice that had clearly uttered these words thousands of times already she told me, "You need to fill out the background check form first, and submit that on your way out." She pointed to the blue sheets of paper that she was holding. "Then you need to get in this form by the end of the week. Make sure you supply a detailed description of all your work experience, and accurate names and phone numbers of previous employers. We also need three letters of recommendation, which should have been written no more than a year ago. Submit those with your application, an official copy of your college transcripts, a current teaching license, and your essay."

"My essay?" I asked.

She pulled out a form from the bottom of the stack.

"You need to write a 1000 word essay about your goals as a teacher, and your personal educational philosophy. Make sure to describe any powerful influences you may have had from within the profession, and you may also want to mention victories you have had as a teacher."

I swallowed, and ignored that I was breaking out in a nervous sweat. "And after I submit all of this, do I get an interview with the principal?"

She laughed. "After you submit these forms, if they meet with our approval, you will be called in for an interview with our district hiring supervisors. They will ask you basic questions regarding your educational experience and practices. If you pass this initial interview, then you will be admitted into the Minneapolis school district hiring pool."

"What does that mean?"

She sighed again, and continued on as if she was speaking to a small and stupid child. "It means that if, after all the displaced teachers who already work within the district have bid for positions, there are still openings in your area of license, that principals will have access to your application, and can call you in for an interview if they so desire."

"Okay, so before I spend hours on my application, let's make sure I get this. There is one job open in language arts, and that job is only open if there aren't any other language arts teachers already in the district who want it?"

"That's correct," she said. "And to be honest, the chances of that are slim. We've had a lot of budget cuts this year, so a lot of our good teachers were laid off."

"Thanks for your help," I said. I walked off, leaving the thick stack of applications still on her desk.

"It's hopeless," I told Carolyn once we were down in the car. "Reality is setting in. I'm going to lose the deposit on my apartment in Duluth since I'm not giving them adequate notice, I'm going to have to live with a stranger down here, my job prospects are poor; I mean, remind me again of why I'm doing this?"

"Because," said Carolyn, "you need to do this for yourself. You'll regret it someday if you don't."

I was sure she was right, but I made no reply. After a moment, she said, "Don't worry. I'll help you. Things will work out, you'll see."

"Thanks, Carolyn."

"Anytime." Although I did not say it aloud, I wondered why it was so important to Carolyn that I move down here. She had Charles, and I'd always had the impression that she had a wide circle of friends whom she knew from work and the theater. Why did she need me?

We drove back to her place to grab something to eat, and found a message on her answering machine. Carolyn pressed play and a deep voice projected itself.

"Hello, this message is for Faith. This is your condescending and lewd mechanic Ethan, from Honest Abe's Garage. I took a look at your car, and you were a little low on oil, and, oh, your rear-sway bar is about to snap. We definitely don't want that to happen. But I would (pause) love to give you a brand new rear-sway, which should cost around two hundred bucks. Otherwise, though, I would say that you're in (pause) really good condition. But I don't want to mess with your parts without your consent, so, uh, call me back and let me know what you need. However, I went ahead and (pause) replenished your oil. That's on me. Anyway, give me a call. So yeah, it's Ethan, 555-6721. Talk to you later, Faith."

Was he laughing with me or laughing at me? I couldn't tell.

"Oh my God, that's your mechanic?" Carolyn had made her way toward the kitchen, which meant she was still close enough to have been able to hear the entire message. "What's with the sexy flirty voice?"

"You think his voice is sexy?"

"Yeah! You don't?"

"I think it's kind of sleazy. Did you hear him talk about replenishing my oil and messing with my parts? Don't you think he sounds a little depraved?"

Carolyn laughed as she reached into the fridge. "Oh Faith, lighten up! He was only joking." She pulled out bread, celery and mayo. I knew without asking that she was making tuna, so I grabbed the can from her pantry, and she handed me the can-opener.

"How do you know?" I asked. "Maybe he's really like that."

"Like what? He was talking about your car."

"Carolyn, you heard the message. It was clearly sexual."

"So what if it was?"

"Well, how do I know he isn't like that with all of his female customers?"

"You don't. But who cares if he is? I mean, didn't you say he was cute?"

"Yeah. He's kind of cute. I guess."

"Is he or isn't he?"

"He is. If you like his type, yeah."

"What's his type?" Carolyn asked, as she finished chopping the celery. I handed her the bowl with the tuna so she could add the celery and the mayo.

I went to pour us some iced tea as she put together our sandwiches. "Wavy dark hair, olive skin, green eyes..."

She cut me off. "And his body?"

"Pretty good. He's not very tall, but you can tell he works out." Against my better judgment I decided to include this next piece of information. "He looked good in the coveralls he was wearing. Especially his butt."

"Does he have mechanic biceps?"

"Yeah, he does."

"So who cares if he picks up on other women!" she cried. "You're not looking for another serious relationship, you're looking for a rebound fling! Go there, have sex with him in the garage! Get oil all over yourself, and run your hands all over his muscles and through his wavy dark hair! It will do you good. Hell, I'd go and do it for you if I could. But as it is, I'll have to live vicariously through you. Just make sure he wears a condom."

"Right, I'll keep that in mind." Thing was, if I could wiggle my nose and turn myself into a brash and brave person (like Carolyn), I would have already been having burning, blistering garage sex with

Ethan. But I was still myself, and I didn't have the power or the temerity to change. So I felt more like an uptight English teacher than a wild seductress as I picked up the phone, and I vowed simply to talk in a reasonable way about my car.

"Honest Abe's." Ethan had answered on the first ring.

"Um, hi Ethan. This is Faith. Returning your call. You called about my rear sway bar…

"Faith! Hey, how's it going?" He spoke like we had been friends for years. And he still used that sexy voice, but maybe that was how he naturally spoke.

"I'm fine," I said. To be polite I added in, "How are you?"

"I'm good, thanks for asking. Hey, I want to apologize again for my attitude yesterday. My ex had stopped in not long before you got there, and I was taking my frustration out on you. Sorry about that."

I had to ask. "Is that why you said you shouldn't be joking about relationship problems? "

He chuckled. "Yeah. Why is it so hard to be friends with someone after the romance is over?"

I wasn't sure if he posing a rhetorical question, or if he truly wanted my opinion. "Um… I'm the wrong person to ask."

"Oh yeah? You aren't still friends with the guy who dumped you?"

"No. No, I'm not."

"Why? Is it because you're still too hurt and angry, or do you have no interest in him as a friend? Because I don't think we usually pick people we have a lot in common with to date. You know what I'm saying, or is that just me? Maybe I need to find a woman with whom I have more in common."

His correct use of the word "whom" (so few people bother with that sort of thing nowadays) tickled me, but I wasn't sure I wanted to be having this conversation. I didn't even know him, yet he confused me. Plus Carolyn was avidly listening as she chewed her sandwich. The whole situation felt more like an episode of *The Twilight Zone* than say, *The Bold and the Beautiful.* But his silence on the other end of the line prompted me to answer back.

"Well, I think you have to do what feels right at the moment. It's impossible to know how something's going to turn out."

"Unless you're psychic."

Okay, on this, it was my duty to enlighten him. "Well, even then, it's not actually possible. Most psychics just have an idea of things that might happen, they don't really know. That's a common misconception. Actually, it's as hard for a psychic as it is for anyone to make heads or tails out of their interpersonal existence. Human beings are such an inconsistent variable, there's no absolute certainty when it comes to matters of the heart." I had more to add, but catching sight of Carolyn's glare prompted me to shut up.

There was a long moment when neither of us spoke, then Ethan broke the silence.

"Thanks. So anyway, do you want me to go ahead and replace your rear sway bar? I have one here already in the shop, so with parts and labor, it should cost you around one hundred fifty bucks."

"Um, okay." I don't know anything about cars, so I figured I had better take his word for it. Besides, if he were trying to rob me then he would have come up with something far worse than needing to replace the rear sway bar.

"Great," he said. "I can go ahead and do that for you this afternoon. If you want to pick your car up today, it should be ready by five."

"Okay, I'll be by at around five."

"Sounds good, Faith." I did like how soft his voice sounded when he said my name. "I'll see you then." He hung up.

From the kitchen Carolyn said, "Well?"

"Good news," I said. "It's just my rear sway bar. My car will be ready by five."

"Great, so you'll see him tonight. What are you going to wear?"

"I was thinking I'd wear my black see-through tank top, and a thong." I walked into the kitchen, grabbed a plate, and began to eat the remaining sandwich.

"Hmm, that's a good start, but what else? Do you want to borrow my short jean skirt?"

"No," I said. "I am simply going to wear the tank top and thong. Why mess around with mixed signals?"

"You know Faith, you make fun, but mark my words, this Ethan will make a great rebound guy for you."

"No he won't. He's not interested. I could tell by how he sounded on the phone just now. He was all business. There was nothing there."

Carolyn pondered for a moment before she spoke. "Maybe he was responding to how you sounded on the phone. The way you were talking, you sounded like a school-marm."

Carolyn knew how much I hated being called that. "Shut up! I did not! Anyway, I'm not even interested, okay? I don't want to think about men right now, I have too many other more pressing concerns." That was a lie. Whether I wanted to be or not, I was actually very attracted to Ethan. But looking at the situation intellectually, I knew it was wrong of me to pursue him. He was getting over someone, I was getting over someone; that's not a superior combination.

"Pressing concerns, my ass! What concern could be more pressing than getting laid by a cute car mechanic? Huh?"

"How about finding a job and a place to live?"

"Yeah, well, maybe doing it with Ethan would put the rest of your pressing concerns in perspective." Again, I had to wonder if there was something wrong in Carolyn's own life that might explain her sudden interest in turning me into a slut. But I didn't feel like asking.

Instead, I said, "Give it a rest, okay Carolyn?"

"Fine," she said. "But at least let me do your hair and makeup before you go to pick up your car."

❋　❋　❋

The next morning my first waking thought was, "Where am I going to live?" My second thought was about Ethan. My third was a realization that I'd had two whole thoughts before Peter and Lacey jumped into my head. Not perfect, but I was making progress.

However, the hours between when Carolyn and I discussed Ethan over tuna salad and the next morning had not transpired as I had wished. First of all, when I went to pick up my car from Ethan, I was not in my most confident place. I blame Carolyn for this, since she insisted on making such a big deal of it, dressing me up and doing my hair and makeup. I was wearing her denim mini-skirt, which hung only a couple of inches below my crotch. With it I wore a simple black cotton tank top, and black leather sandals. My hair had been curled and sprayed, but hung loose around my shoulders, and I had on way more makeup than I was used to wearing. My instincts told me I was about to make a mistake, but my skin didn't hurt, nor did my toes itch, so I wasn't sure.

When I walked into the office, Ethan was there behind the desk, looking even cuter than I remembered. With his jeans and white t-shirt he looked like he could easily fit into any era post 1950s. His short sleeves exposed the tan skin of his arms, and I noticed that he had a small tattoo of a yin-yang on his left bicep. The light he was sitting under highlighted his prominent cheekbones and slightly large nose, but his casual attitude was the most noticeable thing in the room. He was reading a magazine, and the thick black rimmed, Elvis Costello type glasses he wore only added to his hipster look.

"Hey," I said. "What are you reading?"

He looked up, and it took a second for the recognition to spread across his face. Then he gave me a crooked smile. "Hello Faith." His voice sounded like warm maple syrup over Sunday morning pancakes.

I faltered. What the hell was I doing? I couldn't even decide if I was after him or not. He was the first guy who had piqued my interest since Peter, but even if he was actually interested, the last thing I should do was get involved with another flirtatious guy who confused me. I was setting myself up for hurt. Besides, it was too soon to be in another relationship, and I'm not the casual sex type. So I decided to actively resist sending signals of any type.

"I'm here to pick up my Mazda 323," I said in my strict teacher voice (and thus my least sexy voice).

"Yeah, I remember." He put down his magazine, and walked towards the wall where he kept the keys. In an after-thought he turned to me, and said, "Uh, I was reading *Harpers*."

I blurted out the first thing that came into my mind. Bad idea. "Wow, you read fashion magazines?"

He responded. "No, you're thinking of *Harper's Bazaar*. This is *Harpers*, part of the liberal press."

"Right, yeah, I knew that. I always confuse it, I assume because the titles are so much the same, you know? Maybe they ought to change the name of one of the magazines, to distinguish them. Like, rather than being *Harpers*, it could be *Sreprah*, which is *Harpers* in reverse. That would be a lot less confusing." Pause. Ethan looked at me like I was as odd as I felt. "So, um, are you like this liberal political guy then? Or is it your cousin's magazine?"

He gave me another crooked smile, his eyes crinkling at the corners. "No, it's mine. I like to read up on both sides of the issue."

"Oh, so do you watch Fox news for the conservative side?"

"I don't watch a lot of television."

The phone rang. "Excuse me," he said, picking it up. "Honest Abe's!" he answered. "Hey." His voice immediately lost its previous enthusiasm. He turned his back to me, the tension growing in his voice as the conversation progressed. "Yeah, I can't talk right now. (pause) No, I have a customer. (pause) Yeah, I really do. (pause) What, do you want me to put her on? (pause) Look, I'll call you back. (long pause) That's completely unfair. (pause) No. (pause) No! (another long pause) Look, I'm calling you back. Goodbye."

He slammed down the phone and turned back towards me. He was now wearing all of the tension that had been in his voice; his shoulders were hunched and his smile was gone. He didn't make eye-contact as he spoke, his voice now projecting cyanide rather than syrup.

"Sorry. That will come to one hundred and fifty bucks. On the nose."

I handed him my credit card. The silence between us as he ran my card through was uncomfortable, but I had no idea what I should say. So again, I stupidly said the first thing that popped into my brain. "Do you ever wonder where that expression comes from, 'on the nose'? I mean, did people used to put exact amounts of things on their noses? The English language is so odd, it never ceases to amaze me."

"It's an idiom," he said, as he handed me the slip of paper to sign, along with my credit card.

"What?" I had already lost my train of thought.

"On the nose, it's an idiom." He spoke in the same impatient way he had first spoken to me the day before. I looked up from the desk and realized he wasn't even looking at me. Instead, he was staring at the velvet painting of Niagra Falls on the wall beyond me, boredom planted clearly on his face.

I put my credit card in my wallet and shoved it in my purse. "Yeah, I happen to teach English, so I get that it's an idiom. Thanks. What I meant was, what is the root of the idiom? Idioms don't just make themselves up. They come from somewhere."

"Sorry." He sounded genuine; I think he was responding more to my tone than to my actual words. Then, for the first time since I had gotten there, he actually really looked at me. "Hey, where are you off to? You look nice."

It was too late. I already regretted my behavior and his response to it. Since it's easier to blame others than ourselves, I took my frustration out on him.

"Just tell me where my car is," I said tersely, and he responded quickly in return.

"It's outside, right around the back."

"Thanks." I started to walk out.

"Hey, let me know if there are any more problems with it. I'll take a look – no charge. Those older foreign models can be a little tricky."

"That won't be necessary. I'm sure it will be fine." Even if it wasn't fine, I knew I would never bring my car back here. This guy was too into mixed signals and ex-girlfriends to be good for me, and I was too into him to be able to exercise superior judgment. Furthermore, my intuition was failing and that scared me. I needed to leave. I had my hand on the doorknob and was about to go when he stopped me once more.

"Uh, who was it that said, 'It's a constant struggle to see what's in front of your nose.'?"

I turned to face him. "I don't know."

"That's not it exactly, but it's something like that. Some twentieth century author, I can't remember who."

"I truly have no idea. I've never heard that quote before."

"Oh." he said. "Well anyway, he probably said it after 'on the nose' became an idiom, but it's interesting anyway. If something is on your nose, or even right in front of it, it is impossible to see. You're too damn close. You know what I mean?"

"Sure."

He brushed his dark hair away from his forehead, and continued. "So why would we use 'on the nose' to describe something that is exact? How can something be exact when we can't even see it clearly enough to have perspective on it?"

Perhaps Ethan was as big a geek as I was. I stood there for a moment, trying to think of something profound to say in return, but came up blank.

"Well anyway, let me know if your car gives you more trouble. I'm running late, and I sort of need to call someone back." He was up, organizing the stuff in his office, perhaps in preparation to leave for the day.

"Your ex?" I inquired.

He stopped what he was doing, and looked at me in shock. Then his face relaxed. "Oh yeah, I mentioned her before. Yeah. She was sort of angry, so I better call her back."

"Good luck."

"See you around."

＊　＊　＊

When I got back to the apartment I relayed the story to a disappointed Carolyn and an amused Charles.

"You're being too sensitive." said Carolyn. "He was just preoccupied because his ex called while you were there. If you had been a little more friendly something would have happened."

"Just because she called doesn't mean he doesn't want to do you," said Charles. I think that was supposed to cheer me up, but it didn't. I was sure that Ethan wasn't interested, even though Carolyn insisted he was. Otherwise, she said, why would he offer to look at my car again for free?

"He was probably worried that he didn't fix it right, and he wanted to have all of his bases covered before I called the better business bureau on him."

"Come on," said Carolyn. "With an attitude like that, you're never going to move on from Peter."

She was right on that count, but it's hard to get your attitude to change simply because you want it to. And truth was, I still missed Peter. Sure, I knew that ultimately I was better off without him, but my heartbreak refused to disappear so easily. In my weakest moments I allowed myself to fantasize about him coming back to me. In these fantasies he would admit how foolish he had been, how much he loved me, how much he needed me. Of course, at first I would refuse him, but after many apologies and groveling attempts to win back my heart, I would finally relent, and we would have a tearfully bittersweet and passionate reunion.

I knew such thoughts were like a high protein diet – instantly gratifying yet ultimately dangerous to your heart. I wanted to believe that even if Peter came back, I wouldn't accept him. After all, there was the whole Lacey issue. But I was scared I would never love another man as much as I had loved him.

I was desperate, and in more ways than one.

For desperate was also the perfect word to describe how I felt as I called the names on my roommate referral list.

"Hello, is this Sky?"

A raspy voice answered. "Yeah, this is Sky."

"Um, hi, my name is Faith. I got your number from roommate referrals?"

She waited a good five seconds before she responded, "Oh, yeah, hi."

"Hi. So are you still looking for a roommate?"

"Yeah, I'm still looking. I haven't had any luck so far in finding someone good. It's amazing how many freaks there are out there."

"Oh yeah? That's too bad. Well, you're the first person I've called, so I haven't had that experience yet...."

"Uh huh. Look, I have three questions I always ask the people who want to move in with me. The way you answer will determine whether or not you're okay. Are you ready?"

"Um, sure."

"Great. Question number one. Do you believe that wild animals have souls? If your answer is yes, does that mean that killing them is murder? Make sure you answer honestly."

"Isn't that actually two questions?"

"Just answer." she demanded.

"Sure," I said. "I don't know. My sister Margaret does, she works for Green Peace, and refuses to eat meat."

"Yeah? That would help me out a lot if it was your sister who wanted to move in. Seeing as how it's you, we'll move on. Question number two..."

"Wait," I said. "I can expand on question number one. I only need a second to think it through."

But Sky had no time. "Question number two. Which of the following is the cutest: a. puppies, b. kittens, c. bunnies, d. babies, e. turtles."

"Um, it depends. I've seen some ugly babies and some cute turtles, you know? But that doesn't mean that turtles are cuter than babies in most cases. It's hard to say."

Sky let out an exasperated sigh. "But generally. Obviously there are exceptions to any rule, but I need to know which you would prefer in most situations."

I gulped. I felt like I was on a game show, and a million dollars was at stake. "Okay. Kittens then."

"Great. Final question. Have you ever been or would you ever consider being in a threesome?"

I wasn't sure I heard her right. "When you say threesome, do you mean, like in bed?"

"No, I mean as in 'The Three Musketeers' type threesome."

"Look," I replied. "I appreciate you taking the time to talk to me, but I don't think that this is going to work."

"Fine!" she yelled. "You're just like all the rest of them!" and with that she hung up on me.

I told myself it was no big deal. She was only the first person I talked to. There were bound to be some weirdos out there, and it was up to me to weed them out. The next person on the list was a guy. I admit, the idea of moving in with a man I didn't know seemed too much like the premise of the bad Lifetime suspense movie, but I called anyway.

I called, and he picked up on the first ring. "Thith ith Thteve," he said.

"I'm sorry. Is this Steve Robbins?"

"Yup!" He said. "Thith ith Thteve."

Oops. His lisp was so pronounced that I hadn't been able to understand him at first, and I was worried I had already insulted him.

"Oh, hi Steve. My name is Faith, and I'm calling because I got your name from roommate referrals. I understand you're looking for someone to share your apartment?"

"Yup. How thoon can you move in?"

"Oh. Um, don't you want to ask me some questions first? Find out what kind of person I am before you let me be your roommate?"

"Thure. Leth thee. Are you a therial killer?"

" Ha ha. No, I'm not a serial killer."

"Do you abuth drugth?"

"No, I don't do drugs, unless you count caffeine and ibuprofin."

"Will you theal my thuff?"

"I'm sorry?"

"Will you theal my thuff." (Pause. I still couldn't understand him, and had no idea what to say.) "Will you theal my thuff? Will you theal my thuff?"

"Oh!" I finally got it. "No. I won't steal your stuff."

"Great," he said. "How thoon can you move in?"

I would like to believe that his lisp had nothing to do with it, that I was turned off simply because he didn't get to know me before he asked me to move in. I can't say for sure. However, there was no way in hell I was moving in with this guy.

"I'm sorry Steve. There are several more people I was going to call. Why don't I get back to you?"

"Thure," he said. "Juth let me know."

The third person I called was Micheala, and at first she seemed halfway normal. She said she had had several inquiries already about her place, and she was meeting in person with each one. This seemed like a nice contrast to Steve, so I agreed to meet her at a coffee shop the next evening.

When I walked in she was already there, drinking a large latte and entering something into her palm pilot. I recognized her by the description she had given me on the phone: extremely thin, with black hair wound tightly into a bun. She was a ballet dancer, and every inch of her looked the part. She had even dressed in a pink cardigan and a thin black wrap-around skirt. Everything about her was impeccable, from the way she drank her latte without letting a drop rest on her chin or mouth, to her French manicured nails. I introduced myself and sat down.

"Faith," she said, "it is so nice to meet you." She spoke slowly, accentuating her vowels and clipping her consonants so that she nearly adopted a British accent. "Let me explain my process. I have a few questions I am going to ask you, and I am going to record your answers in purple. You will notice," she held up a notebook with writing in multiple colors scrawled across its pages, "that I have already interviewed several people. Each person was assigned a different color, that way I could keep track of who said what fairly simply." She clicked her multi-colored pen so it was writing in purple ink, and added my name to the bottom of a list on the first page of her notebook. She spoke as she wrote. "Faith equals purple." She then looked up, sure to make careful and steady eye contact with me. "After I am done interviewing you, I hope you will have some questions for me, which I promise to answer sincerely.

"Now, there are a couple more people I need to interview after you. I plan to be done with interviews by the end of the week, on Friday. Saturday I will need to step away from the whole process, so I intend not to think about it, but rather take a break. Sunday I will look through my notes, and decide who I will be calling for a second interview. I plan to have second interviews done by Wednesday. Since my expectation is that I will only give two to three people second interviews, I expect I will have come to a final decision by the end of next week. Any questions?"

Yeah. Why was it easier to get a job with the Minneapolis school system than it was to become Micheala's roommate? However, seeing as how she was still the most normal person I had spoken to so far, I shook my head no so we could proceed with the interview.

"Would you object to a rotating cleaning schedule?"

"Oh, no, not at all." I was starving, so I took a bite of the scone I had ordered. Naturally, a bunch of crumbs escaped and fell down the front of my blouse. Micheala's eyes narrowed, and I immediately brushed them away. One crumb then flew (it was kind of breezy in there) and landed on Micheala's pink sweater. "Sorry," I said, as she brushed it away. I put down my scone. "Anyway, my college room-mate and I had a cleaning schedule. That way we knew stuff would get done. I'm not too good at remembering to clean, but if there's a sign up, I'll do it."

She nodded. "Um hmm." Her long fingers reached into the port-folio that rested on the table, and she pulled out an elaborate chart.

"Here is a sample of what I was thinking. It divides the duties into categories: bathroom, kitchen, living room, hallway, and then into subcategories: refrigerator, tiles, carpet, closets, toilet, curtains, heating vents, woodwork, and knick-knacks. It goes without saying that we would each be responsible for our own bedrooms. But the other duties would rotate, according to the schedule." She pointed to the chart's key. "Assume you are roommate B, and I'm roommate A. Every category that is in green you would do on Saturdays, and every subcategory that is in blue you would do on Mondays, Wednesdays, and every other Friday."

"That's a lot of cleaning." I said. I wanted to ask why she got to be roommate "A," but thought better of it.

"I'm going to be very upfront with you Faith; I am a neat and orderly person. I am also creative, but I need order before my creativity can thrive. If you want to move in, you need to be okay with that."

I had been living with Carolyn and Charles for nearly two weeks now, and as great as they were, the apartment was small, the walls were thin, and we all needed privacy. So I replied, "I understand."

She asked me dozens of questions, ranging from my family history to the type of poster art I preferred. I wanted to like her, but as the interview progressed I didn't need for my skin to hurt to know this was a bad match. By the end of the meeting I knew I didn't want to get picked by her, so I admit I was looking at my watch and shifting in my seat quite a bit.

"Um," she said. "Is there something wrong? I'm detecting a hostile undertone from you."

I had been there for over an hour, answering her questions. But I took the easy way out, and lied. "No, no hostile undertone. I'm just late for something. Sorry; I have to go and color coordinate my sock drawer." I never heard from her after that.

And on it went. It seemed that each person I spoke to was weirder than the last.

"Why don't you get a place by yourself?" Carolyn wanted to know.

"I don't even have a job yet. Nobody is going to rent to me without proof of income." Besides, rent was so much more expensive here in Minneapolis than it was in Duluth. I was already losing a lot of money with the move; I couldn't see committing to my own apartment until I was sure that I actually had a future here.

Finally, after several more days of staying with Charles and Carolyn, I got a hold of Missy. After a brief phone conversation where we exchanged basic information about ourselves, she invited me to come see her place, which was not far from Charles and Carolyn's.

Her building was a medium-sized brownstone that housed about twenty units. It was on the same block as an organic coffee shop called "Cafe Panoply," and a new-age bookstore and incense shop called "Crystal Clear."

I knocked on the door to her apartment, and was pleased when a normal looking person answered. Missy was of average height, with brown hair and dark coloring. She made the most of her neither remarkably large nor small figure by wearing light khaki pants cinched in at the waist with tapered legs, and a tan blouse tucked in. She smiled, and her tone was friendly.

"Hi, you must be Faith. Come in." Her apartment was neat, and although her decor reminded me of a hotel room (lots of cornflower blue, with embroidered pillows and paintings of country scenes) it wasn't awful by any means. The carpeting was wall-to-wall beige, covering a huge living room with big windows that let in lots of light.

"This is a great place." I said, looking around. Actually, it was generic enough to not be distasteful. Everything that was necessary was provided, with the kitchen off to the side and two bedrooms down the hall. Plus, it was in a great area; Charles and Carolyn would be close by.

"How long have you been looking for someone to move in?" I asked

"Actually, I just started. I wasn't expecting to need a new room-mate, but my best friend and I had a falling out...." her voice trailed off, and she looked kind of sad.

"I understand. My best friend and I recently had a falling out too."

She smiled, and said in a perky voice, "Great! So we have something in common." She started towards the hall. "Let me show you the bedrooms." We got to the smaller of the two first, which was empty. "This would be your room."

"Terrific," I said. It was rectangular in shape, with one window and a closet that took up most of one of the longer walls.

"It's not huge," said Missy, "but if you don't have a lot of stuff, it should be fine."

"Oh sure," I replied. "Most of what I have would fit in here."

"Well, it's not like you would be confined to this room. You're more than welcome to use the rest of the apartment as well." She continued on down the hall until she reached the other bedroom. "And this is my room."

Her bedroom contrasted with the rest of the apartment. It was actually decorated in a distinct way. The walls were painted red (later she said that she gotten permission from the landlord to do that), and decorated with three framed black and white posters of people kissing. At least one looked familiar. It was of a sailor grabbing his girl right after WWII had ended.

"I hope you don't mind cats," she said. Upon her pink satin bedspread were two of them. One was small, dainty, and brown, and looked like a purebred, although I couldn't say of what. But she was fluffy in all the right places, with fur gathered around her paws and her neck. The other cat, which was much more ordinary looking, stretched his large orange body across her bed as if he owned it.

"This is Jinny," she walked over to the brown cat and began stroking her, "and that's Thomas." She merely pointed to him, but for me it was love at first sight. I walked over to the bed. He rolled over on his back so that I could pet his massive belly. As soon as I did, he began to simultaneously purr and lick my hand. Then he looked up at me, and I knew. Thomas was in my future.

"I love cats," I said. "My old apartment didn't allow them, otherwise I would have had one myself."

"Oh good. We got off the phone yesterday and it occurred to me I should have asked you about that first thing. Jinny is like my family, so it's important to me that anyone who lives here gets along with her." She was still petting Jinny, lavishing affection on her. "I've had her for years. An ex-boyfriend gave her to me for my birthday. As you can probably tell, the boyfriend is long gone, but Jinny and I are still together."

Jinny looked like she had the personality of a popular Junior High School girl, but she was a very pretty cat. "What about Thomas? How long have you had him?"

Missy looked up. "Oh. Well, I never actually planned on having two cats. But there was this little market place I used to go to, and the owners had him there and kept him locked up in this cage. So one day I asked, and they said they were planning on taking him to the pound unless someone wanted him. My heart went out; I had to take him home with me. Sometimes I regret it. Don't get me wrong; he's a love. But he and Jinny don't get along too well. I think sometimes he's jealous of her."

I didn't doubt it. If today was any indication of what usually went on, Jinny got all the attention and he got none. I would be jealous too. But on the other hand, Missy had taken him home with her, which is more than most people would do.

"Anyway," she said, "your share of rent would be $445 per month. That includes all utilities except of course, the phone."

"That's cheap!" I said. "I haven't heard of anything in this area that's even close to that."

"Yeah, since I moved they've been renting the vacated apartments for a lot more. I got in at the right time. By law, they can only increase my rent 7% per year."

"Cool," I said, still petting Thomas. He was on his side now, washing his face with his right paw and purring loudly while I continued to pet him.

She continued. "But about the phone. I have a second job, doing some telemarketing from home. What would you think about installing a second line for us to use for personal calls? That way I wouldn't have to worry about always tying it up."

"That's no problem."

She smiled. "Great. You seem easy going. That's always nice."

I smiled back. "You have no idea who I've met while trying to find a roommate. I'm relieved you seem so normal."

"Well, today is your lucky day. I have a good feeling about this. Unless, you want to keep looking and let me know later?"

I looked down again at the bed where Thomas was still washing himself. His huge stomach was spread out in layers of fat, and he was content to take his time in licking all of it. This was the first time since meeting Ethan that I had felt my intuition kick in. Surely I couldn't be wrong twice in a row?

"No, this feels right. How soon can I move in?"

Missy said anytime. So the next day I drove back up to Duluth, rented a U-haul, and brought back all the furniture and possessions I thought would fit into Missy's apartment. The rest I dropped off at Goodwill. It was that easy. I was now a Minneapolis resident, and I had left my old life behind.

Sometimes I wonder what my life would be like if I hadn't made this move. It's easy to reflect back and regret my choices. But hindsight is twenty/twenty, and who's to say what would have become of me had I stayed in Duluth? After all, safety is merely an illusion, and the best way to grow is by making a lot of mistakes. And I had a lot of growing to do.

6

Finding a place to live had been a load off my mind, but that was only half the battle. I still needed to find a job. I had some money saved up, so it wasn't like I was going to go broke right away. But I needed to find something soon, before all the teaching positions for the fall were taken. If worst came to worst I knew that I could always substitute teach, but ick. Being a professional practical joke target just didn't sound appealing.

So I set out, trying to find a school that would hire me. I spent hours filling out applications. I called old colleagues of mine, asking for letters of recommendation. I wrote essay after essay on my philosophy of teaching, and I couldn't even get an interview.

But I was determined to keep my chin up, so I began each morning at the coffee shop two doors down from my new apartment. Cafe Panoply had a friendly atmosphere, with oversize sofas, funky lamps, and pop art in every nook and cranny that would hold it. Plus, every inch of the place had been painted, and the walls, floor, ceiling, chairs and tables were in alternating bright shades of blue, purple, green, and red. Missy never went there, she said the decor was too busy, but I found the place as invigorating as the coffee it served.

It also gave me a sense of belonging. I enjoyed recognizing the other regulars who came in each day when I did, even if I didn't speak to them. One guy I noticed right away. He looked like he was a little older than me, early thirties maybe, but his hair had gone prematurely gray. It was cut very short, and the remaining fuzz stuck up straight on the top of his head. Below was a long narrow face, and eyes I could only describe as soulful.

Yet his demeanor contrasted noticeably with his appearance. He looked like he ought to have been intense and serious, but he was just goofy. Everyday he flirted with the owner and manager, Sally, who had to be a good twenty years older than he was. He would come in grasping his laptop in one arm, march straight up to the counter, and slap it with his free hand.

"Sally!" he would bellow, "get me the usual, and blow me a kiss!" She would laugh, hand him his hot chocolate with extra whipped cream and a rice crispy treat, then obligingly blow him a kiss. Every day he would hand her a ten-dollar bill, telling her to keep the change. Sally later told me he was a computer consultant, and had a lot of expendable income. Sally had come to recognize me, and greeted me each day when I came in, which was usually around 10. I liked to avoid the morning rush.

"Hello Faith, how's the job hunt going?" she would ask in a way that reminded me of my mom. Sally was in her early fifties, and she dressed like an ex-hippie. She wore her graying hair in a long braid down her back, which went well with the Birkenstocks she always wore.

"The same," I would say. "How are you?"

"Tired of these early mornings. I can't ever seem to find a reliable person to take the morning shift. I swear, if I have to continue getting up at 5am every morning, I might as well sell the shop. I'm not a morning person."

Every morning she would say that, and every morning I would reply, "Shouldn't you have thought of that before you opened a coffee shop?"

"Foresight has never been my strong suit," she would tell me. "Here's your coffee. Would you like a scone? I made them fresh!"

Meanwhile, there were some bumps in the road of living with Missy. I didn't realize before I moved in how lonely she was. I still thought she was a nice person, but she was needy needy needy. At first I didn't mind, mainly because Carolyn and Charles were the only people I knew down here, and I didn't want to be too dependent on them. But after a while she became, well, super mega needy.

I couldn't relax if she was at home. She always wanted to be talking, and would force me into a conversation no matter what I was doing. This wouldn't be so bad, accept that there was only one topic of conversation she found acceptable: Missy.

For Example:

"Yeah. I lost 15 pounds by cutting out carbs. And you know, I don't even miss it. I feel so much healthier now." (Missy while I was cooking spaghetti.)

"Faith, you ought to pay more attention to how you dress. Look at me; I try to add sensual elements. People will respect you for it. (Missy while I was getting ready to go out.)

"When I was out of work I decided to change careers. Sometimes you need be willing to bend, Faith." (Missy while I was filling out job applications.)

And so on. Okay, a lot of the time she would include me in the conversation, but usually to illustrate what was wrong with me versus what was right with her.

"Hey roomie!" she called to me one afternoon as she walked through the door. "Watcha doing?"

I was reading a magazine, trying to unwind after a long day of filling out more job applications and redoing my resume yet again.

"Just relaxing," I said.

"Huh, I wish I could afford not to work." She walked into her bedroom and closed the door. In a few minutes she came back out, dressed in biker shorts and a clingy top. "I'm sorry I snapped at you," she said. "I had a very bad day. I hate my job so much."

I had put down the magazine, and turned on the television instead. Dr. Phil was on. "That's okay," I said. "Sorry your day was bad."

Missy stepped in front of the television; I hated it when she did that. "Hey, do you want to go for a walk around Lake Calhoun? It's beautiful out, and my friend Lex should be down there. I ran into him yesterday, and he says he bikes around the lake most afternoons."

Hundreds of people are usually at Lake Calhoun on sunny, warm afternoons, and it is nearly impossible for walkers to find bikers, seeing as how they have to stay on different paths around the lake. But Missy desperately sought people out.

"Nah, I already went for a walk today," I told her, which was true. Not the reason that I didn't want to go, but true nonetheless.

"You never want to do anything with me," she said, and got up to leave.

"Yes I do!" I lied. "I'm tired. I've spent all day job-hunting, and I need to relax a little and do nothing. That's all." I felt bad, but I also knew the main reason Missy wanted me to come was so she'd look popular if she ran into Lex.

"I understand." Her smile was nutra-sweet, but she was trying to be genuine. "Have fun doing nothing. Hey, maybe when I get back, we can go get something to eat. I'm starved, and I heard there's this new tapas bar that's great to meet people at."

"Maybe, we'll see." That meant I needed to come up with a reason why I couldn't go out, and in the time that it took for her to walk around Lake Calhoun. It needed to be good too, since she was on to me.

Laundry? If I put laundry in now, it would be in the dryer by the time Missy got back. But then what? I wasn't sure, but in the meantime, I may as well do a load. I gathered up my dirty clothes, and headed downstairs. When I got down to the laundry room, I encountered a man preparing to dry his clothes.

"Gosh darnit! I'm short a quarter." He said this to himself, unaware I had walked in. I realized he was the guy from the coffee shop.

"Here" I said, as I walked over to the dryer, and handed him a coin.

"Oh. Thanks," he said, and for a moment it seemed that was all he was going to say. But then he looked at me, squinting and holding his gaze longer than most people would.

"I've seen you around, haven't I?" he said, finally.

"Yeah," I responded. "At Cafe Panoply. I see you just about every morning."

"Riiiight!" he exclaimed, "you're the new girl."

"The new girl?"

"The new girl at Cafe Panoply. The new girl in the building. The new girl." He exclaimed this as he threw all of his laundry into the dryer, slamming the door shut for emphasis. I laughed.

"What's so funny?" he enquired.

"Nothing," I said, separating my lights from my darks. "I can't remember the last time I was a new girl. I don't know if I've ever been one."

"Well, then congratulations!" he said, "and welcome to the building."

"I'm Faith."

"Nice to meet you, I'm Bill, in number twelve. So how do you like it here?"

"It seems nice so far."

"Right. Well…" He started to walk away, then turned back once again. "Uh, Faith, which apartment did you say you were in?"

"I didn't. But I moved into number 5."

"With that brown haired girl? Melissa?"

"Well, yeah, but she goes by Missy."

He laughed and shook his head as if in sympathy. "Good luck!" he said, then he walked away.

When I got back upstairs there was a message on our machine. I figured it would be one of the many guys who Missy meets through her dating service (did I mention she does online dating?), but I pressed play on the off chance it would be someone calling me for a job.

"Um. Hello, Faith? Faith, this is Ethan. The guy you yelled at? Wait, that might mean nothing to you… I'm the guy who fixed your car? I was calling to see how it's doing. I hope that your rear sway isn't giving you any more problems, and the problem was (pause) adequately altered. And oh, just so you know, I call all of my customers several weeks after they bring their cars in, it's part of my good customer service strategy. And… I was wondering if you'd like to get a drink sometime. I think you should say yes, so give me a call at home, 612-555-7849!"

I didn't know whether to be shocked, happy or skeptical. Whatever. My list of Minneapolis acquaintances was severely limited. At the very least he could be a new friend.

I picked up the phone and dialed.

"Hello?"

"Carolyn, you'll never guess what happened."

"Ethan called."

"How did you know?'

"Because he called here first, and I gave him your new number."

"Oh. Right, I suppose that makes sense. So what did you think when you spoke with him? Was he polite, or did he act full of himself?"

"I don't know." Her own voice sounded rather flat. "What's wrong?" I asked.

"Nothing, it's not anything. Charles and I sort of had another fight, but it's not a big deal."

Then there was a knock on my door. "Carolyn, hold on a minute, there's someone at the door. I'll be right back."

Standing in my doorway was Bill from the laundry room. "I always repay my debts," he said, and handed me a quarter. I was surprised that he went to the trouble.

"Oh, thanks. You didn't have to do that."

"Well, I'm an old fashioned guy, and I don't believe in being in obligation to a lady."

"There really was no obligation, but thanks again. I'm on the phone, so I should go."

I closed the door before he could answer, and picked the phone back up to speak with Carolyn. "So what happened?" I asked her.

"Nothing. It's not a big deal."

"Carolyn..."

She sighed. "It wasn't even a true fight. We had another talk about marriage. He said he knew he wanted to get married soon and have kids because he's always wanted to have a family. All I said was that's an easy thing for him to want, because it wouldn't change anything for him. But for me, it would. I would wind up never leaving here, and having kids would make it rather hard to go out on auditions. Meanwhile, who would be taking care of those kids while he went out and did his music? You know?"

"What did he say?"

"He said if that's what I think, then I don't know him very well, and thanks for the vote of confidence. Then he stormed out. I have no idea where he is."

"Well, what are you doing right now? Other than waiting for him to come back?"

"Nothing. But I should stay here."

"Why?"

"Because he might be even more upset if he comes back ready to talk, and I'm not around."

"But sitting around the apartment moping is only going to make you feel worse. If you wait for him too long and he doesn't show, after a while you're going to start feeling angry, and that will make everything worse. Isn't it better to go and get your mind off things?"

"I don't know."

"Oh come on Carolyn, let's go for one drink. It will make you feel better, and it will get me out of having to spend the evening with Missy."

"So that's how it is? Why don't you just tell her no?"

"I did. I've told her that several times already. She's starting to take it personally. I think it's better to be gone when she gets back. But I could come over..."

"No, that would be awkward if Charles did show up." She took a deep breath and exhaled. "You know, I don't like sitting here, waiting for him. You're right. Let's get a drink."

❋ ❋ ❋

I once read a poem that compared men to busses. The basic idea is they're the same. You wait and wait for one, feeling like it will never show. Then, all of a sudden, just when you've given up, three appear at once, and you have no idea which one to get on. Well, while Carolyn and I were sitting at the C.C. Club (a grungy but popular bar in our area), completely unconcerned with the many guys who surrounded us, we were being checked out. Two guys approached the table, one of whom Carolyn already knew.

"David! Hey, how are you?" She addressed the taller of the two. He looked a little like Charles, blond and broad, but his hair was cropped very short, rather than in dreadlocks like Charles' was.

"I thought that was you." He reached over and gave Carolyn a hug. "It's been such a long time! How have you been, babe?"

"I've been good. How about you?" She smiled up at him. I hadn't seen Carolyn smile like that since college, when we used to go to keg parties together. It was her "come get me" smile.

"Oh, I'm hanging in there." His friend standing next to him cleared his throat. "Oh, sorry Max. Uh, Max, this is Carolyn. She and I were in a play together at the Guthrie."

"Nice to meet you," he said to her. He turned to me, but before I could introduce myself, Carolyn broke in. "And this is my friend Faith. She and I went to college together, and she moved down here a few weeks ago."

They both smiled, muttered things like "cool!" or "great!" and nodded their heads. For an uncomfortable moment nobody said anything, but then Carolyn relented.

"Would the two of you like to join us?"

"Sure!" said David. "Hey, what are you two drinking?"

"Vodka tonic, light on the tonic." said Carolyn.

"Miller Light." I said.

David reached into his pocket, and handed Max a twenty. "Why don't you go buy these ladies another round?"

Max smiled and said sure, and walked to the bar as David sat down next to Carolyn. I wondered why David couldn't get the drinks himself, but it soon became clear he was wasting no time in getting close to Carolyn. He already had his arm around her. Carolyn, who had finished her second drink, relaxed into his embrace.

"So, tell me really, how have you been?" He leaned in and spoke to her as if they were the only two people in the room.

"I've been kind of restless," said Carolyn. "How have you been?"

He ignored her question. "Restless? Why have you been restless? I thought you were the girl who had it all."

She laughed, and sucked on an ice cube from the bottom of her drink. "No. I am not that girl. I am the girl who has it all, but wants more."

"Well hey, there's nothing wrong with that." He inched even closer to her than he already was. "You know, I always thought you were too good for this place. Have you ever thought about hitting New York or Los Angeles? See how you do there?"

She squealed like a call-in prizewinner on a radio morning show. "Oh my God! I can't believe you asked me that! Because I've been thinking about it, really seriously."

I tried to interrupt. "Carolyn, you've been thinking about it seriously? I thought it was just something that you were considering."

She waved her hand as if to dismiss me. "You know what I mean. Same thing." Her attention turned back to David. "So, you think that I ought to go for it, then?"

"Yeah!" he said. "I mean, I am. I'm leaving for New York in a month. Hey, I know! You ought to come out there and stay with me. That way you can check it out. What do you think?"

"Sure! That would be great!"

"Carolyn!" I nearly shouted, "Don't you think you ought to talk to your boyfriend, Charles, about this? You know, the one who wants to marry you?"

Her eyes squinted and reprimanded me before her words dug in. "Actually, Faith, I think I'm an adult, and can handle my own life. Thanks though."

Max came back with the drinks. He handed them to us, and sat down next to me.

"So," he asked, "what did I miss?"

Nobody answered him. Instead, David leaned over and whispered something in Carolyn's ear, and they both started to laugh. She then whispered something in his ear, and they both laughed again. Max and

I looked at each other, as if to concede how unpleasant the situation had become. As Carolyn and David continued their own private little conversation, Max addressed me.

"So, you just moved here, huh? What do you think so far?"

It was difficult to divert my attention away from Carolyn and David. However, I was raised to be polite, so I turned to face him and answered his question.

"It's fine. I don't have a job yet, but other than that, things are okay."

He took a swig of his drink. "What sort of a job are you looking for?"

"I'm a teacher."

"Oh yeah? My sister's a teacher. She teaches fifth grade. What do you teach?"

"Well, nothing right now, but I'm looking for a job in high school English."

He smiled, and I noticed he was actually kind of cute. He had a clean-cut look about him, with brown hair and a close shave. He was good looking enough to be a model actually, but his appearance was better suited for a J.C. Penny circular than the Abercrombie catalogue.

"Wow," he said, "you must be brave. I could never deal with teenagers everyday."

I shifted in my chair, further away from Carolyn and David, trying to block out their continuing laughter. "I get that comment a lot when I tell people what I do. But truly, it's all relative. Sure, there are bad days when you work with kids, but at least I don't go to work everyday feeling like I'll get fired if I don't make some quota. I think teaching is a lot less scary than say, selling something." From behind me I could still hear their giggles, but it was getting easier to ignore. I took a swig of my beer. "So what do you do?"

"I sell things," he said with a laugh.

"Really?"

He laughed again. "Really. Well, actually, I sell time for a radio station. You know, advertising time? It's not so bad."

"Yeah, and I would think there's something almost cosmic about that, selling time."

He noticed my drink had left a wet spot on the table, so he took his napkin and reached across to wipe it up. "I work for an 80's station. There's nothing cosmic about that."

"Do you have certain quotas that you have to fill?" I asked.

"Well, sort of..." Max was beginning to explain, when David interrupted.

"So hey guys, I think we're going to get out of here." He gestured towards Carolyn as he said it.

I had to risk it. Even if it meant Carolyn would be angry with me.

"Guys, could you excuse us please, for a moment. I need to talk to Carolyn alone."

She gave me another glaring look, but said nothing. David hesitated, but Max came to my rescue.

"Sure," he said. "Come on Dave, let's go outside for a sec."

Carolyn sat slouched in her seat as she watched the two of them leave, purposefully not looking at me. I waited until they were gone, and then I asked her.

"Carolyn, what in God's name are you doing?"

She still would not look at me as she answered. "Oh, don't get moralistic on me. You have no idea what my life is honestly like. And weren't you the one who said we should go get a drink in the first place? That I shouldn't be at home, waiting around for Charles?"

"Yeah, but I didn't mean...." How to finish this sentence? "A few hours ago you were afraid to leave your apartment for fear of hurting Charles. Now you're going to cheat on him?"

She turned to face me in anger. "Faith, who said I was going to cheat on him? Do you actually think I would do that?"

Actually, I did think that she would do something like that. She basically said so herself when she was trying to convince me to go after Ethan. But delicacy was necessary at the moment. "I don't know, but I can say that David out there thinks that, or at the very least, he is hoping for it."

Her gaze shifted down, so that she was now staring at her drink, as if it somehow held an answer to the dilemma she was facing.

I continued. "Look, I'm not going to judge you. I think that maybe you're upset and you've had a couple of drinks, and you're not thinking too clearly. That's all. I don't want you to do something that you are going to regret."

"Right," she said. When she looked up at me, her eyes were as sad and lost as a kindergartner's at the bus stop. "Faith, to tell you the truth, I haven't been thinking too clearly for the past few months." She was fighting tears as she said, "I have no idea what I want anymore. I mean, I love Charles, I do. I suppose I thought if I could have some fun, blow off some steam, things would be better."

"Carolyn, I'm sorry, but I think that that's a bad idea. I really, really do. You don't want to hurt him, do you?"

She sighed and looked around the room. "Let's get out of here," she said. She got up to leave, and I threw some money down on the table, a tip for the waitress who had been serving us before the guys came along. Carolyn beat me outside, so when I got there, she was already talking to David.

"Yeah, I'm going to head back. Maybe some other time."

"Is your number still the same?" he asked her.

"Um, yeah, yeah it is." There was now nothing encouraging in Carolyn's manner at all. But she didn't tell him not to call either.

Max turned to me. "So Faith, it was nice meeting you. Maybe you want to go out for a drink again sometime?"

For a moment I didn't know what to say. I had been too focused on what was going on with Carolyn to put much thought into Max. Plus, Ethan had called. And Max was no Ethan. But after quick reflection, I decided maybe this was a good thing. He seemed stable, and nice. Not exciting, but interesting, perhaps.

"Sure," I answered him. "That would be great." I reached into my purse for a pen, but found no slip of paper to write upon.

"Here, write it on my hand." He held his arm out, and I did as he had requested. After I was done, he said, "Now it's official. You're branded on my skin, and in my heart."

I laughed because he expected me to. But actually his humor was uncanny enough that I instantly questioned my wisdom in giving him my number. Oh well – too late. After making Carolyn promise to call me later, I headed back. When I got there I was pleased to find that Missy was not yet home. I plopped down on the couch to pet Thomas, who awoke with a meow, and stretched lazily as I stroked him. I was enjoying this moment of peace and quiet so much that when the phone rang, I chose not to answer it. Instead, the answering machine clicked on.

A male voice spoke. "Hi, it's me. I want you to know that I'm thinking about you." Click.

The message had to be for Missy. I didn't recognize the voice; it was too deep to be Ethan's. But was it really? Unsure, I listened to it again, and then I listened to Ethan's message to compare them. It didn't sound like him, but I wasn't one hundred percent sure.

Or what if it was Max? Now that would be disturbing. But he hadn't seemed disturbed, at least until that last comment. I dialed star 69 to find out who had called, but the number had been blocked. Great.

I told myself that I was making too much of this. The call had to be for Missy. Deciding to dismiss all thoughts from my mind, I headed off to bed, where it took me forever to fall asleep. However, it wasn't the message that kept me tossing and turning, it was the actions of the evening running through my mind. In retrospect that seems ironic. Then again, it's those whom we love that bring about the worst kind of pain. There's no great mystery as to why, but the events that were about to unfold would remain elusive to me for a long time.

7

When I awoke the next morning I remembered I had left my laundry in the washer the night before. When I went down to finally put it in the dryer, I found that someone had already taken care of it, and my clothes were folded neatly on the table off to the side. I smiled but felt my cheeks turn red; most of what was in that load was bras and underwear.

I took my stuff upstairs and put it away. I figured the person to thank was that guy Bill, so I wrote a note thanking him and slipped it underneath his door.

I spent the rest of the morning once again working on my resume and looking for jobs. But it was hard to concentrate because most of my mental energy was used thinking about Ethan. How long should I wait to call him back? Was he truly interested in me, or is he simply a flirt? And what about his ex-girlfriend? Should I be getting involved with someone who, like me, is on the rebound? Shortly before 10:00am I was diverted however, when Missy came in.

"Hey, what are you doing home?" I asked her.

She looked as if breathing were a chore. "You will never believe what happened to me this morning," she said, as she sat down slowly on the couch, as if to say it was hard for her to do so. "I decided to go for a short walk before work, and I got run-over by a dog!"

I was run over by a dog once, when I was two. It was so traumatic I still remember it. However, at the time I was about two-and-a-half fett tall. I couldn't fathom how Missy, who is at least 5'4," managed to let a dog run over her.

"How did you get run-over by a dog? Was the dog really big or something?"

"No, it was small. I was walking, and it ran out in front of me, so I tripped. When I fell, I landed on my shoulder and my wrist, and I could instantly feel that something was wrong. I've been in the emergency room all morning. They say there might be nerve damage."

"Missy, that's terrible, but then the dog didn't literally run over you, right? Because the way you made it sound...."

She jumped up from the couch. "You weren't there Faith! I felt like I had been demolished. It was awful. And quite frankly, it would have been nice to have someone to drive me to the hospital, rather than driving myself. That was not easy."

Missy's face was all pinched up, and her eyes had narrowed into little slits. She stood with her hands on her hips, glaring at me. This was the first time I experienced her anger, and already I knew to tread lightly.

"I'm sorry Missy. But I was here, you could have woken me, I would have taken you."

"I didn't want to interrupt you, you were out so late last night." Forget that she had gotten home last night after I had. She sounded as grouchy as a spoiled child.

"I'm sorry. Carolyn called, and she and her boyfriend had had a fight. She needed to talk. Otherwise I would have waited for you to get back, and invited you along."

"So you just take off, expecting me to finish your laundry for you?"

"What?" I was shocked. "You finished my laundry? How did you know I was even doing any?"

"Because I went to do some of my own, and I recognized your clothes in the washer."

I almost started to say thank you, when an unpleasant thought occurred to me.

"You recognized my underwear?"

Missy's face went blank for a moment, her look of anger transitioning into one of confusion. But only for a moment, then she resumed her aggressive pose.

"I helped you move in, remember? Personally, I would never have left the box with my underwear without a lid, but it's not like you have that much to hide. Hanes Her Way and all."

"That's not all I own! There was some Victoria's Secret in there too!"

"Whatever."

"Anyway, you didn't have to do that. You could have left them on top of the machine, I would have finished them later."

She turned towards the kitchen, and walked to get a glass of water. "A simple thank you would be nice," she said, as she turned on the faucet.

Better to let the whole thing go. "Oh, well, thanks. Would you like some quarters for the dryer?"

Her glare told me the mere question was an insult. Then without warning or seeming cause, her face turned from anger to sorrow. It reminded me of watching a mime at a street fair – how quickly and drastically her expression changed. Unfortunately however, Missy was not as quiet as a mime. She began to sob. In the flash of a second she turned the water off, and threw the glass in her hand down on the floor, breaking it to bits. Next she was gasping for air, as I stood watching, too shocked to go and comfort her.

"What am I going to do?" she wailed. "I'll have to quit my job! How am I going to live?" She screamed this up towards the ceiling, and then lowered her head and her voice at the same time. She looked around her, gradually realizing the scene she had created. It didn't take long for her to regain her composure; she grabbed a paper towel, wiped her eyes, then retrieved the broom from behind the fridge and began to sweep up the mess she had made.

"Sorry," she said, without looking at me. "I didn't mean to be so dramatic. Sometimes when I've had a bad day the tension builds up, and I lose it for a moment."

I had to take a deep breath. Talk about tension.

"That's okay," I replied. "We've all been there. Do you need help cleaning that up?"

"Sure," she said. "I suppose I shouldn't push it." She handed me the broom and the dustpan, and walked back out into the living room. So much for "helping."

"Thanks," she called out. "I appreciate it. But hey, now we're in the same boat, huh? Jobless and all."

I finished cleaning up the glass and walked back out into the living room. She was sitting next to her cat Jinny, playing with her tail.

"Why are you going to quit your job?"

"The doctors said nerve damage! I can't do the same repetitive motion all day, sitting at a desk and typing." Missy did data entry. "But I can't survive simply on my phone sales either."

"On your phone sales?" It took a moment before I remembered. "Oh yeah, that's right. You do telemarketing. But I've never actually heard you selling anything. You always go into your room and close the door."

Missy flashed a smile through her remaining tears. "That's because what I'm selling is me."

"Huh?" Call me dense; I didn't get it.

So she put it simply. "I do phone sex. That's my telemarketing. But I can't do it full time, they're only willing to give me part time work. No, I'll have to figure out something else as well."

Never mind that Missy had used a lot of force to break that glass. Never mind that no doctor had actually said to her that she did have nerve damage, and would have to quit her job. These were not the issues foremost on my mind.

"You do phone sex? For money? From our apartment?"

She sighed. "It's not like you ever would have known if I hadn't told you."

I plopped down on the chair across from the couch where she was sitting. Revelations such as this needed to be taken sitting down.

Missy laughed. "Lighten up, Faith. This isn't a case of guilt by association."

"But don't you think you should have told me before I moved in?"

"Why?" she asked. "What difference does it make?" Before I could answer, she continued on. "Anyway, I did tell you. I just didn't tell you what it was I telemarket."

"Well, that's a fairly significant piece of information to leave out, Missy!"

"Oh, relax!" she snipped. "I have my own line, so it doesn't even concern you. Now, if you'll excuse me, I need to call some lawyers."

"Lawyers? Why?"

"Why do you think? I want to sue the owners of that dog."

※　※　※

I ended up calling Ethan that afternoon, and we went out a couple of nights later. When he picked me up I was pleased to notice he cleans up nicely.

He was wearing khaki painter pants and a crisp white shirt, which looked good against his dark coloring. I was glad I hadn't dressed too formally though, seeing as how he hadn't either. After much deliberation, I had decided to wear my black stretch hip huggers, paired with a white cotton blouse with a red floral print, and red suede flip-flops to complete the ensemble. I have to be careful how much red I wear, because too much of it clashes with my hair. But I wore my hair up that night, even though both Missy and Carolyn told me not to.

Ethan didn't seem to mind. His eyes lit up with appreciation when I answered the door. "Hey, you look great!" he said. Now my face was red too. At least it matched with everything else about me. We went to this bar downtown called Brit's Pub, where you can sit on the roof and watch lawn bowling tournaments. And although there were threatening clouds on the horizon, we decided to take our chances rather than sit inside.

We ordered our drinks and made a lot of small talk.

"How long have you lived in Minneapolis?" I asked.

Ethan took a swig of his Summit and placed it back down on the table. "Since I was five," he said. "We moved here from Belgium."

"You're kidding," I replied. "Why?"

"My dad's American, and he couldn't find decent work. He had met my mom when he was traveling with a Fullbright. Then he got a temporary work visa to teach American Studies at one of the universities. But his visa ran out, so we moved here."

"What about your mom?"

"She's an artist; she can work anywhere."

"What kind of art?

"Paintings. I'll show you her pieces at the art institute sometime. She has a couple on display."

The art institute is connected to the children's theater in the southern part of the city. It has a national reputation, so I was impressed. I was also happy. He was already suggesting another date! "Yeah, that would be great. I've actually been meaning to get over to the institute."

Then there was a lag in the conversation. Ethan examined the label on his beer, ripping off the corner that had risen from condensation. I took a sip of my gin and tonic, and swirled the ice with the straw.

"So are you an American citizen?" I asked.

"I actually have dual citizenship"

I laughed.

"Why is that funny?" he inquired with a smile.

"I don't know. It seems ironic—a man who idolizes Abe Lincoln isn't 100% American."

His voice was soft, intimate. "But I don't, that's my cousin. However," he raised one eyebrow, "I do admire Abe Lincoln."

"Well," I replied, smiling, "what's not to admire? He was honest, fair, extremely intelligent...."

"Just like any good car mechanic should be."

"So, are you a good car mechanic?" I was expecting him to make another joke about how he had serviced my car, but he didn't. Instead he leaned forward, and took my hand in his.

"Let me put it this way," he said. "I'm only 50% American, but if that's mutually exclusive with being a good car mechanic, then I serve as the perfect example for both."

I had no idea what he meant. It didn't matter. His voice had that Sunday morning pancake quality again. Combine that with how he was holding my hand in his, he could have been reciting the phone book and I'd still have been thrilled. I smiled and savored the moment.

"So, Faith, what's your story?" He looked down at my hand that he was holding, and began to play with my fingers.

I struggled for an answer. I wanted to reply with something witty, but my mind drew a blank. So I settled for honesty. "Well, I'm here, and everything is so new. I'm trying to make sense of it all."

He considered this, looked up at me, and nodded his head. "You said that you just moved down here. Where did you move from?"

"Duluth."

"Why did you decide to do that?"

I didn't want to launch into the whole explanation, it was way too soon to bare my soul. I had already said too much when I had yelled at him that day in the shop. "I felt disconnected. My life felt so predictable. I needed a change. You know?"

He nodded again. "Sure, I know. I feel that way everyday."

"Really? That's funny, because you strike me as a person who seems fairly content with yourself."

He let go of my hand, leaned back, and took another swig of his beer. "Content, maybe. But satisfied? No."

"What's the difference between being content and satisfied?"

"There isn't much of a difference, it's more a matter of degree. When you're content you have what you need, it's like a five out of ten on the happiness scale. But being satisfied, that's having your desires fulfilled – like an eight or higher on the scale of happiness."

I smiled. "I thought only English teachers thought about the distinctions in meanings of synonyms."

He drummed his fingers on the table, and I met his gaze. He was grinning. "No, some car mechanics do too."

"Tell me about how you became a mechanic."

"You don't want to hear about that, that's boring."

"Why? Don't you like it?"

"Sure, it's fine. It's good money. But it wasn't what I had planned.

See, I didn't do very well in high school because I didn't do any assignments I wasn't interested in. Not that I didn't read."

"Were you the type of student who read just about anything except the required material?"

He laughed. "You mean that there are others like me? Yeah, I was like that. But anyway, I couldn't get into a decent college, and my cousin Andy, who owned the garage, said he would train me for free. I figured it would be a good job until I decided what it was that I really wanted to do. But now, ten years later, Andy moved to Portland, the shop is mine, and I'm still figuring out my next step."

"But it sounds like you're set. You're not even thirty yet, and you own your own shop. Why do you need a next step?"

"I'm sort of bored." he said. "And you're right. Here I am, 28 years old, and I've fallen into something I don't care much about. I've got to figure out what it is I do care about, before it's too late." He tilted his head up and looked at the sky. "Wow, those clouds are ominous looking. Are you sure you don't want to go inside?"

"No, I like it out here."

He laughed as if I had made a joke. "You're not one to be intimidated, are you Faith? I like that about you."

I wasn't sure that he actually had the right perception of me, because I feel intimidated all the time. But if he wanted to think that, I sure wasn't going to stop him.

"So are you glad you moved here?" He asked.

"Yeah," I responded. "Things have gone well, I guess."

"That doesn't sound too convincing."

"No, no. It's just that my roommate, Missy, is a little odd."

Ethan scrunched up his face. "Missy... is she a little shorter than you, brown hair, likes to wear tight clothes?"

"Yeah, that sounds like her. How do you know her?"

"I go to that coffee shop on your block, and I used to see her in there a lot. She mentioned that she lives in your building."

"Oh, that's weird, she told me she never goes there because she doesn't like the decor."

"Maybe it's a different Missy then," he said. Then there was another pause. I took another sip of my drink, finishing it this time. "So, besides your roommate, how is everything else going for you?" he inquired.

"Well, I haven't been able to find a job yet."

"You teach high school, right?"

"Yeah, high school English."

"And you like it?"

"I love it."

"Why?" He leaned forward again, resting his chin in his hand, his elbow on the table. Again he practiced that intense gaze with strong eye contact. Either he was honestly interested in hearing about me, or he's an expert at playing the game. But I was certainly willing to play.

"Because it's never boring. There's always a better way to do things, you know? I'm always challenging myself to come up with a better lesson plan, or a more creative way of tricking them into learning something. And I like the kids." I laughed. "A lot of times it's me who ends up learning something from them." A couple of fat raindrops fell onto our table. "Hmm... it's sprinkling."

Ethan's response was to shrug his shoulders. Then he spoke. "I envy you – how you feel about teaching. I wish I felt that way about something."

"So if money and training were no option, what would you want to do with your life?"

"Arragg!" He cried and laughed at the same time, looking back up at the sky. Then he once again locked his eyes with mine, and said with a smile, "I hate that question. Because I have no idea."

"Why? Because there isn't enough that you're interested in?"

"No, because I can't decide what I'm most interested in. That's my problem. This world is far too full of possibilities to spend your life stuck in a garage, fixing other people's cars."

"Well, then maybe you should bust out of here. Go travel and see the world."

He leaned in closer. "Maybe I should. Would you like to come?"

Then there was a flash of lightening and a clap of thunder. All of the people who were sitting at tables around us got up to go inside. But Ethan simply reached up, and opened the umbrella that was attached to our table. We both had to scoot our chairs in to be underneath, so our knees were touching. The rain had certainly started to fall, but sitting next to Ethan, I was sheltered from it.

"Is this okay?" He asked. I nodded. It definitely was. This close I could enjoy the smell of his skin combined with the fresh laundry smell of his shirt. I had the urge to reach up and brush away that lock of hair that had again fallen onto his forehead, but my inhibitions prevented me from doing so.

"So, how about it?" he persisted. "Want to come traveling with me?"

I gulped. "Um, don't you think it's a little soon to ask me that? You don't even know me."

"That's true. But I know that there's something about you." As he leaned in to kiss me my brain was screaming, "Don't let him! He's a player! Stop!" But at the same time, my toes were itching so much they tingled, and tingling in my toes was only the beginning of the story.

Then his lips were on mine. His kiss was firm yet gentle. He placed one hand on my knee, using his other hand to run his fingers through my hair. And as our mouths opened to each other, all thought exited from my mind. I was aware only of how good being close to him felt, until I was brought harshly back to reality when the waiter said, "Excuse me folks, but we need you to move inside. There's danger of a lightening strike."

Ethan broke away from me and laughed. "It's already happened."

8

The next morning I smiled as I woke, remembering how my date with Ethan the night before had gone. After we went inside, we stood at the bar for a while, waiting for the rain to stop. Once it had, we walked through the wet streets of downtown. The storm had cleared only temporarily however, and when it started to rain again, Ethan pulled me underneath the roof of a large church and began kissing me again.

It was like we were in movie or a perfume ad. I can't remember ever having such a good time on a first date. Maybe we knew each other in a past life or something, because usually I get all nervous and uncomfortable, but with Ethan, I could totally be myself, minus all my usual stupid and awkward moments—well, most of them anyway. And I didn't even think about Peter once, which is sort of amazing. But then later, when Ethan was dropping me off, things took a slight turn.

We were standing outside my apartment building. "I'd invite you in," I said, "but Missy might be home, and I'm not ready to expose you to her yet."

He smiled and shrugged his shoulders. "That's okay, I have an early day tomorrow, I should get going anyway." My stomach turned with his words. He didn't want to be asked up?

I played it cool. "Okay. Well, thanks for everything. I had a great time."

"Me too Faith. I'll call you." He reached up and stroked my

cheek, gazed into my eyes, then turned tail and ran. Okay, he didn't exactly run. But he didn't kiss me again, and there was no mention of another date, only the promise of a phone call, which we all know is guy-speak for, "You will never hear from me again."

But then, I couldn't deny the date had gone well up until that point. I went upstairs to my apartment, and had a pleasant night's sleep, with Thomas purring by my side. He was the best kind of guy to share my bed with anyway; he didn't hog the covers, and his only demand was to cuddle.

The next morning I had been awake for about twenty minutes; I was lying in bed, petting Thomas and replaying the events of my date with Ethan in my mind, when the phone rang. I was far too content to get up and answer it—petting Thomas had that effect on me. So I let the machine pick it up again.

"Hello, it's me. I hope you had a good time last night. I'm still thinking about you. I guess this proves that intimacy is priceless."

It was the same voice that had left that mysterious message before. Was it Ethan? I wasn't sure. It sounded like it could be his voice, but why wouldn't he identify himself? He referred to last night, so maybe it was him. But then, what was with that weird comment about intimacy?

I tried star 69 again, and again the number was blocked. I looked to see if Missy had come home last night, and it looked like she hadn't. Probably she had spent the night with whomever she had gone out with. I vowed to ask her about it later, I had forgotten to do so with the last message.

The phone rang again. Startled, I jumped a little and caught my breath, but still managed to answer it on the second ring.

"Hello."

"Hello. Is Faith there?"

My breath caught in my throat. It was a male's voice. "This is she," I whispered.

"Faith, hi, it's Max. From the other night at the bar."

Disappointment permitted me to breath freely. I should have known instantly that it wasn't Ethan, but oh well. "Hi Max, how are you?"

"Great. So you do remember me?"

"Of course. What's up?"

"Not much. I was wondering what you're up to later on today. I thought maybe you'd want to go out and get something to eat."

"Gosh, I can't. I already have plans." That was a lie, but it was possible to play hard-to-get with Max.

"Oh, sure," he said. "I figured it was probably too short notice. How about sometime next week?"

I contemplated for a moment, and decided it's never good to put all your eggs in one basket. Going out with Max could serve as a good distraction while waiting for Ethan to call. Plus, he seemed like a nice enough guy. Why not?

"Okay," I told him. "How about Thursday?"

"Thursday sounds great. I'll pick you up at seven."

I gave him my address, and we made small talk for a couple of minutes before we hung up. Afterwards I went into the kitchen to make myself some breakfast. There I found a note:

Faith —

Could you please try and do your share of the housework a little more often? Between physical therapy, meeting with my lawyer, and looking for a job, my hands are tied. The bathroom needs to be cleaned, and it wouldn't hurt to vacuum either. Thanks roomie!

Sincerely,

Missy

❋   ❋   ❋

I hated it when she did that. Missy often left notes for me when things were bothering her. I much preferred to just be told; that way I could respond. But when I told her this, Missy simply explained leaving notes was her way of communicating. However, I had to admit I hadn't been doing my share of the housework. So after some coffee and toast, I set to work cleaning the bathroom. I had about finished when the phone rang again. I went to answer it, and this time it was Carolyn.

"Hey, how did your date go?"

"Great. Well, pretty great." I told her about what happened, right up to the end, when things had seemed weird.

"Maybe he didn't want to rush things," she said. "I still think he'll call. A guy doesn't kiss you twice on the first date unless he's interested."

"I hope you're right."

"I am, don't worry. And if he doesn't call, all you have to do is find something else wrong with your car, then you'll have an excuse to see him again."

"Great Carolyn. Wouldn't that would make me seem a little desperate?"

"So what? You are desperate, aren't you?"

"Actually, no. You remember that guy Max, who's a friend of your friend David? He called and asked me out. We're going out next Thursday."

There was silence on the other end of the line. After a moment she spoke. "I didn't know you were interested in Max."

Carolyn had an edge to her voice, like she was annoyed or something. I didn't understand why. "I don't know that I am," I explained, "but he seemed nice enough. He asked me out, and I figured, why not?"

There was another tense pause. "Yeah, but don't you think that's leading him on? If you're not honestly interested, you shouldn't go out with him."

"Carolyn, what are you saying? You've never gone out with someone just for fun? Anyway, maybe after spending more time with him, I will be interested. Who knows?"

"I thought you were interested in Ethan."

"I am. But come on, what are the chances of that going anywhere? I mean, he's good looking and fun, but I doubt he's trustworthy."

"You never know," she said. "Maybe you're underestimating him."

"I hope you're right. But I still don't see what the big deal is about me going out with Max."

"It's not a big deal!" she snapped. "Forget it. Do what you want. You always do anyway."

"What's that supposed to mean?"

"Nothing. Never mind. Forget I said anything. Look, I have to go. I need to be at work in twenty minutes, and I'm not even ready."

"Okay, well, I'll talk to you later."

"Yeah, talk to you later."

We hung up, but I couldn't stop thinking about our conversation. I couldn't stand to have her mad at me, and had no idea what had even set her off. And what did she mean, I always do what I want? Was she one more in a long line of people who believed I was self-involved?

I was sitting, as if in a trance, mulling over these questions, when Missy walked in.

"Hey," I said. "How are you? Feeling any better?"

"I'm doing okay." She mumbled in a martyred tone.

"I got your note, and I cleaned the bathroom." I was getting really tired of conflict, and was now desperate to please someone, even if that someone was Missy.

Missy walked into the bathroom to perform an inspection, and came out after a couple of moments with a scowl on her face. "Thanks for doing that, Faith, but you didn't get around the toilet, and there are still streaks all over the mirror. Did you even try to clean them?"

"Um, I was going to, but the phone rang right as I was finishing up. Sorry, I forgot I hadn't done the mirror yet."

"You need to finish what you start, Faith."

If Carolyn hadn't just snapped me at I might have defended myself, but as it was, I was too vulnerable for another argument. Then I remembered the phone messages. I almost asked Missy about them, but decided against it. The mysterious one had to be for her; I probably was self-involved, thinking it was for me. I decided then and there to let the whole issue go.

❄ ❄ ❄

Several days went by, and nobody called me. I left a couple of messages for Carolyn, but she did not call back. Since moving down to Minneapolis her friendship had become even more important to me than before, so any amount of conflict with her was scary. The other person who hadn't called was Ethan. This was as sadly predictable as clicking on one of those "You're a Winner" pop-ups on the web, only to find it's a sham, and you're just like everyone else. Our date was just too good to be true, and it had only been a matter of time before he figured out I'm not exciting enough for him. Besides, we had no future. Sure, he was cute, but we had very little in common. No, it was good that he hadn't called. That's what I told myself, anyway.

In reality, my feelings about him were more complicated. I liked him, but I thought it was too soon for me to become involved with someone new. It would be better to be rejected now, before I had indubitably fallen for him, instead of months down the line, when he'd really be capable of breaking my heart. The way I saw it, if my heart was broken again, it could be damaged beyond repair.

However, when Thursday evening approached I worked to put myself in the right mindset for my date with Max. I was lucky he had called. He seemed liked the safe-bet sort of guy I had dated pre-Peter. That's what I needed. Forget the sensitive artist type, or the sexy mechanic. A normal guy I could take or leave fit my mood to the tee.

Max took me to Planet Hollywood in the Mall of America. As we sat across from each other, drinking elaborate cocktails, surrounded by pictures of Arnold Schwartzanaeger and Demi Moore, I found myself with nothing to say. He seemed to be having the same problem. But after studying his menu for several minutes, he closed it and attempted to engage me in conversation.

"So, what do you think of the mall? I thought since you were new here, you might want to see it."

"Oh, it's great. It's huge. I can't believe how big it is." I sounded like I was reading dialogue from a porn movie, but it was the best I could do. And it was big, that's for sure. There were four floors, each about a mile long in circumference. The bottom level had an amusement park with a huge roller coaster, visible from most points in the mall. But there was a reason why I hadn't gone to the Mall Of

America yet, and that was because I'd had no desire to go.

"Do you come here a lot?" I asked.

"Sometimes. It's nice if you want to get out of the city."

"And escape to suburbia?" I said, as a joke.

"Sure." Max's face was serious, and he put down the glossy drink menu he had still been fiddling with. He leaned forward and grabbed my hand. "I would love to get a place outside of the city at some point. I mean, the suburbs are so much cleaner, and safer. Plus, the schools in Minneapolis are lousy. If you're going to have kids you want to be living in the suburbs."

Holding hands with Max over drinks felt nothing like it had with Ethan. I gently pried my hand away from his, and started fishing for something in my purse, so it would seem like the reason I pulled away. I found some chapstick and put it on. After I was done I looked up, and he was still gazing at me, obviously waiting for me to respond.

"Um, I suppose. I mean, I've done some research on the schools here while looking for a job, and I know what you mean. But I still like the city. I just wish it wasn't so expensive. I would love to be able to live on my own."

"Yeah, me too." He had a roommate! Thank God – a common topic to discuss.

"Oh, does your roommate drive you crazy as well? Mine sure does. She leaves me all these notes every time she's annoyed about something, she runs a phone sex business from our apartment, and lately she's been freaking out because she got run over by a dog."

"What do you mean, she got run over by a dog?"

I started to answer, but he cut in. "Wait, never mind. I think I'd rather hear about the phone sex business." I laughed and explained the whole situation.

"Well," he said after I was finished, "my situation isn't quite that extreme. But David has women over all the time. Our walls are thin. It gets annoying."

"David from the bar? He's your roommate?"

"Yeah. I thought you knew that."

"No, I don't think you ever mentioned it."

"Oh, well, yeah. He and I have shared a place for a while now. And it's always been the same thing: One woman after another. They never last for long. The fact that your friend Carolyn has lasted for over a week is very impressive."

My stomach dived. All the background noise of the mall and the restaurant closed in on me, and I feared being sick right at the table. The expression on my face must have betrayed how I felt, because Max quickly stopped laughing. "Hey, what's wrong?" He reached for my hand again, and I was in too much shock to pull away.

"Are you sure it's Carolyn that's been coming over, and not somebody else?" I asked, hoping for the impossible.

"Well, yeah, I'm sure it's her. Why? What's wrong?"

"What's wrong?" I yelled, and more than a couple of heads turned our way. "She has a serious boyfriend who loves her! He wants to marry her, and she's throwing it all away! And on a creepy guy like your roommate! It's so completely screwed up, I can't even begin to tell you how wrong it is."

"Well, it's not like she's going to leave her boyfriend for David. He's never even heard of the word commitment." Max said this with a fake little laugh.

"You know, if you're going to make light of this..." I was so upset I was having trouble forming words. "Forget it, I'm out of here."

I stormed out of the restaurant and into the mall. I instantly felt lost. I would have to catch a bus or get a taxi home, but I had no idea where to do that. I was looking around for a mall directory when Max approached me.

"Hey, are you alright?"

"Gee, do I look like I'm alright?"

He scratched his forehead as if he was solving a complicated puzzle. "No. And I understand that you're upset. But I don't understand why you're upset with me."

He actually looked kind of sweet standing there with such a concerned and confused expression on his face. "I'm not upset with you," I conceded.

"Then let me take you home." He reached out his hand, and

this time I took it willingly. We walked to his car, and drove back to my place in silence. When we got there, he came in without being asked. Then, for reasons I'll never be able to explain, I cried on his shoulder for a long time.

I'm not particularly religious, and until several months ago, I don't know that I honestly believed in things such as sin or betrayal. I always naively assumed that true betrayal lies within; when you do something wrong, you are merely betraying yourself by going against your own conscience or desire. But now I think wronging others is a much bigger sin than wronging yourself—but it's impossible to commit one of these sins without committing the other.

9

Suppose you're driving back from a camping trip, the first trip you've ever taken together. You stop at a rest area, and after coming out of the bathroom you can't find him. But soon you discover a trail leading to a scenic overlook a few feet away from the park building. You assume correctly he walked down, because there he is, getting a fantastic view of Lake Superior's rocky cliffs, the wind causing his hair to stick out in all directions.

It is cold, and your thin jacket doesn't protect you from the harsh elements. "Hey," you shout into the wind, "are you ready? It's freezing out here."

He doesn't turn to look at you, but keeps his gaze focused down the shore. "Come here for a second." He motions forward with his arm.

"Peter..."

"Come on. Just for a second."

You walk the narrow path towards him. As soon as you are within his reach, he grabs you in a hug, then unaffected by onlookers, gives you a leisurely kiss. After several moments he pulls away, and with gentle hands turns you around to face the lake.

He whispers in your ear. "Isn't it beautiful?" Your emotions are so powerful they take on a life of their own. A moment before you felt disgusting after camping for several days, only thoughts of a hot shower occupied your mind. But now every ounce of you is consumed with him.

He remains behind you, his arms wrapped around your stomach. You feel as safe and warm as when your mom used to give you hot chocolate after you played outside on snow days. He whispers in your ear, sending a balmy shiver down your spine. "Don't say anything in response, okay? I don't want you to say anything. But I want you to know … I love you."

You don't say a word; instead you answer him with a passionate kiss. And after the moment is over, you get back in the car and drive home to reality. But you carry the experience with you, ecstatic with the proof that love can be perfect, even if only for a glimmer of time.

When Peter broke up with me that memory shattered as if he had purposefully taken my favorite childhood mug—the one "Santa" gave me with my name painted on it, and threw it against a cold stone floor. But I hadn't given up my romantic notions of love. Love may not exist for me, but it did for other people. After all, look at Charles and Carolyn.

Finding out Carolyn was cheating on Charles was almost as devastating as being dumped by Peter for Lacey. Like I said, I couldn't explain that to anyone, including Max. He was really nice that evening, and although I apologized for crying so much on our first date, I was sure the whole episode would scare him off.

He said he'd call, but I figured I would hear from him about as soon as I'd hear from Ethan, as in, the week after never. If things didn't turn around soon, I was doomed to be alone for the rest of my life. All of my friends had left me, no guys were interested, and to top things off, I couldn't even get a job interview.

I resolved to take the bull by the horns, so to speak. My big summer paycheck was not going to last forever, so I decided to get a job doing something other than teaching. Maybe when the school year started I would sign up as a substitute teacher, in hopes of landing a permanent job through the back door. But for the time being, I needed a routine. I needed somewhere in this city I could call my own.

I'm amazed it took me so long to think of it. But one morning when I went into Cafe Panoply for my regular cup of coffee, Sally made her usual comment about how she needs someone for early morning shifts. This time I responded differently.

"Sally," I said, "you don't have to sell the place. I'll work the early morning shift."

She stopped filling up my cup mid-way, and turned to me. "You? You want to work here? Do you know how to work in a coffee shop?"

"Yes!" I said, with more bravado than necessary. "I have all sorts of experience from when I lived up in Duluth." So what if my experience was limited to what I learned from Peter working in a similar setup; Sally didn't have to know that.

She looked as if she didn't know what to say. "I don't know Faith. Are you sure it's what you want? You're a trained professional. Don't you think you're a little beyond working here?"

I laughed. "Sally, I could kiss you for calling me a trained professional. I don't think I've ever heard anyone refer to a teacher that way!"

She was obviously flustered, and started to arrange the pastries on the shelf below. "Well, you are a trained professional. You shouldn't think so little of yourself."

For a moment I thought I was going to cry. It had been a long time since someone had been so nice to me. "Sally, all I know is I feel more at home here than anywhere in Minneapolis. I need a job, and you need someone you can rely on. I can't promise you I'll stay forever, and I'll need a few days off in July for my parents' stuffing convention, but I do want to work here. So, how about it? Will you give me a chance?"

Sally raised herself back up, and when she looked at me, it was with a grin on her face. "I thought you'd never ask." Then she walked out from behind the counter, and gave me a hug. We were in the middle of our embrace when Bill walked in.

"Sally!" his deep voice boomed, "do I have competition? I thought I was your favorite customer!"

She let go of me and smiled. "Don't worry, you still are. Faith is going to start working here, so she'll no longer be a customer. Do you know Faith?"

He placed his laptop down the nearest table. "Oh, yes! Faith and I go way back. Welcome to Cafe Panoply, Faith." He held his hand out to mine, I assumed to shake it. But once our hands made contact he drew mine to his mouth and kissed it lightly. All I could do was laugh at his goofiness.

"Don't mind Bill," Sally said. "He's a huge flirt."

Bill responded. "That may be true Sally, but you're always my favorite girl."

I walked back to my apartment, my dark mood partially lifted. At least someone wanted me, even if it was only to work behind a counter. Besides, maybe I would meet people working there. Things were looking up.

When I got to my door I found something had been left outside of it. It was a nightlight, the cheap kind you can buy at the drug store. There was no note, but it was obvious by the way it had been propped up against the door that it had been deliberately placed there.

Then, when I got inside, there was another message. "Hey, it's me. I hope you like your present. Maybe it will help to shed some light on all your issues." It was the same voice as the last two times. Determined not to freak out, I told myself it had to be a friend of Missy's. Yet I wasn't sure if Missy had any friends.

I went and sat down on the couch, still holding the nightlight. Maybe if I sat and stared at it, holding it in my hand, I might pick up some sort of vibe. I figured it was worth a try. I studied every angle of the light – its cheap plastic construction, its Walgreen's label, the way the upper part was modeled like a miniature lantern. I felt nothing, though. My skin didn't hurt, my toes didn't itch; no visions came to me. Oh well, even when my powers were at their strongest I'd never been able to pick up much through objects.

When Missy got home a few minutes later I asked her about it. After playing her the message, and showing her the nightlight, she had no real insight into the situation either. Missy had been using the line I put in for her personal calls, in order to keep her "telemarketing" separate, so she had already heard the messages.

"I figured those messages were from someone you knew," she said, fiddling with the nightlight. "Hey, do you mind if I keep this? I was going to buy one for my room anyway."

"Keep it – that's fine. But Missy, are you sure? You have no idea who it could be?" She shook her head. "What about your customers? Could it be someone you talk to on the phone?"

"No," she replied cheerily. "The agency I go through promises complete anonymity. There's no way my customers can trace me."

"Then who is it? Don't you think it's a little creepy, this guy is calling, and he knows where we live?"

"I wouldn't worry about it Faith." She seemed to be in an awfully good mood. "It all seems rather harmless to me. Anyway, I have exciting news!"

"Oh, yeah?" I said, reluctant to change the topic of conversation.

"I found a new job!" she announced, and for a moment she looked like she was going to start jumping up and down. "I'm a dancer! Can you believe it? I've always wanted to be a dancer, and now I am one! I started last night. I went in, and they said they'd try me out, and so I stayed and danced that night, and at the end of the evening, they hired me!"

Hmmm... I knew Missy wanted me to be as excited for her as she was, but something was off. Still, I tried. "That's great Missy, I'm glad that you're happy. But... where did you say you're going to be dancing?"

"De Ja Vu." she said, and her face glowed. De Ja Vu was a popular "gentlemen's club" downtown. Their slogan, painted on their door, was "1000 pretty girls and three ugly ones."

"So, um, when you say dancing, you mean you're going to be, uh, stripping."

Her smile faded. "Well, yeah, if you want to put a label on it!" she snapped. "But have you ever tried it, Faith? It's not as easy as it looks. It takes a lot of skill, and a lot of strength." Then she paused for a moment, as revelation spread across her face. "Hey, you're looking for a job! You should try it! You can make good money, and we could work together! It would be great! Do you want to go down there with me tonight? I'll introduce you..."

I cut her off. Thank God I could now say this. "Actually, I got a job. But thanks anyway."

"Oh, you got a job? Where?"

"Right down the street, at Cafc Panoply." I said this with a smile, but apparently Missy was about as happy for me as I was for Missy.

"You're going to work at a coffee shop? But you'll make next to nothing there! You won't believe the money you can make as a dancer. Why, last night I got over a hundred in tips alone."

"I know, but this is temporary, until I find a job teaching."

"Why not work temporarily as a dancer?"

"Because," I retorted, "no school will hire me to teach children if they knew I took my clothes off for money!"

With that Missy's face fell, and I instantly regretted my words. "I'm sorry Missy. I didn't mean... It's not the right thing for me, that's all."

"Never mind," she said. "Tell me, why is serving people coffee so much better than dancing naked?"

Perhaps she had a point, I mean, who was she hurting by being a stripper? Before I could articulate my thoughts, she went into her room and slammed the door. My eyes glanced down, and I noticed she had left the nightlight abandoned on the coffee table. In a half-hearted gesture of apology I picked it up and left it propped outside of her bedroom door, much the way I had originally found it.

❄ ❄ ❄

The next morning I was trained in at my new job. Sally walked me through all of my responsibilities. She went through everything from watering the plants to taking out the garbage. Most importantly, I was to double check that the drawer in the cash register was starting out at an even hundred by counting all of the money. I was sure it was all fairly simple, but Sally went through it all so quickly I was afraid I would forget something important.

I had never actually worked in a coffee shop, but I knew a lot about it after being with Peter for two years. He talked about his job all the time, and one night for fun, he snuck me into the shop after closing to teach me to make drinks on the espresso machine. That first morning I tried hard to remember what he taught me, while I tried to forget the memory of slinging milk foam at each other, and how he had grabbed me, and then we kissed all of the spots on each other's bodies where the milk landed. "Move on," I told myself. "Focus. All you need to do is forget about love for a while, and focus."

Actually, I was handling my first morning rush quite well. I was keeping up with the drink orders, and maintaining a pleasant attitude, even when customers were rude. Of course, since it was my first day Sally stayed to help me, which I was glad of. That is, until Ethan happened to walk in.

I didn't notice him at first. It was around 8:30, and I had just finished serving a customer a scone and a double skim cappuccino when I heard his trademark drawl. "Faith," he said. "When did you start working here?

I looked up and there he was, standing before me, with a shocked but not unhappy expression on his face. He was as cute as ever in his work shirt, worn jeans, and dark rimmed glasses. His hair was still wet from his morning shower, and it was slicked back from his forehead, with one stray curl hanging down. He was freshly shaven, and I could smell his aftershave from where he was standing.

"Hey Ethan, what's up? What can I get you?" I plastered a fake smile on my face, aware of Sally watching me.

His smile seemed more genuine than mine, but I wasn't buying it. If he wanted to see me, he could have called, and he hadn't.

"When did you start working here?" he asked again. "I'm here every morning, and I've never seen you before."

"This is my first day."

"Wow," he said, "So what about teaching? Have you given up on that?"

I wanted to answer. Engaging in friendly conversation with someone who understood me was something I desperately needed after the week I had had. But flirting with a man at a coffee shop was too familiar a feeling, even if I was the one now standing behind the counter. I had to avoid the inevitable pain I knew would come from associating with Ethan.

My voice was like bright blue antifreeze. "I've given up on a lot of things." I said this as I looked long and hard into his eyes. "Can I get you anything? I'm very busy, so I actually can't talk."

He stepped back as if he had been slapped. But he recovered quickly, and handed me his stainless steel travel mug. "Fill it up with the French Roast, please." I did so, and handed it back to him. As he dug into his pocket for some change there was this seven and a half hour long silence between us. He paid for his coffee, but before he turned to leave, he said, "Good luck, Faith. See you around."

I assumed that meant goodbye. That was spectacular. No more waiting around, wondering if he was going to call. Now I knew he wouldn't. And as I'd already told myself, if he wasn't the wrong guy for me, this was definitely the wrong time.

I worked in a daze for the next five or ten minutes, too consumed with my own thoughts to notice much around me. "Miss! Excuse me, I'm in a hurry here." An impatient customer pulled me out of my reverie: a skinny woman in her early thirties, dressed all in black. From her dark hair done up in a French twist, to her manicured burgundy nails, everything about her appearance was impeccable and composed. She looked like the exact antithesis of how I felt.

"Sorry. What can I get you?"

"I need a large skim half decaf latte. Double on the espresso. Lots of foam, but don't over-heat the milk. I hate that."

"Sure." I went over the to espresso machine. Now, lets see, how did Sally say you make something half decaf? I looked over to ask her, but she had gone in the back.

"Is there a problem?" said my customer, tapping her nails against the counter.

"Not at all!" My reply was all sugar. Forget the half decaf thing.

This woman was already high maintenance enough, so I decided to save myself, and the people whom she worked with some trouble, and I made her latte all decaf. As I did this I made sure that my back was covering the espresso machine, but it was impossible to prevent her from having a perfect view of me steaming the milk.

Her eyes interrogated me, and then her voice did as well. "Don't you think you've steamed that enough? Remember, I don't like it too hot!"

"It will be done in a moment!" Her blazing stare made me nervous. I couldn't get the milk to foam at all, and it was probably already way too hot for her. I should have dumped the milk and started over, but a line had formed, and other people had become impatient. I poured the hot, flat milk in the cup, and put a lid on it, hoping she wouldn't notice.

No such luck. As soon as I handed her the cup, she took the lid off to inspect it. "Where's the foam? Were you not listening to me? This is not what I wanted at all. You need to do this over."

Groans and impatient sighs came from the people behind her. "Look, why don't I just not charge you for this one? There's a line..."

Her flat laugh cut me off. "You certainly won't charge me for this, nor for the next one, which you will make correctly. I am not going to let your incompetence ruin my morning."

My inclination was to run out of that coffee shop and never come back. But instead I turned around and tried to make her drink again. This one turned out no better. "I'm sorry," I said. "It's my first day...."

"So in other words, you don't know what you're doing. Jesus! Where's Sally? Sally!"

Sally came out from the back. She said in a calm voice, "Did you need something, Glenn?"

"Yeah, I need my coffee. This inept girl messed up my drink twice, and she was rude to me as well."

My mouth fell open. "Sally, I'm sorry, but I was not rude!"

Sally put her hand on my shoulder. "Faith, that's enough for today. I'll see you tomorrow."

"But, there's still two more hours in my shift! Don't you want me to stay and help? There's a line..."

"Sally!" At Glenn's command, Sally's head snapped towards her direction. "I'm already late. Please! I need my drink."

"Faith, just go. We'll talk tomorrow." Sally said this softly, but I was in no way reassured. I left, more frustrated with myself than anything.

And then, when I thought my morning could not become any worse, I saw her standing at the front door of my apartment building, buzzing in vain to be let in. Before I could turn around and hide, she turned and saw me.

"Oh. There you are. Do you have a minute? We should talk."

My shoulders sagged as I walked towards her. "Sure Carolyn. Let's talk."

10

We walked up the stairs silently. When we got inside I was disappointed for once that Missy wasn't home. Then maybe this conversation could have been postponed. Thomas was asleep on the couch, his big orange belly turned up and out, begging to be petted. However he got up as soon as we approached, as if he could feel the tension we had brought into the room.

Carolyn reminded me of a toothache drowned in Novocain. She was wearing a short loose dress, her hair was up and her makeup done. But she was pale underneath the artificial color on her face, and her eyes were flat.

I didn't ask her to sit down, and I didn't sit myself, other than leaning against the arm of the sofa. Carolyn walked over to the window and looked out. With her back to me, she said, "How did your date with Max go?"

I refused to make it easy for her. "Fine. Why do you ask?"

Carolyn turned around, her arms crossed over her chest, as if to shield herself. "Did he talk about me at all?"

"Yeah, he did."

"Oh. I sort of figured, when I hadn't heard from you..."

"Carolyn, in case you forgot, I called you twice since you accused me of always doing what I want. You didn't return either call, so I gave up. Yeah, Max told me about you and David, but that's only one of the reasons why I didn't contact you. You accuse me of being self-centered when you're the one who is only thinking about yourself!"

Facing me, Carolyn picked at the hem of her dress, and avoided looking me in the eye. "This has nothing to do with you, Faith. I am kind of messed up right now. I'm sorry though, okay?"

Her vulnerability should have caused my heart to melt, but instead my temper exploded. "No, not okay. How can you do that to Charles? He loves you, Carolyn! He trusts you! How can you betray that? And how can you look to me for sympathy, when you know that.... that I was like Charles not too long ago? I trusted someone, and he hurt me, for no real reason! And now you're doing the same thing to this fantastic guy! I'm sorry, but I can't take your side on this one!"

Carolyn stood up straight as her arms fell to her side. "I see. And you're not even interested in hearing my side of the story? Did it ever occur to you that Charles and I aren't so perfect? I tried to tell you that before, but you didn't want to hear it, because it was too important for you to believe otherwise."

"How would you know what's important to me? Don't give me that. I moved down here, partly because it was important to you! And now this happens...."

"Yeah," she cried. "It happened. I cheated on Charles, not on you! And if you could get down from your moral high horse for one second, you would see I'm your friend who needs help!" Carolyn threw herself into a chair, and her head fell into her hands. "I know what I did was wrong. And I ended it, okay?" She took a deep breath. "And if you want to judge me, fine, I suppose I deserve it. But don't turn away from me."

I sat on the couch across from her. "Then help me understand why, Carolyn. Why would you cheat on Charles?

"I can't tell you why. I don't know why I did it. I just know that Charles and I want different things."

"That's the exact reason Peter gave for breaking up with me."

"Well, sometimes it's a legitimate reason."

"No, I don't believe it is. If you want different things, then you talk about it. Jumping into someone else's bed is not the solution!"

"I didn't jump, Faith. This was a long time coming."

"I still don't get how you can justify..."

"I'm not trying to justify it Faith, I'm trying to explain!" Carolyn yelled this to the ceiling. "You said you wanted to hear it."

I slumped back. "Fine, go ahead." Carolyn reached out and placed her hand on my arm.

"It's different, Faith. And I'm not Peter. Please, I'm begging you, hear me out."

I took her hand from my arm, and placed it in my own. I squeezed it, which was about the best that I could do at the moment. "Okay, I'm listening."

She exhaled, and began. "Well, I would read about the theater that's going on in New York, and I would hear from friends who were there, and I began to resent Charles for keeping me here. Maybe it's unfair, but it's how I felt. And after that fight we had, you know, the night you and I went out? He was very angry when he came home and I was gone. I apologized many times, tried to talk to him, but all he would do is pout. Then two nights later, David came into Palomino."

Palomino is the restaurant where Carolyn works. "Did he know that you work there before he came in?"

"I mentioned it to him at the C.C. Club. Anyway, I had been having a terrible night, Charles was barely speaking to me earlier that day, all of my customers had been rude, I had dropped a tray of food, gotten yelled at by the manager; it was bad. Then David showed up, offered to buy me a drink after my shift. I said yes."

I squeezed her hand again. "Okay, I can understand you going out for a drink. But did you have to sleep with him?"

"No, but I wanted to. I KNOW that's selfish. But being with David made it seem like it was possible to have the life I had always planned for myself, that maybe I could break out of here, and be someone else. I thought if I was capable of cheating on Charles, I was capable of leaving him as well." Carolyn's voice grew husky and her eyes teared up. "But I don't know if I actually am. Yet every time I try to talk to him about how I feel, he shuts me down or changes the subject. He's afraid to discuss our relationship."

"Carolyn, it's up to you then, to force the issue."

"That's easier said than done. The last thing I want to do is hurt Charles. But I'm thinking I should just break up with him."

Even though I knew she had been about to say that, shock delayed my simple reply. "Are you sure?"

"No. But I can't not tell him about David. It isn't honest. And how can I think about a future with Charles if I can't even be honest with him? But if I told him, he'd break up with me anyway, so...."

"Maybe you should tell him, then let him decide."

"Right. Maybe. But either way, it's going to be awful."

Carolyn reached for the box of tissue Missy kept on the coffee table. After she blew her nose and wiped her face, she looked at me, and noticed for the first time I was still wearing my apron from the coffee shop. "Hey, why are you wearing that apron?"

"It's a long story. A lot has gone on since we last talked."

She forced a smile. "Oh, well, do you want to give me the highlights?"

"No. Lets talk more about you. "

My short-lived career as a barista, my stripper roommate, Ethan, Max, the fact I was maybe being stalked: I could wait to tell her about all of it. Today I was determined to do nothing but listen.

❋　❋　❋

The next morning at 6:00am I returned to the coffee shop, fearing Sally would tell me I no longer had a job. When I walked in I found her humming to herself while restocking the paper products.

"Hey Sally, how are you?" I said, bracing myself for the worst.

She looked at me with a smile. "Faith! Good morning. Ready for another day of drudge work?"

"You mean I'm not fired?"

Sally finished stuffing napkins into the dispenser, picked up the box they come from and walked towards the back. "Of course you're not fired. Glenn is always like that. She treats every person who works here the same. Why do you think I have so much trouble keeping employees?"

"Oh." So I wasn't the only one who had been terrorized by that evil girl! "Well, if she's always like that, why don't you tell her that she's banned from the shop? I can't imagine anyone would miss her. She was plain awful!"

Sally paused at the door, and the smile she had been wearing faded from her face. "I'd miss her. You see, Glenn is my daughter."

I instantly apologized to Sally, saying things like, "I'm sure I just need to get to know her better," and, "It's my fault. She was probably having a bad morning, and I made it worse." Sally nodded and accepted my words, but I worried she was just too nice to actually express her anger.

I scratched my head in confusion over the whole matter. How had someone as kind as Sally spawned someone as evil as Glenn? I found this especially troubling since I had been looking to Sally for a bit of maternal-like comfort every now and again. Plus, this meant that I would be seeing Glenn on a daily basis, and I couldn't complain if her treatment towards me continued to be dreadful.

My thoughts were interrupted by my work duties. "Faith, can you go get the baked goods and lay them out," Sally asked from the back. I did so, and afterwards I brewed the coffee. Soon I was absorbed in the task of running a coffee shop, and once we opened and customers came, there was no time to further discuss or apologize for my earlier mistake.

And, despite everything, my second morning of work went fairly well. I was keeping up with the drink orders, and even had a little time to make conversation with the customers. A lot of them were around my age, so I pegged a few as potential friend material. Not that I was looking for dates. Listening to Carolyn's tormented confessions the night before had only strengthened my resolve that love was not for me, at least not for the time being.

So it didn't matter that I hadn't seen Ethan come in that morning. However, it did matter that I would have to deal with Glenn again. When she approached, she wore the same air of impeccability and aggression as she had the day before. The only blessing was this time, there wasn't a line.

She marched right up to the counter, and simply said, "Same as yesterday. Get it right today, okay?"

I had been wiping the counter, so I put down my sponge, and mentally tried to dissolve the butterflies in my stomach. "You wanted a double skim latte, heavy on the foam?"

"Isn't that what I said? And foam means foam, understand?"

I looked briefly to make sure Sally was nowhere within earshot before I made my sarcastic reply. "Actually, no. Please explain it to me."

Without missing a beat, Glenn retorted, "It means you need to learn how to do your job. I realize it's hard for Sally to find intelligent people for this type of work...."

"Excuse me," I said. "Yesterday was my first day, I was still learning. And I happen to be very intelligent. In fact, normally I work as an English teacher. This is only temporary, so I'd appreciate it if you would ease up on me a little."

Glenn smirked. "You're a teacher? Well that's one reason why our educational system is in crisis."

I said nothing—I decided it was better to keep my cool. And I did myself proud. I had just finished making the perfect latte, not too hot with a lot of foam, when Ethan walked in. I concentrated and kept my mojo working, and I even managed to hand Glenn her drink without spilling it. However, she wasn't even paying attention.

"Ethan! Here you are! I'm so sorry we missed each other yesterday!" She spoke as if she was a completely different person – one who didn't eat kittens for breakfast.

"Yeah, I think I got here a little early." He put his arm around her waist and kissed her on the top of her head. Motionless, I stood there, unable to do anything but stare.

"Hi Faith, how are you this morning?" Ethan still had his arm around Glenn, but stood facing me.

"You know her?" Glenn asked.

Ethan's cheeks were slightly flushed, and his words weren't emitted with their usual confidence. "Yeah, I fixed her car a few weeks ago. Glenn, this is Faith. Faith, this is Glenn."

"His girlfriend." Glenn added. Then, maintaining her benevolent bearing, she extended her hand to me and said, "It's so nice to meet you."

I wanted to pour Glenn's perfect latte all over her overly made-up face. I certainly didn't want to shake her hand. But I was worried that any action, or non-action against Glenn, would be interpreted by Ethan as jealousy. So I shook her hand. "Likewise," I said.

Ethan handed me his stainless steel mug. "Can you fill this up with the French Roast?" he asked. Then he spoke to Glenn. "Why don't you go find us a table?" She complied, and Ethan stood alone at the counter while I filled his mug with coffee. The dispenser was nearly empty, and the coffee dripped out in a slow trickle. Ethan shifted his weight from foot to foot, but said nothing. After what seemed like hours his mug was finally full.

I handed it to him, and said, "So do I charge you, or is free coffee a perk of dating the owner's daughter?"

He pulled out his wallet and handed me three one-dollar bills. "Here, put the rest in the tip jar."

I took one of the dollar bills and put it in the cash register. The other two I held out to him. "That's okay. I'm not *that* hard-up."

His hand stayed by his side. "Look, I get that you're upset with me, and I'm sorry I couldn't call you like I said I was going to. But there are things about my situation you don't understand. I'm going to be coming in here a lot, so it would be good if we could at least be friends."

I placed the bills down in front of him, but he still did not pick them up. "Don't worry. You're a customer. It's my job to be friendly to you and your girlfriend. Just don't assume it's anything more than professional courtesy."

"She's not my...." Ethan broke off, and with a burst of frustration, grabbed the bills and shoved them in his pocket. "You know what, never mind. I'd explain everything to you, but why waste my breath? You obviously don't want to hear it." He stomped away, and joined Glenn at the table where she sat.

"He's cute, isn't he?" Sally's words from behind startled me. "I saw you talking to him yesterday. He's charming, but a real heart-breaker."

I picked the sponge back up to finish wiping the counter I had been working on before Glenn had come in. "What do you mean, isn't he dating Glenn?" I tried to sound casual, even though I felt anything but.

"Yeah," Sally sighed. "Be careful, okay?"

"Sure." What did she mean? Careful how? Careful as in, don't steal my daughter's man? Careful as in, he'll hurt you so stay away? I would have asked, but I didn't want to upset Sally anymore than I already had. Besides, a new customer walked in, so I pushed Glenn and Ethan to the back of my mind.

But I puzzled over why I hadn't seen any of this Glenn/Ethan stuff coming. Maybe it was like I was Superman and Ethan was kryptonite – he deleted any psychic ability I may have had. Then again, I couldn't be sure it was Ethan. Maybe it was Minneapolis in general, or perhaps it was all the heartbreak I had recently been through.

I was reminded of this time at the dentist's office when I glanced at *Reader's Digest*, and read a true account of this guy who had been struck by lightening twice. After the first time he was struck he gained an ability to communicate with animals, sort of like the pet psychic. He made a lot of money from it. Then two years later, he was struck by lightening again, and he completely lost his ability to know what animals were thinking.

Perhaps Peter dumping me was my first bolt of lightening, only in reverse. The pain he inflicted caused me to lose my powers, and what I needed was to be shaken up again to get them back. Then again, in that same issue of *Reader's Digest* I took this MENSA quiz, and found out I'm a genius, which I doubt is true. So I suppose I shouldn't take that other article too seriously either. Besides, I was about to make an incredibly accurate prediction, whether I wanted it to happen or not.

$$11$$

That night I dreamt that I was on an all female jury, and the other members were Missy, Carolyn, and my sister Margaret. The person who was on trial was Ethan. I don't remember exactly what he was on trial for, but the judge was Judge Judy. And she kept yelling, telling us we can't judge someone until we've walked a mile in their shoes.

I thought that was both a clichéd and hypocritical thing for her to say, because I've watched her show, and she judges people all the time. But none of us said anything except for Margaret, who stood up and replied, "Well, I've walked a long way in my own shoes to get here, and I'll judge whomever I please, thank you very much."

Judge Judy scowled at Margaret, and at first I was worried she'd get her head bitten off. But no.

"You are a brave young woman, Margaret," Judge Judy said. "I hope you do better in Minneapolis than the rest of these young woman are."

"Don't worry," said Margaret. "I plan to."

Then I woke up. My skin and my toes itched simultaneously. My body didn't know if this was going to be good or bad, but I knew without a doubt Margaret would be showing up at my door later that day.

"Surprise!" she exclaimed, at 6:38 that evening, when I opened the door to find her standing there, along with three suitcases. Margaret doesn't own a lot of stuff, so it meant she was staying for a while.

"Did you bring everything you own?"

"What kind of welcome is that? Aren't you even surprised?" Margaret grabbed two of her bags, and shoved past me into the apartment. "Can you grab the other one?" she said, over her shoulder.

The bag she had left for me was the largest and the heaviest. I picked it up and followed her in. "Of course I'm not surprised. I had a dream last night. I've known all day you were coming."

"Faith, you need to give this psychic bit a rest."

"It's not a bit, Margaret. I dreamt we were on a jury, and you announced to Judge Judy that you walked to Minneapolis."

"But I didn't walk, I drove."

I took a deep breath. "That's not the point. I'm just saying I knew..." Why was I even bothering? "Look, never mind. What are you doing here?"

"Why? Was that not explained in your dream?"

"Margaret..."

Margaret strolled into the kitchen. "I got sick of my Green Peace job. All those college kids I supervised were such brats! I couldn't take it anymore." She opened the refrigerator and grabbed some leftover pasta, then sat down at the kitchen table, where she proceeded to eat it with her hands. "And the job market in Duluth is impossible! So I thought I'd find something down here. You don't mind if I crash on your couch for a while, do you?"

Of course I minded. Margaret and I had never been close, and my life was complicated enough without throwing her into the mix. "You know Margaret, I wish you had called first before just coming down here, expecting to move in."

"What difference does it make, if you already knew I was coming?"

"Last night I dreamt you were coming, that doesn't mean I could communicate with you in time to tell you not to come."

Margaret smiled in victory. "Well, then maybe you ought to work on your telepathic abilities, because here I am."

I said nothing, instead I kicked the suitcase closest to my foot, wishing I could kick Margaret instead. Living with her was sure to drive me over the edge.

As if she could read my thoughts, she said, "Oh, come on Faith, what's the big deal? It will only be for a few days, until I can find a place of my own. Don't be selfish about it."

The door opened, and in walked Missy, decked out in bright pink stretch pants and a leotard. Since she had gotten her new job she only ever dressed in workout gear, even if she was just going out to run errands. "Hey roomie! How are ya?" Missy looked to her left, and spotted Margaret. "Oh, you have a visitor, who is this?"

Margaret shot up, and rubbed her hand against her worn pant leg to remove the remains of pasta. She then walked across the room to Missy, her hand stretched out, ready to shake. "Hi, I'm Margaret, Faith's little sister. It's so nice to meet you."

Missy shook Margaret's hand. "Oh! You're Faith's sister. Well it's nice to meet you too. I'm Missy."

"Yes, I know. Faith has told me all sorts of wonderful things about you." Margaret held out her arm, indicating the apartment Missy had recently cleaned. "And this is a lovely place you have here."

"Well, thanks." Missy eyed Margaret up and down, noticing her messy brown hair, self tie-dyed t-shirt and second hand, ill-fitting men's Levi 501s. She looked down and saw Margaret's bags. "Are you going to be staying here?"

Margaret smiled and shrugged her shoulders. "Actually, I don't think so." She threw an almost neutral glare in my direction. "Faith seems to have a problem with the idea. But it was so nice meeting you. I am going to be staying in the area, so maybe we can have coffee sometime."

This was typical Margaret. On the surface she's an organic-granola-love-all-living-things type, but underneath it all is the mind of a politician. I previously told her Missy was needy and that she was dying for friends, so Margaret came in here and flattered her and said she wanted to do stuff with her. And it worked. Missy's gaze switched from Margaret to me.

"Faith! Why don't you want Margaret to stay with us? There's plenty of room! Margaret, you can stay on the couch for as long as you like!"

"Oh, I don't know. I don't think that's the best idea. I mean, if Faith doesn't want me to..."

"Margaret," I said, "It's just that things are sort of hectic, that's all."

Missy laughed. "How are things hectic? You work at a coffee shop. You're not dating anyone. If you ask me, you need more of a life. Maybe having your sister down here will help."

I went into the kitchen, and poured myself the remains of a bottle of wine opened the other night. With my back to them, I answered. "Thanks, Missy, but I didn't ask you. And by the way, I won't pass judgment on your line of work, if you don't pass judgment on mine."

"What kind of work do you do, Missy?" Margaret and I hadn't talked on the phone recently, so she honestly didn't know.

"Oh, I'm a dancer."

"Wow!" gushed Margaret, "how exciting!"

"And I do some telemarketing from home. It pays the bills."

"How enterprising of you."

Missy smiled brighter than our fluorescent ceiling lamp. "Thanks, I like to think so." She spoke to me. "Faith, I don't see why she can't stay. Don't you think you're being a little selfish in saying no?"

I didn't answer right away, because I had decided chocolate ice cream would go perfectly with the wine I was drinking. I retrieved some from the freezer, and ate it straight out of the carton. I knew that would annoy Missy.

"That's exactly what I said!" exclaimed Margaret. "We must think alike."

Missy giggled. "Then I don't care what Faith says. It's my apartment too. You'll stay here as my guest."

The battle was over and I had lost. So I backtracked. I had been accused of selfishness so much lately it was beginning not to faze me, plus, a house divided against itself cannot stand. I was relatively sure the same held true for apartments.

"Margaret," I said while trying to unclench my teeth, "obviously you're welcome to stay. However, with my new job I need to be up at

5:30 every morning. So no noise late at night, okay?"

"Sure." Her look reminded me of my high school students, an expression they would wear when trying to convince me they hadn't cheated on a paper, even when I had proof they had. Her widened eyes gazed directly into my own. "I won't get in your way at all. You'll hardly even notice I'm here."

"And if you want to make noise at night, you can come out with me!" said Missy. "You can come watch me dance. It will be great!"

"Oh, I would love that!"

Carrying my wine and ice cream, I went into my bedroom and opened a book. It had been another long day, and I had another early morning to wake up to. Better to leave them to each other, since my presence obviously wasn't needed.

I woke up feeling sorry for myself. It would be my fourth morning at the coffee shop. The previous day had passed without incident. When Ethan and Glenn came in I treated them like I would any other customers. They didn't say much of anything to me, which suited me just fine. But later that day I had the chance to ask Sally what she had meant about being careful around Ethan.

"Oh, you know. He's one of those guys; he'll break your heart without a second thought. I wish Glenn would have nothing to do with him, but unfortunately, that isn't happening."

"How long have they been going out?"

"A few months. They met here, actually. He owns a shop rather close by, so he comes in a lot. Anyway, they started dating, and Ethan swept her off her feet. Things were going great, until Glenn got pregnant."

"What? Glenn's pregnant?"

"Not anymore." Sally struggled to get her next words out, as I silently cursed myself for feeling relieved. "She had a miscarriage. But when Ethan found out she was going to have a baby, he broke up with her."

"No way."

"It was awful," continued Sally. "Glenn was heartbroken. Then, when she had the miscarriage, she was even worse. I thought my poor girl was going to fall apart. It was all I could do not to shake the life out of that boy myself. The final straw, however, was when Ethan wanted to get back together once he heard she was no longer pregnant."

"Oh my God!" My head was reeling—Ethan was the evil one and Glenn was to be pitied.

"And what really blows my mind, Faith, is that she took him back! I'm not sure exactly what the status of their relationship is. They don't seem to be as close as they used to. But they meet here every morning. I told Glenn he was no longer welcome, but she raised such a fit that I caved in. I'll be polite to him, but that's it. And if you're smart, you'll stay away from him. I'm telling you, Faith; he's bad news. If you want a boyfriend, go after Bill. He's nice, stable, and has a good job. I keep hoping Glenn will find him attractive."

I nodded my head in agreement and left it at that. There was no point in complicating the situation even more by telling Sally about my date with Ethan. I vowed to myself to put all thoughts of Ethan out of my mind, once and for all.

But on that morning of my fourth day, he came in a couple of minutes early, without Glenn. Sally had left, having decided I was doing well enough on my own to handle the place. Ethan walked up to the counter, and handed me his stainless steel cup. Without a word I filled it with French Roast and handed it back to him.

"Have you found a teaching job yet?" He asked as he gave me a dollar for the coffee.

"No." I replied.

"Well, I hope you don't mind, but I gave my aunt your number. She'll probably be calling you. She runs a charter school in South Minneapolis, and she's looking for an English teacher. I told her about you, and she said she wants to do an interview."

It isn't easy to give someone the silent treatment when that person is trying to give you exactly what you want. I gave up with little fight.

"What did you say about me?"

"That you seem smart, and honest, and you're eager to find something. Oh, and that you love teaching. That's important to her. She wants people who are passionate about the profession."

"Wow. Well, thanks." In spite of myself I was flattered. "I appreciate you thinking of me."

"Let me know if anything comes of it."

The door opened and in walked Glenn. "Hey babe!" She sauntered up to him, wrapped her arms around his waist, and aiming for his lips, gave him a big kiss. But Ethan quickly moved his head so the kiss wound up on his cheek. If what Sally had said was true, why wasn't Ethan more eager for her affections? Glenn didn't seem like a desperate person, but then, didn't I have evidence of how deceptive appearances can be?

"Honey, can you go grab us a table? The place is kind of crowded this morning."

"Sure thing." Ethan grabbed his coffee and released himself from Glenn's arms. "Good luck," he said to me. "I hope it works out."

"Yeah, I'll let you know if it does." He had walked away, and I said to Glenn, "Do you want your usual this morning?"

"Yes, and I need you to listen to me." Glenn leaned into the counter, and spoke in a waspy female Godfather voice only I could hear. Tapping her bright red nails against the counter, she said, "I don't know what the deal is between you and Ethan, but stay away from him. If you don't, I guarantee you will regret it."

And here I was almost feeling sorry for her. "Is that a threat? Did you just threaten me?"

Glenn pushed the sunglasses she had been wearing up to the top of her head. Her eyes bore into me. "Take what I said however you want. But keep in mind, if you go near him again you will be sorry."

This is what my life had degenerated to. Now, the intelligent thing to say would have been, "Don't worry, I'm not even interested in him." But for some reason, I opened my mouth, and these words flew out: "I'll go near him if I want. And I might. He is a pretty good kisser after all."

Smoke blew out of her ears. Well, not really. But had she been a cartoon character it would have. However, after an instant's worth of transparency she regained her composed veneer.

"I see," she said, as if I simply told her the day's weather forecast. "Make my drink and bring it to me when you're done."

Perhaps what I said pissed her off, but if so, oh well. I couldn't take it back now. I made her drink, and even though there were a couple of people waiting at the counter, I took it over to her.

I should have seen it coming from a mile away. Just as I was approaching their table, Glenn reached out her foot and tripped me. I lurched forward, then in an effort to regain my balance, I lurched back, which caused me to fall flat on my behind, spilling coffee and foamed milk all over my chest and stomach. The worst part was I landed on my tailbone, which not only hurt like a cow in labor, but momentarily knocked the wind out of me as well.

"Oh my God, I am so sorry! Are you okay?" Glenn's words dripped out of her like saltwater taffy, but nobody noticed how insincere she sounded.

I coughed and hacked before I could speak, and my words came out in a jumbled burst. "You tripped me!"

"I didn't mean to! God, I am so sorry! Let me help you up!" She stood and reached her hand out to me. I swatted it away and got up on my own.

Coffee trickled down my front, and tears of pain stung in my eyes. "Don't lie, Glenn!" I turned to Ethan. "She threatened me!"

Glenn hiccupped, widened her eyes and batted her lashes. "Faith, believe me. It was an accident. I am so sorry. I don't know what you mean, but I would never threaten you." She started to cry. "Now you probably think I'm some sort of terrible person!"

Did somebody say Tony Award? Everyone, including Ethan, was buying this performance. Ethan walked to the counter to grab a towel, and then helped me clean up. But he kept his head down, making eye contact with no one. "You believe me, don't you Ethan?" Glenn whimpered.

He nodded his head, still not looking at her, and handed me the towel. "Are you actually okay?"

I wasn't going to tell him my rear end was screaming in agony. At the very least my tailbone was badly bruised, and I could not have asked for a less dignified injury.

Why couldn't I have sprained my ankle? Then he would have had to carry me, or something. "I'm fine." I hobbled towards the counter. Ethan followed me.

"Go easy on Glenn, okay? She's a little fragile right now." Glenn was the fragile one? Had he noticed I could no longer stand up straight? My throbbing bottom brought back my clarity, and I laid into him.

"Oh, and whose fault is it that Glenn is fragile?"

"What exactly are you implying?"

"I think you know."

"Um, actually, I don't."

Now was not the time to get into this. Customers were waiting, I was in pain, and somehow I would have to get through the rest of the morning. I didn't have time for any more drama. I shook my head at him, and turned toward the man who was first in line. Before I could wait on him, Ethan interrupted.

"Uh, Faith? Could I talk to you for a minute?"

"Ethan, there are people waiting."

"I know, but you're upset, and I don't want to leave things this way."

"I'm not upset, I'm in pain, and I have a lot to do. So please, just go."

Glenn had walked up to the counter. "Come on Ethan, let's go somewhere else for coffee. I've already ruined her day. I don't want to make things any worse."

She tugged on his arm and led him away. He looked once over his shoulder at me, but I broke his gaze by focusing my attention on the customer who had been waiting. I was surprised to find it was Bill. I hadn't even noticed him come in.

"Bill, I am so sorry. Did you want your usual?"

He grabbed a paper napkin from the dispenser and handed it to me. "Here."

"Thanks." I wiped away the tears still in my eyes.

"You really hurt yourself, didn't you?"

"I think I bruised my tailbone."

"That's happened to me before. You'll want to ice it. And you'll need a donut pillow."

"Thanks. Now, what I can get you?"

"Are you sure you're okay to work?"

I had to be. I wasn't going to call Sally. She would be hearing Glenn's version of the story anyway. It was probably better to downplay my side by not making a big deal of it. Sally was going to believe her daughter no matter what anyway.

"Yeah, I'm fine." Before I could turn around to make Bill his hot chocolate, he stopped me.

"Actually, I don't need anything today." He leaned his hands against the counter, then hoisted himself behind it. With a smile, he said, "Don't want to set a bad example, eating and drinking on the job." He gently nudged me over, taking my place at the cash register, and spoke to the next customer. "Hi, what can I get you?"

"Bill, what are you doing?"

"I'm helping you out. Don't worry; I know what I'm doing, sort of. You can give me direction if I need it. But this way you won't have to move around as much."

My rear end was smarting. I looked at the clock: four more hours of agony. Time was sure to go faster if I accepted Bill's help.

"Thanks," I mumbled, holding back tears once again.

Why is it that kindness is so apt to make us cry? Perhaps for the same reason love often does: strong emotions often become intermixed, like the roots of weeds and flowers, impossible to separate, feeding off each other.

12

When I got home, Margaret was on the couch, like I thought she would be. She was watching Missy strip. I scuffled in, carrying the donut pillow Bill retrieved from his apartment before finally leaving me at the coffee shop. He wanted to stay and help longer, but had an 11:00 appointment downtown. "You're going to need this," he assured me. "Just give it back when it doesn't hurt to sit down anymore."

Neither Missy nor Margaret noticed my entrance, for they were both preoccupied. Missy was dressed in a pair of jeweled thong underwear, a huge beaded triangular necklace that covered most of her chest, and a tiara. She was gyrating to something by Mariah Carey, and Margaret was a captivated audience member. Neither of them acknowledged me until after the song was over.

"Faith! Hey, what do you think? I was showing Margaret my new routine. I've been working on it really hard."

Margaret answered before I could. "I think it's fantastic! You look so hot! Don't you agree, Faith?"

"Sure." I walked to the kitchen to get some ice.

"Honestly? Because you didn't get the full effect, since I don't have a pole to work with."

"No Missy, it was great!" said Margaret. "I especially liked that bendy thing you did. And your outfit is awesome." Margaret was laying it on awful thick with Missy. She already had a place to stay, so enough already.

"You like the outfit? I was going for a Vegas showgirl look."

"Oh, it totally works."

"And you want to know the best part?" Missy glowed. "It's all tax deductible. Everything beauty-related for me is now: Facials, manicures, lingerie, you name it. Since it's all connected to my job, all I have to do is save the receipts and I can write it off."

I walked into my bedroom, and laid stomach down upon my bed. I was unsuccessfully trying to balance a bag of ice on my sore spot when Margaret walked in.

"Faith, are you okay?"

"Do I look okay?

"What's wrong?"

"I fell on my tailbone, and it hurts." I knew how silly I looked, but I was not in the mood to be teased. "Don't laugh, okay?"

"Why would I laugh?" Margaret approached my bed, and sat gently down by my side. She took the bag of ice from me, and placed it on the spot I had been reaching for.

"Is that where you want it?"

"Yes. Thanks." Having her hold it there did actually help. I let out a grateful sigh.

"What happened?"

"I was at work. This mean awful girl who happens to be the boss's daughter and the girlfriend of this guy I went out on one date with threatened me. And stupidly, I talked back to her, so she tripped me and made it look like an accident."

"Why did she threaten you?"

"She wants me to stay away from her man."

"Wow, Faith, your life is like a soap opera."

"No. If my life were a soap opera, I would have hurt something else—definitely not my ass. And the worst part is it happened several hours ago, so I had to work like this through the end of my shift. And the pain has only gotten worse."

"Maybe I should take you to the emergency room."

"No. It's not broken or anything. I simply need to ice it for a while. I'll be fine."

"But what if it is broken?"

"It isn't. And even if it was, so what? It's not like they can put a cast on your tailbone."

I guess Missy had been listening in the whole time. From the door to my room I heard her say, "Faith, I know you don't have insurance, so if you're worried about the money, don't be. You can totally get workman's comp for this. Do you want me to talk to my lawyer for you?"

"That's okay. My insurance from my teaching job doesn't run out for another month."

"But even still, you could sue. Especially if your tailbone is broken."

"It's not broken. If it was there is no way I would have been able to finish my shift. But thank God Bill was there."

Missy walked around towards the other side of the bed, and crouched down so she was looking me in the eye. "Bill? You mean from our building?"

"Yeah. He's so nice. He stayed and helped me serve coffee, and he lent me his inflatable donut pillow so I can sit down. He even blew it up for me."

"I didn't know you knew Bill," Missy replied.

Maybe it was the pain I was in, but Missy had a strange look on her face—like she had eaten something gone bad.

"Yeah, I know Bill. He comes into the coffee shop all the time. Why?"

Missy's expression changed as she forced her normal demeanor back on. "No reason. Just don't believe him if he starts talking crap about me, okay?"

"Why would he do that?"

"No reason!" Missy shot back up and left the room. She could be so odd; besides, if Bill happened to "speak crap" about her it would be believable.

Margaret spoke next. "Oh hey, there was a message for you. Some guy called. It's on the answering machine."

"Who was it?"

"He didn't say. He only said you should stop teasing him, or something like that. It was kind of weird."

Even though it pained me to do so, I got up and went into the living room to listen to my message. It was the unknown voice I had come to recognize. "Hi, it's me again. You're still on my mind. You have to stop teasing me like this, or stay out of my way. I don't know how much more of this I can take." Click.

Missy was in her room getting dressed, so I slowly made my way over to her. "Missy, are you sure that message isn't for you? You heard it, right?"

"Yeah, I heard it. But that's your phone line. I have my own line, remember?"

"But we said you could use my line for personal calls, just not the 'telemarketing.' Did you maybe give that number out to someone, and then forget?"

"I suppose it's possible. But I really don't think so. I think those messages are for you, Faith."

"But I have no idea who it could be."

Margaret was hanging out at the edge of the room. "What about that guy whose girlfriend tripped you?" she asked.

"Ethan? I don't think so."

Missy finished dressing and turned to face me. "Well why not? I think Margaret could be right. The guy has a crazy girlfriend. Who is to say he's not crazy himself? Plus, isn't he the one who left you a sexy message when he asked you out?"

"Yeah, but…"

"It sounds to me like it could be the same voice," said Missy.

"Faith went out with a stalker!" cried Margaret.

"No I didn't! It's not him."

"How can you be so sure?" inquired Missy. "And what about that light bulb? Huh? He's a mechanic, and light bulbs are, well, they sort of have to do with mechanics."

"No they don't. And he left me a nightlight, not a light bulb. If it was even left for me, which we don't know that it was."

"Faith, why would Ethan leave it for me? He doesn't even know me."

Actually, according to Ethan, he did know her from the coffee shop. But because I was sure of Ethan's innocence, it wasn't worth it to bring that up. "You're missing the point. It's simply not him." Suddenly something occurred to me. I went and listened to the message again. The machine said it was left at 10:38 a.m., which was about an hour after Ethan had left the coffee shop. "Hi, it's me again. You're still on my mind. You have to stop teasing me like this, or stay out of my way. I don't know how much more of this I can take."

Whomever it was told me to stay out of his way, which was strikingly similar to what Glenn had said to me today. Maybe Missy was right. But if she was, I didn't want to think about it right then. I didn't know how much more of this I could take.

"God, I need a drink," I muttered, loud enough for Margaret to hear me.

"Great! Let's go out. I've been dying to since I got here. Where should we go?"

Missy emerged from her bedroom. "We're going out? Cool!"

❇   ❇   ❇

As it was only half past one when Missy and Margaret decided we were going out, I was able to stall them until later that evening. But once seven o'clock rolled around there was no escape. They insisted I come, and wouldn't even accept my bruised tailbone as an excuse not to go. "Bring your special donut pillow," said Margaret. "There's no shame in it."

That was easy for her to say. She wasn't the one who was sitting at a bar table, a foot higher than everyone else, balanced on a round inflatable pillow shaped like a toilet seat. We were at Joe's Garage, a local hangout known for their tasty chicken wings and strong cocktails. We were sitting on their rooftop patio, enjoying a view of Loring Park (which Mary Tyler Moore walks through in the opening credits of her show.) I had decided the only way to get through the evening was to become so drunk that the pain and humiliation caused by my predicament no longer bothered me.

I was on my third cosmopolitan, and for the first time all day, I was feeling good. Actually, I take that back. I was feeling good for the first time in months. There was a light yet warm gooey feeling in my arms and legs, and it was as though a huge boulder had been lifted off the top of my brain. Finally I was able to express myself; I had been set free from the burdens that had plagued my psyche for months.

"But who needs men anyway? What are they good for? Nothing! Look at me, for example. I had a man and he left me for my best friend. So I move down here, and what happens? I meet another man with a crazy girlfriend who is out to get me. It's better to stay alone." I had been lecturing Margaret all evening with words I was convinced were profound. I banged my arm on the table for emphasis as I made my next point.

"I mean, who the hell is this Glenn girl to trip me anyway? What did I ever do to her? If I were smart I would have kicked her ass!"

Missy answered. "Her name is Glenn? Isn't that a guy's name?"

I stopped and thought about it. "I suppose it is. Maybe that's why she's so screwed up – she's angry she has a boy's name!"

Margaret, who was drinking Dr. Pepper, had been listening the whole time with a patient ear. "I wonder how she found out about you and Ethan. Do you think he told her?"

"Don't know." I slurred. "But what was there even to tell? We kissed, that's all. Unless..." a revelation suddenly came to me, "unless, maybe she knows he's stalking me! Maybe she's been helping him! I read about this sort of thing in *Cosmo*! It's like one of those sick and twisted codependent relationship games where the girl feels more important because she's enabling the guy in his dev-cee-ush-nesh!"

"I don't think so, Faith. If she were helping him, then why would she tell you to stay away from him? That would mean that she was encouraging his fascination with you while trying to end it simultaneously."

I ignored Margaret's rational analysis except for the one part I was interested in. "Do you truly think he's fascinated with me?"

"Can we talk about something else, please? This is all we've talked about since we've gotten here." Missy was sitting across from me, dressed in a buttoned white tailored jacket with nothing but a bra underneath, and a matching short skirt. Since beginning her new career, her goal was to look sexy at all times. She had been scoping out the place, and was disappointed Margaret and I weren't interested in trying to pick up guys along with her.

"No! Tonight it's all about me, got it? Go ahead, say I'm self-involved and see if I care. Ha! I don't care." I must have been swaying a little, and I made a quick movement to grab my drink off the table. In the process I nearly fell off my cushion, and had to catch myself before I toppled off of my chair altogether.

"Faith, maybe we should get you home," said Margaret.

"No! Tonight it's all about me, and I want to stay." I burped, and for a moment became more lucid. "I need to figure it out."

"Figure what out?" inquired Margaret.

"You know!" I waited for her to answer back, but she didn't. Okay, maybe I wasn't all that lucid after all. "You know. I need to figure out my roman... my roman-ack... my love life. Why don't I have one anymore?"

"I thought you didn't want one."

"Huh?"

Margaret sighed and continued gently on. "A minute ago you said you didn't want one."

"Didn't want what?"

"A love life."

"Of course I do! Everyone does. I'm only human, Margaret. I have needs. I need to know why Peter stopped loving me. How Lacey could do that to me. Why Ethan would rather be with that evil Glenn than me. I don't get it. What's wrong with me?"

My sweet little buzz was swiftly turning sour, but in my intoxicated state I was convinced the only cure was to drink more. I called the waiter over to our table. "Gimme 'nother cosmo!" I croaked.

"Sure," he said hesitatingly. "Do you think maybe she's had enough?" he said softly to Margaret.

"Hello!" I cried. "I'm right here. I can hear you. And I'm fine. I don't need some man to tell me when I've had enough. I want another drink, so please bring it to me."

I must have talking louder than I realized, because a guy across the bar answered me back. "Hey pillow girl! Shut the hell up, or I'll give you a real pain in the ass."

"Oh yeah! I'd like to see you try!" I was ready to leap off my stool and pick a fight, but Margaret grabbed my arm and muttered a severe sounding "Faith, no!" Then Missy interceded.

"Actually, the drink is for me," she said to the waiter with a wink. She leaned forward seductively so he could see down her jacket. "And don't worry. It's my last one, then we're getting her home." Missy had the art of sex appeal down, and those simple words did the trick.

After he had left she turned to address me. "You're going about this all wrong," she said.

"Huh?" I uttered.

"You get crapped on by the men in your life, and then you whine about it. Then it happens again and you wonder why. Don't you see that you're creating a pattern for yourself? You have to stop the pattern by breaking the cycle."

The liquor was squashing my brain as I struggled to understand Missy's words. "How do I break the cycle?"

"By telling them off. Stand up for yourself. Tell them you aren't going to take any more. Once you get in the habit of doing so, you'll exude an aura of confidence, and the guys you meet will know not to mess with you."

Missy's words reached past the murkiness of my mind and made perfect sense. "You're right. I have to stand up for myself. I'll do it right now. Can I borrow your cell phone?"

Margaret's eyes widened. "Faith, I don't think Missy meant you had to stand up for yourself right this minute, did you Missy?"

"Sure I did. Why not right now?" Missy reached into her purse and handed me her phone. As she did the waiter came and placed my drink down in front of her. I reached across the table and took it, swigging it down with a gulp.

"There's no time like the present!" I cried. I dug into my wallet to find the business card with the number of Ethan's garage on it. Before I could lose my nerve I dialed the number, and was actually disappointed when I got the answering machine. But I went ahead and left a message anyway.

"Hi Ethan, it's Faith, you know, the girl whose car you serviced. I wanted to tell you that you and your crazy girlfriend can stop stalking me, okay? And by the way, I wouldn't have greasy garage sex with you if you were the last mechanic alive. So stop calling me, stop following me, and you can have your nightlight back. Because the only issue I have is with you, and you can tell Glenn that if she trips me again I'm going to kick her ass so hard she'll be sitting on a donut pillow for the rest of her God forsaken life." On that triumphant note I hung up, and looked to find Margaret's horrified expression, and Missy's proud one.

I chose to pay attention to Missy and to ignore Margaret. "That was fun!" I said to her. "Now I'm gonna call Peter."

"Faith, I don't think that's a good idea. At least wait until you're sober." Margaret said.

"Marg-a-ret! You don't get it. If I wait until then, it will never happen. And I have to break the cycle." I punched in the number I had committed to memory a long time ago. This time there was an answer.

"Hello," said the familiar voice on the other end of the line.

Hearing him sobered me instantly. All my inhibitions came rushing back, and I was tongue-tied.

"Hello?" he persisted.

I had witnesses, so I couldn't chicken out now, even though my instincts were telling me to. I tried to disguise my discomfort with forced gaiety.

"Peter, hi! It's Faith. How are you?"

"Faith?"

"Yes Peter, it's me. How have you been?"

"Uh, I've been fine."

"And Lacey? How is she doing? Are the two of you still

together?"

"Lacey's fine."

"So are the two of you still together?" I hated myself for asking, hated myself more for asking twice, but I couldn't help it. I needed to know.

There was a pause, and then Peter took on his own tone of bravado. "Actually, I'm surprised that you haven't heard."

"Haven't heard what?" The room was spiraling, but I remained entirely still. Could it be they had broken up?

"Lacey and I became engaged last month."

"WHAT?!!" I yelled loud enough for every person in the bar to hear, and there was a moment of silence as all conversation surrounding me ceased, and every head turned in my direction. I barely noticed. "You're engaged? You've only been together for a couple of months. How could you?"

"I.... I love her, Faith."

"Yeah, well you said you loved me. Was that a lie? Huh? We were together for two years and you never saw fit to propose to me, not even once! When we broke up you said you weren't marriage material. And you run off with my best friend and get engaged after two months! How could you? How could you do that to me?"

"Faith, I'm sorry if I hurt you, I am. You've got to know that was never my intention. But understand this. Lacey and me getting engaged, it has nothing to do with you. We both just want to be happy."

I broke out in a cold sweat. My stomach was firing out warning signs that it had had enough, and I felt like I wanted to die. All I could think was, "Now it really is over."

"I hate you Peter. And you need to know this; I have never said that to somebody and meant it, never until now. I hope you and Lacey have a miserable life together. Goodbye." I hung up the phone and stumbled to the bathroom. Thankfully I was able to control myself until I got there. After that the evening became a haze of pain, puke, and tears.

13

I don't remember a lot about getting home, but I was later told by Missy and Margaret that they practically had to carry me out to the car. After a while I passed out. I woke up several hours later in my own bed, grateful to find that someone had the foresight to place a bucket by my side.

In the early morning I was lying in bed, somewhere in between sleep and consciousness, when a memory passed over me so vividly it was as if I was reliving it.

❉   ❉   ❉

Remember a Thursday night, senior year of high school, two weeks before prom. The phone rings. You pick it up and all you hear is crying from the other end of the line.

"Did you know?" she wails. "Tell me you didn't, because if you did, you would have told me."

"What are you talking about?" You say. "Tell me what's wrong."

She gulps down some air. "Trey has been dating Amanda Robbinsdale behind my back for the last two weeks!" Her crying resumes. "Promise me you knew nothing about it!"

You honestly don't, which is a shock. Your high school is small, and word gets around so efficiently that every student's life is an open book. She has no reason not to assume you would know about Trey

140

and Amanda. You look down at your American History textbook. Right before she called you were trying to memorize the important dates and events from World War Two. Now they seem as utterly unimportant and far away as the idea of one day setting up a retirement fund.

You close your book and move from your desk chair to your bed. Trey had seemed like a nice, John Cusak type of guy, and she was so into him. You try to soothe her with your words. "Of course I didn't know. I would have told you if I did. Are you sure it's true? I have a hard time believing it."

"Oh, you can believe it. Trey told me himself. He wants to break up, and he and Amanda are going to the prom together!"

"I am so sorry." With the prom approaching so fast, this, in your minds, is a tragedy of epic proportions. At seventeen you have no perspective, no knowledge of what the world will someday hold.

"What am I going to do? I've got to get him back. I can't let him go to the prom with Amanda."

"Well, what did you say when he told you? Did you try and convince him not to?"

"Yes, but it didn't work. He said he likes her better. I don't get it. What's wrong with me? I thought he loved me. Otherwise I would never have, well, you know."

You do know. She had lost her virginity to Trey about a month before, and it was a huge deal, especially because she had been raised a Catholic. But she had decided she was in love with Trey, had even convinced herself she would someday marry him. That was how she justified her actions. "And you'll be my maid of honor," she said when she told you the whole story after the fact.

You had gone along with her delusion, even though you suspected it was one at the time. But now you no longer can. Sometimes the toughest part of being a best friend is the need to be honest. "I don't think you should try and get Trey back," you say.

Instantly her voice turns to granite. "What! Are you kidding? Of course I should. He's my soul-mate. Don't you get that?"

You fear your next statement will cause her to direct all the anger she feels towards Trey onto you, but you forge on nonetheless. "If he was your soul-mate, I don't think he'd be doing this to you."

"What do you know? You've never even been in an intimate relationship. You've never even had a boyfriend for more than a couple of weeks. Love isn't always perfect, and neither are the people we love."

Ouch. Leave it to her to shamefully remind you of your lack of experience, i.e., of your virginity. She is a woman of the world, and you aren't. How could you possibly presume to give her advice?

"Look, maybe I'm wrong, but I'm still going to tell you what I think. There are other guys out there for you, and maybe you'll have to go through a few of them before you find 'the one.' But you're pretty, and fun, and you're a great person. What guy in his right mind wouldn't want you? Someday you'll meet the guy you are going to marry, and I'll bet you'll just know. And everything will fall into place, and you won't believe you ever even considered marrying Trey."

There is a pause on the other end of the line, while she blows her nose and wiped away more tears. Then in a trembling voice, she asks, "And when that happens, will you still be my maid of honor?"

You can feel your own tears starting to form. "Of course. I can't imagine it any other way."

❄   ❄   ❄

I forced myself back to reality, back to a time when the unimaginable had come true. Had Lacey known when she first met Peter he was the one? How long had Peter harbored feelings for Lacey without my knowing it? I used to pride myself on my perception, so how had things gone so wrong?

My head was pounding, and my throat was as dry as cotton. I wanted to get up and have a drink of water, but I was afraid moving around would be too painful to make it worth it. I decided it was better to let myself die a slow and painful death from dehydration when there was a knock at the door. Neither Margaret nor Missy answered it, so I had to assume they weren't home. I stumbled to answer the door after the second round of knocking, and opened it to find an increasingly familiar and friendly face.

"Hi," Bill said. "Sorry if I woke you up, but I thought you might need your purse, and I didn't want to leave it outside your door." He held it up, the contents of which included my wallet and my keys, plus my favorite lipstick. Not a good idea to lose that.

"Wow, I had no idea I'd even lost this. You've come to my rescue again, Bill. Thanks so much."

"You look like you had a bad night last night."

"Yeah, I had a few too many. I don't remember much about getting home." I took my purse from him, thankful to have it back. "So where did you find this?"

"In the entryway. I hope you don't mind, but I looked inside to see whose it was."

"Of course I don't mind, I'm very grateful." As I said this I noticed he wasn't looking at my face, but at my chest. I looked down at myself and discovered why. I still had on my outfit from last night, but my puke-encrusted top was undone nearly down to my bellybutton, revealing a lacey bra underneath. I grabbed my shirt closed, while feeling the blush spread across my cheeks.

"Sorry," he said. "I didn't mean to..."

"That's okay, Bill. It's my fault." Pause. Neither of us had anything more to say, yet we both still stood there. "Look, I would invite you in, but I need to wash up."

"That's okay, I need to get going." He turned to leave, then thought better of it. "Oh, and I don't know if you noticed, but somebody left something for you outside your door."

"Huh?" I looked, and lying on the floor by Bill's foot was a cheap rain poncho that looked like it came from a drug store. Attached to it was a note.

This should protect you from the storms that are approaching.

How ominous! It was the type of simple metaphor I tried (without much success) to get my students to understand. But at that moment, I was too hung over to care. Then something occurred to me. Bill was starting to walk away, but I yelled out to him.

"Hey, Bill!" He stopped and turned around. "When we first met, you said something about Missy. What did you mean?"

He ran his fingers through his thinning hair, his mouth frowning in confusion. "I said something about Missy? What did I say?"

"You said 'good luck' when I told you I was her roommate. But the way you said it made me wonder what you meant."

With a smirk, he approached, making the distance between us so small he could speak softly. "I meant, well, she can be a handful. But I'm sure with you she will be fine."

"But why do you say that? Do you even know her?"

"No, not really. I used to be friends with the old manager here, and he used to tell me stories about how demanding she is. And one time I was hanging out at his apartment, and she came by and started cursing him out because her toilet needed fixing. I thought I was going to have to call the police or something, that's how intense things became." He looked over his shoulder, careful no one could overhear him. "Be careful, that's all. Don't make her mad. And if she gives you any trouble, let me know. I'm right down the hall." He patted my shoulder with a brotherly type gesture. "Have you tried tomato juice and vanilla ice cream?"

"I'm sorry?"

"Tomato juice and vanilla ice cream. Perfect for hangovers." He walked away again, this time for good. "Take care, Faith," he called over his shoulder.

"Thanks again for my purse." I yelled back to him. He was by now nearly at the end of the hall. He raised his arm in a goodbye gesture, then turned the corner and was out of sight. With my purse in one hand and my new rain poncho in the other, I went back inside my apartment and looked in the freezer. I didn't think we had any tomato juice, but vanilla ice cream would hit the spot.

There wasn't any vanilla, but there was some chocolate-chip cookie dough, which I decided was close enough. I wedged the container out from under the frozen chicken breasts, grabbed a spoon, and dug in. As I stood in the kitchen eating, details of my evening out came rushing back to me, and I struggled to decide if it would be better to kill myself now, or give myself a few hours to put my affairs in order.

My head and my rear end were competing with each other to cause me the most grief. I made a fool of myself twice in one evening with my ill-advised phone calls, and I didn't even want to think of what the ramifications would be. My professional life was non-existent, and I wished I never had a personal life to begin with. And, to top it off, somebody was stalking either me, or my phone-sex operator/stripper roommate. I cursed the day I decided to move down here.

The cold, sweet ice cream did taste good though. At least I still had the pleasures of food left; that was something. I found my donut pillow and sat down to consider my options. Moving back was now impossible. I needed to be far, far away from Peter and Lacey, and from the memories attached to them. But what was I going to do here? Missy was right, I had no life, and any life I did have I quickly destroyed.

Thomas walked into the room, jumped up on my lap, and instantly started purring. I gingerly put down the ice cream so I could pet him. Here was somebody who loved me, despite my flaws and my mis-steps; he didn't even care if I was still wearing clothes I had thrown up on. Maybe that was the answer. I would become one of those reclusive fat women who had a lot of cats. Nobody could ever hurt me because I wouldn't get close enough to let them, and I could eat whatever I wanted because I no longer needed to impress anyone.

The phone rang, and my stomach fell. I was afraid to answer it, for it could be any number of people calling to give me a hard time. Or it could be the stalker. Or, it could be Ethan's aunt, calling about that job interview; on the off chance that Ethan hadn't yet called to tell her I am certifiably insane.

"Hello?"

"Hi, is Faith there?" It was a guy, but it was neither Peter nor Ethan.

"This is Faith." I said it in a professional tone. Maybe Ethan's aunt had a male secretary, you never know.

"Hey Faith, it's Max."

Max! Great. I tried to keep the disappointment out of my voice. "Oh hi, Max, how are you?"

"I'm doing good. How are you? Are you feeling better?"

He was obviously referring to our evening together, when I had mercilessly cried on his shoulder for way too long. I wanted to forget about that. "I'm great! Couldn't be better."

"Well, that's good to hear. Have you talked to Carolyn?"

"Yeah, we talked."

"Oh, that's good. Because I wanted to tell you that David mentioned something, I hear she broke it off with him. I thought that might make you feel better, in case you didn't know."

"Oh." What a sweet gesture. "Thanks Max, I appreciate your calling to tell me."

"Well, that's not the only reason I called. I had a good time the other night…" He had? Was he crazy? "…and I was wondering if you'd like to get together again some time."

I couldn't tell if my skin was hurting out of sympathy for every other part of my body that was in pain, or if it was a warning signal I ought to have been paying attention to. Ah well, he was a nice guy, and he was still interested even after what I had put him through on our first date. I couldn't look a gift horse in the mouth, now could I?

"Sure Max. That would be great."

We made arrangements to go out in a couple of days. I had just gotten off the phone and was hobbling towards the bathroom when somebody buzzed to be let in. I assumed it was Margaret, who had probably gone for a walk without a key. But a couple of seconds later there was a knock on the door, and I opened it to find a teary eyed Carolyn staring back at me.

"Charles and I broke up," she said. Then she collapsed into my arms, crying, but not for long. She looked up, and examined the vomit-enhanced collar of my blouse. In the bewildered voice of a child, she asked, "Um Faith, why are you wearing this?"

❄ ❄ ❄

I explained everything to Carolyn: the engagement, my hangover, my bruised tailbone, Glenn and Ethan, and the possibility I was being stalked. She was very sympathetic, but she (understandably) insisted that I take a shower before we commenced to commiserating. We went over and over the sad details of both of our lives, trying to figure out how things had gone so wrong. We came up with no answers, but we did manage to ingest a hell of a lot of calories.

Carolyn and I sat on my couch, eating the remainder of the ice cream, and every thing else we could find in the freezer, all of which was Missy's. (I promised myself I would replace it later.) I have always been blessed with a strong stomach, so even though I was sick the night before, it did not prevent me from eating out of misery. Plus, I had to do it for Carolyn. I couldn't let her pig out on her own, now could I? I contemplated the last of the pizza rolls. Did I need them? Seeing as how I had puked up everything that I had eaten the night before, yeah, I did. As I stuffed one into my mouth, Carolyn asked me for what had become the millionth time, "Do you think that I did the right thing by telling him?"

I chewed, trying to figure out how I could answer her question so this time she would accept my answer. "Carolyn, you did what you had to do. You wouldn't have been able to live with yourself, not telling him. How could you build a lasting relationship, feeling that way?"

"I know, but he was so hurt. I'll never forget the look on his face when I told him; it's been burned permanently onto my brain. I wish I could go back and erase it all, all of it. Why didn't I listen to you? You should have made me listen to you, Faith."

"Carolyn, I don't even listen to my own advice most of the time. How was I supposed to get you to?"

Carolyn sawed off another piece of the frozen Sara Lee pound cake, which had to be stale. She took a small bite, and with a pained effort, chewed and swallowed. "I tried calling him at his mother's house. She wouldn't even let me talk to him, wouldn't even say she would tell him that I called. Instead she told me to stay away from the apartment tomorrow afternoon so he can come get the rest of his stuff."

"Are you going to stay away?"

"I don't know. I don't know what I would to say to him, even if I could get him to listen. Maybe I should give him some space."

"Well, what do you want? I mean, if he was willing to forgive and forget, would you go back to the way you were, and give up your idea of moving from Minneapolis?"

Carolyn pushed the last of the pound cake away from her, and sat back on the couch. She leaned over and gently stroked Missy's favorite cat, Jinny, who rolled over on her back in a request to have her belly rubbed. Carolyn petted her, seeming to focus all of her mental energy on that task, as if she was in deep concentration. "I can't answer that, I just don't know. All I can say is I wish this hadn't happened. I wish I wasn't such an idiot."

Without thinking, I quoted what Lacey said so many years ago. "Love isn't perfect, and neither are the people we love."

"Did you get that from a fortune cookie?"

"Carolyn!"

"Sorry."

"It happens to be true, no matter how trite it may sound. Maybe you should forgive yourself first, before you try and figure out what you want or what you're going to try and do."

She looked up at me with such a sad expression I felt like crying myself. "That's easier said than done, Faith. Besides, that's hardly apt advice, coming from you."

"What do you mean?"

"Have you forgiven Peter and Lacey? If you're so accepting of love's imperfections, then why can't you forgive them?"

"Well, like you said before, my situation is different."

Carolyn reached again for the pound cake she had pushed away. As she attempted to sever another piece from the frozen chunk, she said, "The situations are actually very much the same. I only said they weren't to make myself feel better. Peter and Lacey betrayed you, I betrayed Charles. How much more basic can you get?"

I didn't know what to say. I considered finishing off the last of the strawberry cheesecake which was sitting on the far left corner of the coffee table, but that would mean getting up. I was too comfortable on my donut pillow to make it worth the effort. "I'll tell you what," Carolyn said, "I'll forgive myself about Charles if you forgive Peter and Lacey."

"That hardly seems like a fair deal, Carolyn."

"Yeah, I know, and I'm the one who it's unfair to. It's a whole lot easier to forgive others than it is to forgive yourself."

I was not convinced. After the anger I experienced last night forgiveness was the last thing on my mind. But Carolyn was never one to give up easily.

"Faith," she said, as she leaned towards me, "Wouldn't you feel so much better about life if you could let go, just be happy for them? Think about how good forgiveness would feel."

"Well sure, if it was that easy. But it's not."

"But don't you see, that's exactly my point. I know it's not easy, which is why you need to find a way to forgive them, for the both of us. Because if you do, then it will show me that it's possible. Like if you can do it, so could Charles, and so could I."

"I don't know. All of a sudden I have the happiness of five people resting on my shoulders. Besides, it's not like they ever asked me to forgive them, they barely even apologized for hurting me."

Carolyn reached out and stroked my hair, which was still drying from the shower I had taken while she defrosted the food. "Faith, I know things haven't been easy for you lately. But I'm asking this of you mainly for your own good. Maybe they don't deserve to be forgiven, but you deserve to be able to move on, and forgiveness is the first step. Say you'll try, for me. Please."

How could I say no? She was the one true friend I had left. "Okay, I'll try. I don't know how I'll do it, but I'll try."

14

L ater that evening, alone in my bedroom, I made a list. If I was serious about forgiving Peter and Lacey, then I would have to be methodical about it. My lists are more like lesson plans, actually, because that's how I think. It read like this:

Goal: Forgive Peter and Lacey

Procedures:

1. Focus on remembering the good times/how knowing them has benefited my life.
2. Remember they are human, with flaws/weaknesses.
3. Find new people to love, or redirect more love to people already in my life.
4. Love myself more (?) (I wasn't honestly sure about that one, but I left it in because I thought that it sounded good.)

Assessment:

1. I will be able to function in relationships like an adult rather than as a self-absorbed lunatic.
2. I won't think about them all the time.
3. I'll be able to trust someone enough to fall in love with him.
4. I will be able to be friends with Peter and Lacey, and be a part of their lives.

I was also unsure about that last one. Did I still want to be friends with them? I never saw the benefit of being friends with an ex, but I suppose I could see the value of staying friends with Lacey, my oldest friend since childhood. And if I were going to be friends with her, I would have to at least tolerate her husband.

I put the list away. It was enough of a first step to have written it. Besides, I had to be at work the next morning, and my stomach lurched every time I thought about seeing Glenn and Ethan. Maybe I should quit. I had only taken the job because I thought it would make me feel better about myself. It certainly wasn't doing that.

The next morning I was still unsure about what I wanted. I hated to give up so easily, but if Glenn was truly set on making my life miserable, perhaps this battle was not worth fighting. I was still sore from my fall two days before, so I sort of hobbled up to the shop, but when I went to unlock the door, I discovered it was already open. I went in and found myself face to face with Sally, who was taking chairs down from the tops of tables.

I didn't know what to expect, so it was with some trepidation that I approached her. "Oh hi, Sally, I didn't know you were going to be in this morning."

She turned, and the look on her face was one of sympathy and concern. "I heard about what happened. I thought maybe you could use some help today. How are you feeling?"

"Not bad," I lied. Actually, while still painful, my tailbone did feel better that day than it had the day before.

"Faith, I feel terrible about what happened."

"You do?"

"Yes. I heard Glenn's side of the story, and then yesterday Bill came in and asked how you were. He told me what actually happened. Why didn't you call me?"

"I didn't want you to be in a position where you had to take sides against your daughter."

Sally sighed. "Well, that's sweet of you, but it certainly wouldn't have been the first time I've been in that position. Glenn has always been a little high strung. She's had a tough life. Her father left us when she was twelve. She took it personally, I still don't think she's over it."

I went over behind the counter to prepare the coffee, listening to Sally at the same time. She continued on. "And in school she had a rough time as well. Her teachers always underestimated her, when in reality she was way ahead of the material they were giving her. They called her a troublemaker, but I think she was bored."

In my teaching career I have heard parents make excuses for their children over and over, and Sally sounded no different. In my mind it came down to one thing, either you were willing to draw the line with your child, or you weren't. Obviously Sally wasn't, and I wondered if that had been Glenn's problem all along.

"But I'm not trying to make excuses for her. I don't care what her situation is, she has no right to treat you like that. I told her if she is going to come in here, then she'll have to be civil, and without that Ethan. It's his fault, he does this to her. I don't trust him. So I put my foot down. He's not welcome here anymore."

While I did not agree with the logic of banning Ethan from the shop for something Glenn had done, I wasn't about to argue, especially not after the message I had left the other night. With any luck, Glenn would find a new place to have coffee, one where she could bring her boyfriend.

And it appeared my wish may have been granted. The morning sailed by, with no problems whatsoever. Bill stopped in at his usual time. "How are you feeling? Is your butt still sore?" I told him it was, but the donut pillow was helping immensely. Then I gave him a free hot chocolate and rice crispy treat.

"You should take your break now, and keep me company while I eat this," he said.

"Okay," I replied, coming out from behind the counter.

"So what's going on with you, Faith?" He asked, as I settled atop the donut pillow.

"What do you mean?"

"I'm not blind – obviously there was something going down between you and Glenn, and it looked like there was something between you and Ethan. For someone who has just moved here you sure managed to get yourself into trouble awfully quick."

"You make me sound much more exciting than I actually am. I'm simply trying to find my place here, you know?"

"Sure, I gotcha. Places can be hard to find."

"Do you ever get lonely, working for yourself?"

He squinted at me, his long nose wrinkling with the gesture. For a second I thought my question had annoyed him, but then he took a huge bite of his rice crispy treat, and smiled with his mouth still full. After he finished chewing and swallowed, he answered me.

"Nah, I'm what you would call a lone wolf. That's the way I like it. I know my place, and it's being on my own. Things are simpler that way."

I contemplated this. "Yeah, that's a good way to live in theory, but me, I get lonely."

"Well, that's what friends are for," he said. "And neighbors – they're a great remedy for loneliness. But friends who are neighbors, that's the best remedy of all."

"I'll keep that in mind." I smiled at him, and got up to get back to work. Before I went back behind the counter, I walked around to his side of the table, and gave him a kiss on the cheek.

❅　❅　❅

Neither Ethan nor Glenn came in, but towards the end of my shift a pleasant looking woman entered and approached the counter. She looked like she was in her late forties, with wavy brown hair and a naturally slim figure. She was wearing no makeup, but she had the sort of face that didn't need it, with pronounced green eyes, dark lashes, and a friendly smile. I found her at once familiar and likeable, and I soon found out why.

"Excuse me," she said, "are you Faith?"

"Yes, I am."

"Hi!" She reached her hand towards me with an enthusiastic smile. I shook it, and was impressed with the firmness of her handshake, and that her hand was warm and dry. I hate limp, clammy handshakes.

"I'm Kristin, Ethan's aunt." No wonder she seemed familiar.

Same eyes, same hair, same easy-going confidence. "I hope you don't mind me stopping in, I understand you're working, but I hate communicating by telephone. It's so impersonal. Do you have a second? Can we chat?"

It was 1:30. Both the morning and the lunch rushes had come and gone. The place was dead. "Sure. Would you like something to drink?"

"Well, I am awfully partial to those Italian sodas. My twelve-year-old daughter drinks them; she got me hooked. Could I have a raspberry-lemon one?"

"Sure." I poured raspberry and lemon flavored syrup, combined it with carbonated water, threw in some ice and a maraschino cherry for good measure. "Would you like a straw?"

"That would be lovely, thanks." I handed her the soda and a straw, and she took a sip. "Perfect. The best I've ever tasted. And Ethan tells me you've been working here less than a week. You must be a quick learner."

I laughed. "Well, I like to think so." What else had Ethan told her? Word about my insane message must not have reached her yet.

"Is it possible for us to sit down? Can you do that, or would your boss get mad?"

"No, it's fine. If a customer comes in, I'll get up, that's all." I led her to a seat. She sat down, and so did I, very gingerly. I wasn't about to grab my donut pillow now. But ouch, it hurt to sit.

"Well," she began, "I don't know what all Ethan has told you, so I'll start at the beginning. I am opening a brand new charter school in South Minneapolis!" She waved her arms triumphantly; it was almost kind of cute. "You do know what charter schools are, right hon?"

"Don't they get government money, but they're run by the administration and the parents?"

"Yes, that's exactly it. It really is the best of both worlds. My charter school is going to be based on the principles of Waldorf education. How much do you know about that?"

I shifted in my hard, wooden seat. This was too important to let my discomfort mess it up. I must focus, and ignore the pain. "Well,

I know that Waldorf education focuses on developing the student's imagination and creativity."

"Very good!" She slapped her hand on the table, then took a long sip of her soda. "Umm, this is tasty. Anyway, yes Faith, you are right, Waldorf does focus on imagination and creativity. But it is also much more than that. One of the reasons Waldorf education started was because Rudolf Steiner, the man who came up with the whole thing, believed teachers ought to be able to teach their students without having to mess with a bunch of economic or government concerns. Now doesn't that sound great?"

I nodded my head and she continued. "Basically, there are three things Waldorf educators are asked to do. Three! Can you imagine? How many hundreds of things were asked of you in the public school system?"

I laughed as if to say, "I know what you mean," and she went on. "Waldorf educators are asked to follow these golden rules." She spouted them off, clearly having memorized them a long, long time ago. "To receive the child in gratitude from the world which it comes from; to educate the child with love; and to lead the child into the true freedom which belongs to man. Faith, as an educator, do you think you can do that?"

My physical discomfort was mounting. I wanted to get up so badly that I was gripping the table to keep myself down. "Sure, yeah, I can do that."

"Well great, that's why I'm here. Ethan is a good judge of character, and he thought you could. But you should be aware, this is not a true Waldorf school."

"Oh no?"

"No. Waldorf usually only goes into the eighth grade, and it is very spiritually based. While we will do things like celebrating the seasons, we are going to focus more on maintaining the student's natural reverence for the wonder and beauty of life. That, along with a full curriculum of science, math, and the humanities." She took another sip of her soda, and nearly finished it.

I grabbed the excuse to get up. "Let me get you another soda!"

"Oh, no dear, that's not necessary."

"Please, it's my pleasure." I was up behind the counter making her another one before she could protest.

"You like to go the extra mile, don't you dear? That's wonderful. I have to say, I have a good feeling about you. When can you come in for a more formal interview?"

"I'm free just about any day after two."

"How about tomorrow?"

"Tomorrow would be great!" The sooner the interview, the less of a chance she will have spoken with Ethan.

"Great! Here's my card. The address is on it. Shall I see you at about 2:30?"

"Sure!"

"Wonderful. Now, how much do I owe you for the sodas?"

"Oh no, they're on the house."

"Well thanks!" She reached to shake my hand again. "Faith, it was nice meeting you. And I look forward to talking with you tomorrow. I'll have to call Ethan and tell him as soon as I get home, he'll be thrilled!" She grabbed her soda, and walked out.

I felt my entire body internally cringe as I wondered if I should even bother showing up for the interview. Ethan was sure to mention something to her. Bill was right, life is a hell of a lot simpler when we keep to ourselves. With a sigh of resignation I grabbed a dishrag and set about to clean the espresso machine. As I scrubbed away at the globs of coffee grounds, I repeated my new mantra to myself, over and over inside my head: lone wolf, lone wolf, lone wolf...

15

Then I told him that if he was going to treat me that way, I couldn't guarantee I wouldn't take *twenty* minute breaks. I believe in mutual respect, without it, what good is the work environment?"

I didn't know if that was a rhetorical question, or if I was actually supposed to answer. I was on my date with Max, this time he had taken me to The Olive Garden, and we were in the middle of bread sticks and salad. He had been talking about work for a while, and I was having trouble paying attention.

He paused long enough that I figured he was actually expecting an answer. "Um, yeah, mutual respect is important." I took a sip of wine, maybe that would help me enjoy myself more. My donut pillow was beneath me, and I felt as if everyone was looking at me. It hadn't helped that Max made a joke about my "booster seat" when we first sat down.

"You're so lucky you don't work in an office,' he said. "There is way too much politics, I'm telling you."

"Actually, there was a huge amount of politics in the Duluth public schools."

"Right. I doubt it's the same thing," said Max.

"No, honestly. You couldn't talk out or complain unless you were tenured, and even then, the administration could punish you by transferring you to a different school or messing with your schedule."

"Yeah, but you get all that time off. That must be great."

"Sure." I took another sip of wine. I had given up trying to convince people that teaching wasn't a cake job. Truth was, I worked an average of 65 hours per week during the school year, and most summers I worked a second job, yet my combined annual salary still was well below that of other professionals.

Max interrupted my thoughts. "So hey, how's the job search going? Have you found anything?"

"I don't know. I have an interview tomorrow."

"Hey, good for you!"

"Yeah, we'll see. It's with a charter school; they're into Waldorf education. The whole thing is a little eccentric. Plus, I don't know if I'm going to get it."

"Why not? Just go in there and impress the hell out of them."

"It's not that simple. You see, I... I have a feeling there's a lot of competition. And I don't have any Waldorf training. It's a whole different ballgame, teaching for that type of school. I'll have to completely rethink my methods."

"Umhmm. What you need to do is go in there with the right attitude. Be confident. Show them who's boss. That's the way to get hired." Max took a bite off one of those huge breadsticks, and a glob of butter and crumbs fell and stuck to his chin. "That's how I got my job," he said, between bites, "by taking command of the situation. That's what employers are looking for."

"They're also looking for someone who is qualified to do the work."

"Faith! You're a teacher! How are you not qualified? You need to get rid of this bad attitude right now, young lady."

"You have butter on your chin."

Max's face fell, his expression changing from one of smug amusement to obvious humiliation. He hastily swiped his mouth with his napkin, while his lack of eye contact punished me with silent recrimination.

"Hey, it's no big deal. I rarely can eat a meal without spilling something on myself."

Then he glared at me. "Would it have killed you to let me know as soon as it happened? Haven't you ever seen people do this?" He wiped his mouth while his eyes now bore into my own. "That's the subtle way to tell someone they have food on their face."

Okay. Time to proceed with caution. "Max, it had only been on your mouth for a couple of seconds. But I'm sorry, I didn't mean to make you feel self conscious."

"Sure. You just thought you would have a little fun at my expense." The waitress brought us our food. She placed steaming plates of pasta in front of each of us, but I realized I had no appetite.

"Can I get you anything else?" she said. How about a different date? Involuntarily, my mind raced back to my evening with Ethan, and a huge wave of nostalgia swept over me. We had only gone out once, but suddenly I missed him so much that I would have gladly lopped off my left little toe in exchange for being across from him, rather than Max.

"I think we're good," said Max to the waitress.

"Okay," she replied. "Be careful, those plates are hot."

"This looks great. I love the Olive Garden's food." Max took a bite from his chicken alfredo. "Mmmm! Tasty, I must say. Very tasty. How is yours?"

I took a bite of my eggplant parmesan. It was salty. Maybe I was biased. Peter used to say all their food was salty; he called it The Sodium Garden. Funny, thinking of Peter didn't bring me the strong reaction the way thinking of Ethan had.

"Faith? How's your eggplant? Is it okay?"

"Yeah, it's good." I knew I ought to be making conversation, but I couldn't think of a thing to say. A bad date regulation silence descended over us. The evening loomed ahead. I looked at my food, and it seemed impossible that I was going to have to eat it. Not that it was that bad, but like I said, my appetite was gone. I took another drink of wine, this time finishing the glass. I wanted to order more, but the memory of my recent hangover discouraged me.

"So have you talked to Carolyn lately?"

Another subject I didn't want to talk about, however unfair that may be. "Um, yeah. She's doing okay."

"Did her boyfriend ever find out about her and David?"

"Well, uh, actually, I can't talk about it."

Max raised his eyebrows. "What do you mean?"

"I mean, I can't discuss Carolyn's private life with you."

Max took his napkin off his lap, folded it and put it back on the table, then placed his fork atop if it. "Oh, I get it." He began in a normal conversational timbre, but soon his voice level raised, attracting attention from the surrounding tables. "I have to listen to her moaning while she's getting it on with my roommate, depriving me of hours of sleep, but her private life is none of my business. I put up with your blubbering after you found out that your friend is more of a slut than you thought, but you can't reduce yourself to talking about her to me. Yeah, that makes perfect sense."

I felt like I was looking at one of those 3-D pictures, where if you let your eyes relax a whole new image will jump out at you. Out of the blue, Max displayed dimensions I had not noticed before, and I was an idiot for never having put two and two together.

"You've been stalking me, haven't you?"

He was silent for a moment. But he quickly regained his composure. "Excuse me," he said, his voice now low, "You can't be serious."

"It's been you. All those phone calls, the notes, the little presents outside of my door."

"I don't know what you're talking about."

"Yes, you do. It started on the night we met. You know, that night that you said you were going to brand my phone number in your heart."

"That was a joke! I make a simple joke, and you accuse me of stalking you! Jeez, get over yourself! Even if I was a stalker, which I'm not, I sure as hell wouldn't waste my time stalking you!"

His face had turned bright red, and his neck was straining against the collar of his fake polo shirt. For a guy who looked like he belonged in a JC Penny circular he sure turned out to be a nut-job. I got up from the table, and grabbed my purse and my pillow. "I'll find my own way home." I leaned into him. "But you need to know, it had better stop.

The phone calls, the letters, everything. It needs to stop."

Snap! If the world was at all just, everyone in the Olive Garden would have burst into spontaneous applause as I strode out of the dining room. No matter—I had put my biggest problem to rest, and exhilaration lifted me as a result. I went outside. This time we were in downtown Minneapolis, so I was able to find a bus without any problem. However, I had to transfer once, and I was still dropped off several blocks from my building. By the time I got home nearly an hour passed since I left the restaurant. When I approached my door I could see from a ways away that something had been left outside it. It wasn't until I got close that I realized that it was a witch's hat. There was a note as well:

I can't imagine this won't fit. Wear it and think of me, because you know that I'm still thinking of you.

My blood went cold. That was practically a threat. I turned the hat over and looked at the tag. It was from a downtown theatrical supply store, not far from the restaurant. Wow, he acted quickly. I started inside, ready to call the police.

The door was unlocked, and the lights were off. Had he broken in? Perhaps he lurking somewhere, ready to jump out at me. I was so gripped by fear that at first I didn't notice there was soft music playing. I looked towards the living room, and saw two glasses of wine and the flaming candles on the coffee table.

I was about to slink away to my bedroom. I would use the phone in there. Then I heard smooching, followed by giggling. I recognized Missy's giggle first, I had come to know it in the past few weeks. But the second giggle was as familiar to me as the back of my hand. In a burst of horrific clarity, I realized that the romantic evening upon which I intruded belonged both to Missy, and my baby sister Margaret.

I was paralyzed with shock and indecision. They hadn't noticed me yet. Should I walk away? Which would be more uncomfortable, saying something now, or later? It didn't occur to me that I could put off saying something indefinitely. Yet I was saved from having to make a decision when Margaret, who must have noticed the light streaming into the apartment from the hall, sat up. Whatever questions my facial expression may have been asking were not ones she was prepared to answer.

"Faith! We didn't you hear you come in! How long have you been home?" She simultaneously jumped up from the couch, wiped her mouth, and straightened her hair and clothes.

Missy sat up at this point too. "Oh, hello Faith. You're back from your date so soon? Didn't it go well?" If Missy was embarrassed by being caught making out with my sister, she didn't show it. But Margaret looked like she was about to cry. I didn't know what to say, so I didn't say anything.

"Faith, why are you back so early? Was your date very awful, or something?" I nodded my head. "That's too bad," she said.

Margaret and I stood there, each of us humiliated for different reasons. After several moments, I found my voice. "I'm sorry to barge in, I didn't know...."

"Don't worry about it." Margaret answered quickly. She was still standing, and walked towards the door, shutting it behind me. The room went dark again, so she reached and turned on the main light.

"We were just hanging out," Missy chimed in. "You don't mind me getting to know your sister better, do you?"

Actually I did mind, quite a bit. I wasn't sure why it bothered me so much. Was it because Missy was female, or was it simply because she was Missy? Perhaps I minded for the uncomplicated reason that Missy was irritating and unstable, and I knew that Margaret could do better.

Before I could answer Missy, Margaret changed the subject. "Why are you holding a witch's hat?"

"It was left outside our door, not too long ago. You didn't hear anything, did you?"

"No! And we've been here a while." That didn't mean they would have heard something, although none of us were going to point that out.

"Well, I know who did it. It was Max. He totally freaked out on me during our date, and when I accused him of stalking me, he became quite belligerent."

"Did he confess?" asked Missy.

"No. But he didn't have to; I could tell it was him anyway. So I left, and took a bus home. But it took me a while to get back because I had to transfer, and in that time he must have bought this hat, driven up here, and left it outside of our door. Isn't that creepy?"

"Yeah, it is," responded Margaret.

Missy got up, and took the hat from me in order to inspect it. I continued, "It's from a store downtown, and we were at The Olive Garden, so all he had to do was walk over." She didn't say anything, and I detected she needed further convincing. "And look, there was a note too!"

I showed her the note. "It's typed!" she exclaimed.

"So?"

"So! So Max went and bought a hat, ran home to type a note, then drove to our place and left this outside of our door, all in the time that it took you to take a bus? Seems unlikely to me."

"I had to make a connection. It took me a long time to get home, so it's completely possible."

"But he didn't confess when you accused him."

"Well of course not, but you should have seen his face! It's Max. Believe me."

"You know what I believe? I believe you are still so stuck on Ethan that you are grasping at straws. You don't want to believe it's him, so you've convinced yourself it's Max."

"Missy, that's ridiculous. If you had been at the restaurant, you'd know what I mean. Max totally started going off on me for no reason, he was creating this huge scene. Believe me, he has a screw or two loose."

"Uh huh. And has Ethan called to defend himself since you left him that message? Have you heard from him at all?"

"I was drunk when I left that message. He probably couldn't even understand what I was saying..."

"You can't get over him, can you? You would rather believe that what you felt with him was real than acknowledge the truth."

Her words interrupted my train of thought. It was one thing to have been rejected by Ethan, but I wanted to regard our one date as pure. I pushed my doubts away and continued on.

"Ethan may not be a prince, Missy, but I think I would know if he was a stalker."

"Sure. Defend him all you want. I'm just telling you what I think." I had the urge to slap her.

"Well, pardon me Missy for not putting much stock in your opinion."

"Guys, calm down. I think the important thing to do right now is to contact the police." Margaret had stepped between us, and put her arm around me. "Why don't we let them know what's going on. We can tell them about both Ethan and Max, and they can figure it out."

Missy didn't look at Margaret, nor did she acknowledge what she said. "Faith, I'm trying to help, and I'm not going to lie to pacify you."

"Well I don't want or need your help! It just so happens I am a very perceptive person, sometimes I'm even psychic! So I think I have a better idea about who is behind this."

Missy laughed. "Get over yourself. You're not psychic, and you're definitely not perceptive. If you were, your life wouldn't be such a mess. All you are is a confused, self-important baby who lies to herself so she won't have to grow up already."

She knew how to push my buttons; I'll give her that. Hearing her talk was as painful as it had been to recently watch the tape of myself singing "Tomorrow" for the 7th grade talent show. My worst fears about myself were confirmed. But I wasn't going to admit that to her, and I wasn't going to give in without fighting back, so I laid into her, surprising myself with the severity of my words.

"Oh, and your life is so together, I suppose? When I look at you, all I see is a lonely tramp, so desperate for attention that you're willing to do anything or anyone, including my sister!"

Margaret's grip tightened around my shoulders. "Faith! Stop!"

"Shut up Margaret." I shook her off. "And for all I know, all of these presents and notes could be directed at you. You're the stripper. You're the one who does phone sex. Why are we even so convinced that I'm the target? Because if either of us is a witch, then believe me, it's you." I began to walk away, but Margaret attempted to stop me.

"Faith, stop. We need to work this out."

"No! It's no longer my problem. Everyone thinks that I'm so self-involved, well okay. Then this is not about me. It's about Missy. I'm officially handing it off to her."

I stormed off to me bedroom and slammed the door. If I was being immature, then I didn't care. I had had enough.

16

S o tell me Faith, what are your main goals as an educator?" Kristin asked me this with the earnestness of a child. I was at my job interview, and so far, it seemed to be going well. Ethan's name had not come up, so I guessed she had not spoken to him. I was able to put the events of last night behind me rather well, and completely focused on the here and now.

I contemplated her question. "Well, that's a hard one, because my goals as an educator are always changing. I mean, there's the obvious answer, which is to teach the students something, to get them excited about learning, to inspire them to be life-long learners. Those are all goals of mine. But how do I go about doing that? My methods, you would say? Those are always changing, or to put it a better way, evolving. I find that each class is different, and each student is unique in their own way. So I have to figure out, I have to gauge how best to reach the students, according to what their needs are. Whether it's stricter discipline, a more concrete lesson plan, incorporating higher expectations, or giving the students more input. It all depends."

Kristin nodded her head as if she was takeing in every single word I said. Kudos to her if she had, because I wasn't at all confident that my teacher rhetoric made any real sense. "I completely know what you are talking about. That is so great that you think that way!" She twirled from side to side in her swivel chair, reminding me of a wood nymph. Her office was decorated in shades of brown and green, with twigs and pots of ivy emerging from every corner.

Kristin herself was dressed in green, a loose sheath of a dress with a matching scarf around her neck, and another one in her long brown hair. I had chosen to wear my usual job interview outfit, a gray linen fitted jumper with a white collared blouse underneath. I hoped I didn't look too corporate.

"Because you see," continued Kristin, "so much of Waldorf education is based on the environment. We are all products of our environment, so it is important that we establish one highly conducive for learning. How do you think you would incorporate this philosophy into your teaching?"

"Well," I said, "I would have to do some research and get some suggestions from you or fellow staff members. Then I would set up my classroom, and as I was teaching I would try and assess how the environment was affecting both me and my students, and um... modify it accordingly?"

"Wow!" exclaimed Kristin. "I love that you're willing to do research. So much of what we do here is dependent on the Waldorf philosophy, so it is imperative that you are open to that. But it seems that you're not only open to it, you're willing to do the leg work yourself."

Leg work? Was I going to have to do a lot of walking while I did my research? I have never understood that term, but whatever. My job was to smile, nod my head, and pretend I understood what both she and I were talking about.

"Okay, I have one more question for you. When you have a conflict with someone, and that could include a student, a fellow teacher, a parent, or an administrator, how do you handle it?"

"Well, I usually like to take some time after it's happened, and step away, you know, so I can evaluate what role I played. After I've done that, I like to talk about it, see if the conflict can be worked out. If it can't, then I need to decide how important it is to solve the conflict, and if I decide that it is important, then I ask for help, like advice, or perhaps mediation. Then I give it another try." Wow. If I truly did that, what a balanced person I would be. "However, there are times when the other person is not going to be in a place where they can work out that conflict. In those cases, I try to be accepting, and forgiving."

"Uhmm hmm." said Kristin. "And this is the routine you always follow? Does it make a difference if it's a student rather than an administrator that you are having the conflict with?"

Does it make a difference whether it's an ex-boyfriend, nutty roommate, or psycho date from hell? No, I treat them all equally by simply screaming at them. That's just my style. "Actually, I try not to let it make a difference. I always make an effort to be as diplomatic as possible."

"Okay Faith! I think that about does it. Do you have any questions for me?"

I was dying to ask her if she had spoken with Ethan, but I thought doing so might seem unprofessional. Besides, if she hadn't, I didn't want to give her any sort of reminder that she ought to. And if she had, how could I possibly defend myself anyway? Instead, I asked her about the difference between her school and public schools, so I would seem interested and engaged. After that she told me she would let me know soon, and I went home.

As I left I realized that although I had gotten a good feeling from Kristen, I had no idea whether or not I was going to get the job. I also had no idea last night that anything bad was coming before I walked in on Missy and Margaret. Maybe my psychic abilities really never had existed; perhaps they were a form of self-absorption. But I refused to believe that someone like Missy was actually more perceptive than I was, so I told myself the same thing that I had been saying to myself for months, that my abilities were simply on hiatus.

I had been dreading going home. But I didn't have my donut pillow with me, and there wasn't anywhere else I could think of to go anyway. Plus, I couldn't avoid Missy and Margaret forever. Might as well get the confrontation out of the way.

When I walked in I saw Margaret on the couch, watching television and petting Thomas.

"Hey, how did your interview go?"

"Fine, she said she'd let me know in a couple of days."

"Well, I hope you get it."

"Thanks." I grabbed my pillow, and sat down next to her. She was still petting Thomas, who was purring very loudly, and alternately squinting up at her and licking her hand.

"I think he likes me, we've been cuddling all day." I laughed and reached over and petted him myself.

"Doesn't he remind you of Whiskers?" asked Margaret. Whiskers was the cat we owned when I was eight and Margaret was six. Tragically, he was run over one day, and it was Margaret who found him dead. I don't think she ever quite got over it, which is probably why our parents never got us another cat. Yet Whiskers had been nothing like Thomas, he was aloof and prone to biting. But why destroy Margaret's memory of him?

"Sure. I can see the similarities," I said. They were both cats after all, so it wasn't a total lie. We sat there for a moment, lavishing our attention on Thomas, who loved every minute of it. But I couldn't stand the silence for too long, so I gave in and asked.

"Where's Missy?"

"She had errands to do before work," Margaret stated simply.

"So, um are you two a... a couple?"

"Would that be so awful if we were?"

"Why can't you answer the question?"

"Why can't you lay off?"

Swell. "I will lay off, if that's what you want. But I think I have a right to know if my roommate and my sister are a couple. So answer me yes or no, and then we can drop the whole thing."

"God, Faith, things sure are simple in your world, aren't they?"

"How so?"

"You're either a couple or you're not. You're a tramp or a good girl. You're gay or you're not."

"Are you gay?"

"Faith!" Margaret looked up towards the ceiling and rolled her eyes. But her eyes met my own as she started in on her next statement. "I'm not like you. Maybe I don't know myself as well. Maybe you have a better idea of what you want than I do. But for me, there are no easy answers. I don't know what I want to do with my life, or whom I want to spend it with. So I thought I would come down here, and just be open to the experiences that presented themselves. Is that so awful?"

"No. But you need to be careful. And I don't think Missy is the right person to get involved with."

"First of all, we're not involved. And second, what do you know? You've always been careful, and yet you still wind up getting hurt."

"That is not true."

"Whatever. Listen Faith, I appreciate your concern, but I can take care of myself. And believe it or not, Missy is not all that bad. She just has different standards than you do. At least she doesn't go around afraid all the time. You could learn a lot from her."

"I don't go around afraid all the time."

"Please! Faith, you are the queen of going around afraid all the time."

Margaret probably thought that because while we were growing up I had been somewhat cautious. I was the type of kid who saved up my allowance for a rainy day, then never spent it all. When we went to the state fair, Margaret always rode the roller coaster while I opted for visiting the pig house. And I was never one for going to parties where I wouldn't know very many people, but that had never bothered Margaret. So she always had more friends than I did, and they admired her for her carefree spirit. But I had changed since high school, and I needed to convince her of that. "I moved down here, that was brave!"

"The only reason you moved down here was because it was easier than staying and dealing with your feelings about Lacey and Peter."

I got up. "I don't need to sit here for this. You're the one who followed me down here, so ..."

"Faith! Fine, be mad. But listen to me. All I'm saying, and believe me, I'm saying it for your own good, is maybe if you stopped looking for your psychic abilities to give you permission to be happy or sad, you'd notice there's a whole world out there, and it's waiting for you to notice it."

"Margaret, that is the biggest load of crap I've ever heard! The world isn't waiting for me to notice it; the world couldn't give two shits about me. It will go on spinning whether I notice it or not, and if you don't realize that, then you're living in a dream world."

"That's honestly sad, if that's what you think."

"I'm being realistic Margaret. And by the way, I don't look for my psychic abilities to give me signs, they just do. And you and Missy and everyone else can laugh at me all you want, but I know what I feel."

"That's my point! You don't! You're so busy examining what you feel that you don't feel anything at all! And the crazy thing is, you don't even admit to yourself that's what you're doing. Instead you use it as a crutch. Like if you examine the pain, you don't have to feel the pain. It saves you from actually acting on your instincts, or going after something or someone you may want. Because doing so would be way too scary for you."

Could she be right? If she was, I certainly wasn't going to admit it, especially not to her. "Look Margaret. We're just very different. Okay? So let's drop the whole thing. You do what you want, and I'll stay out of it."

I started to walk away, but Margaret got up and followed me into my room. "Faith, I'm sorry. But I want you to be happy."

I turned to her. "Well, my way of finding happiness isn't like yours. I can't jump into bed with any-ole-one, I'm not going to change professions every time I feel bored or restless, and I don't crash on other people's couches, being a mooch. I have responsibilities; I'm an adult. We can't all go around with Peter Pan complexes. So go ahead and be yourself Margaret, I won't judge you. But don't judge me either, okay?"

"No. Look. I realize I can be a flake." She gave a self-conscious little laugh, and I was surprised once more at how hard it is to offend her. "I know that I've made my fair share of mistakes. But here's my point. Life isn't a math problem. There is no 'right answer.' There is simply one thing to do, or another, or another. The possibilities are limitless, and you're never going to know what works for you until you try. So why not trust your instincts, and let go a little?"

I shrugged my shoulders and walked away. But I thought about what she said. I didn't know if trusting my instincts was something I was capable of, having always followed signs. But I hadn't been given much to go on lately. The dream I had had about the stuffing convention was the only thing I had left, and I had that dream weeks ago.

So as Carolyn and I prepared to go up North, I searched for some sort of message to guide me. Did my skin hurt? Did my toes itch? Would my dreams provide me with answers to life's complex questions? Maybe the Waldorf philosophy isn't off base, and we're all, in fact, products of the environment. That reduces us to something far more primal than I had ever estimated the human race to be, meaning we rely not on intellect, but on instinct. Yet, how could I not accept this theory? Truth was, I was all out of signs. Instinct was all I had left.

17

Before Carolyn and I left town we stocked up on gas and junk-food. The weather was perfect —clear and breezy, yet there was basically no traffic as we drove up north. The only thing that needed improvement was our attitudes. Carolyn and Charles had been broken up for a couple of weeks now, and she was still acting like Bonnie Tyler songs were running an endless loop inside her head. But every time I brought Charles up she would change the subject. I looked over at her. In her black t-shirt and cutoff jean shorts she looked like she was about eighteen. However, her expression aged her several years, despite her attempt to act cheerful.

"I still think it's so great. You got a real teaching job! And it sounds like such a cool place to teach." We had been over this already, but if that was what she wanted to talk about, fine.

"Yeah, it is great. I feel lucky. I'm just worried. What is going to happen once she finally talks to Ethan?"

"Maybe she already has, and he didn't say anything."

"You would think he would have said something."

"Hmm. Do you think there's any chance he is the one who is stalking you?"

"No."

"But you did at one point. Why did that change?"

I shoved some cheetos into my mouth and proceeded to explain and chew simultaneously. "Because of Max. If it's not him, then it has to be some person who knows Missy. Missy only convinced me it was Ethan because I was drunk. I don't think he would do something like that."

"You don't still like him, do you?" I had told Carolyn the story about how Ethan got Glenn pregnant then dumped her. We both knew it was taboo for me to still have feelings for him.

So I gave her the correct answer. "No!" I exclaimed, perhaps a bit too loud. Yet I couldn't deny that somewhere in me there was still a flame burning for Ethan, and all of my rationalizations could not put it out. I told myself it was residual feelings from my relationship with Peter, or that it was pure physical attraction. I didn't know how to explain it any other way.

"That's good. Because lately, you seem to be using a lot of your energy worrying about guys. Believe me, there are much better things to be concerned about."

"Oh, and I suppose you're an authority on this? You're still awfully concerned about Charles."

"That's not true! I hardly talk about him at all."

"Yeah, but Carolyn, that doesn't mean you don't think about him."

Carolyn squirmed in her seat and took a gulp of her slurpee." At least I'm making an effort to focus on other stuff."

"But don't you think dealing with your feelings would also be healthy?"

"Just because I don't talk about them doesn't mean I'm not dealing with them. We all have different ways of handling things."

"I know, and I have a feeling this weekend will be great for you. A change of scenery can work wonders."

"Let's start by changing the c.d.," Carolyn answered. "This sappy stuff is getting on my nerves." She turned off my Best of Air Supply compilation and switched to Elliot Smith, who may not be sappy, but he is certainly depressing.

I had been walking on eggshells around Carolyn. She was still so sensitive, and I didn't want to say anything to piss her off. However, I failed Lacey by not getting her to talk about her dad, and I didn't want to make the same mistake with Carolyn in regards to Charles.

So I was gently trying to get her to open up.

But Carolyn was a master at changing the subject. "So are there going to be dead animals everywhere at this thing?"

"Sort of. The people who come up are usually preparing for the big taxidermy convention down in Duluth in the fall. But they like to show off their mounts…"

"What's a mount?"

"You know. When they mount their animal?"

"And is it in some sort of freaky pose?"

"It depends. If it's a mount of a deer, then no, it's usually just the head. If it's something like a chipmunk, then yes. But anyway, they like to get feedback on the artistry of their mounts…"

"Artistry? You're not serious."

"Yeah, I am. These people take it very seriously. They have workshops on things like painting and sculpting to improve their skills. And they spend a lot of time critiquing each other's mounts. Because once they're down in Duluth, there are all sorts of cash prizes for the best mounts."

"So we're going to be surrounded by dead mounts all weekend."

"Exactly."

"How representative of both of our love lives."

"Well, anyway. I think we should relax and have a good time. My parents will be expecting us to help and all, but there should still be time to go out and to walk around the lake. It will be great."

Even as I said those words, I had trouble believing them. In the weeks since I had moved down to Minneapolis, a lot had gone wrong for both Carolyn and myself. I suppose I had looked at the stuffing convention as some sort of salvation, a quick fix for all of our problems. But now that the weekend was here, I realized how ridiculous my thinking had been.

We were supposed to be at my parents' place before noon, so as to arrive before any of the guests did. But that would have meant leaving by around 8:00am, and Carolyn is not good at mornings. So by the time we got up there, it was after one. As we pulled in, my mother came out to greet us.

"Well it's about time, Faith! We've already had two people check in, and several people who are staying elsewhere have stopped by. I can tell already that this year is going to be busier than ever."

"Sorry Mom, we got off to a late start." I reached to hug her.

"Well I'm glad you're here." I had pulled away from our hug, but her arms tightened around me once again. "I'm so happy to see you. I miss having you girls close by."

It was good to see her too. I had forgotten how comforting it was to be around my mother. "Well, it's good to be home."

"And Carolyn is here!" My mother let go of me, and reached to hug Carolyn. "It's lovely to see you, and it's been way too long! It is wonderful of you to come up and help us out like this."

"It's good to see you too, Kay. And I'm happy to be here, it will be fun." Carolyn used to come home with me for weekend trips during college, and she got to know my parents well.

My mom smiled at both of us, her beaming red face matching the color of her hair. "You're right, it will be fun. Faith, why don't you two go on up to the orange room, and unpack. Then I need you to come down and help me in the kitchen. Unless, of course, you're hungry. Have you two eaten lunch?"

"We're fine, Mom. We'll put our things away, and be down in a minute or two." I led Carolyn up to the orange room, which was appropriately named for it's burnt orange painted walls, and matching bedspread and curtains. It was also the smallest room in the house, and was furnished with only one full size bed.

"We're both sleeping in here?" Carolyn asked.

"All the other rooms are being used. We're lucky that Dad didn't make us crash on the couch. This is one more room he could have rented out."

"Yeah, but the bed is so small, and I toss and turn."

"Then you can have it. I'll sleep on the floor."

"Faith, don't be ridiculous. You're not going to sleep on the floor."

As soon as she said that, my toes started to itch, but I pushed the sensation away. "We'll figure it out later. Come on, let's go help my mom."

On the way downstairs we ran into my dad, who was helping some guy display his mount in the living room.

"Faith! Come over here and check these out! Tell me these squirrels don't look real!"

Carolyn and I strolled over to where the squirrels were being displayed. One was holding an acorn, with his head tilted in a quizzical, Walt Disney type way. The other was in an attack stance, up on his hind legs, with his front legs drawn and his teeth bared.

"Aren't these great? This has got to be just about the best I've seen."

"Sure Dad. I think you're right." My Dad was always saying this, and that was my standard reply. He wasn't being insincere; he loves looking at the mounts so much he just gets carried away. He even tries to do taxidermy himself. That's how my parents got started having the stuffing convention in the first place. But he's terrible at it. His mounts usually end up with limbs of unequal length or lopsided faces, like taxidermy done by Picasso. Lucky for him though, that doesn't spoil his fun.

"Dad, you remember Carolyn."

"Of course! How are you Carolyn?"

"Fine, thanks."

"You two should meet Harry. He's down from Grand Marais, and he's the guy who did these fantastic squirrels."

"Nice to meet you. Good work too, by the way." I held out my hand to shake his, but my gesture was ignored as soon as Carolyn spoke.

"Nice to meet you, Harry." Carolyn spoke almost at the same time I did, and it was like they were the only two people in the room. Their eyes locked, and I could feel the sparks flying from a few feet away.

Harry took her hand, and shook it firmly. "I'm sorry, but I didn't catch your name."

"No, I'm sorry. It's Carolyn."

"Carolyn. Now that is a lovely name."

Carolyn giggled as her face turned bright red. I couldn't blame her; Harry was cute. He looked like a lumberjack, the type you hoped would offer you his flannel jacket just so you could get a better view of his biceps. Tall with broad shoulders and tanned skin, (which offset his brown hair with golden streaks perfectly), his eyes were his most noticeable feature: Crystal clear blue and piercing, as if he was looking right through you. He was like a bigger, more rugged looking Brad Pitt.

"Um," said Carolyn, "I don't know much about taxidermy, but these squirrels are amazing! I can't believe you did these yourself."

"Well thanks. I take a lot of pride in stuffing the animals I kill."

"Oh, so you killed these squirrels too?" Carolyn is sort of a pacifist.

"You betcha! I love to hunt; I'll hunt just about anything. You ever been?"

"Hunting? Um, no."

"You're kidding! You live around here?"

"Well, in Minneapolis."

"You live in Minnesota, and you've never been hunting? But you've been fishing before, right?"

"Actually, no. I've never been fishing either."

Harry ruefully shook his head. "That's practically a crime! We're going to have to fix that. How about we go tomorrow morning?"

"Um, well, I'm supposed to be helping..."

"We'll go out early in the morning, like at 5. You'll be back in plenty of time to help out."

"Okay. Sounds great."

I was bowled over that Carolyn would agree to do anything in the early morning, let alone fish. I could practically hear her heart beating as we walked into the kitchen to find my mom. On the way in Carolyn grabbed my arm with tremendous urgency.

"Faith! I can't go fishing with him. You have to get me out of it. You'll have to cover for me or something, say that I have some job that I need to do for your parents...."

"Why?"

"Why? Why? Isn't it obvious as to why?"

"But..."

"Faith, if I want to get Charles back, the last thing I should do is go fishing with Harry!"

"Then why did you agree to go in the first place?"

"Oh good, there you two are!" My mom walked into the kitchen. "Faith, I need you to start breading the walleye for me. And Carolyn, if you wouldn't mind chopping some vegetables and preparing the salads..."

She put us to work. It was only after several minutes of being on task that Carolyn was able to sneak over to me to continue our conversation.

"I mean it, Faith, you have to get me out of this."

"If you don't want to go then why did you say yes?"

"Because! My hormones took over for a second; I couldn't say no. Which is exactly my problem. I need you to save me from myself."

"Carolyn, this will be fine. You don't even know where things are with you and Charles. Maybe spending time with someone else will be good for you."

"Spending time with someone else is exactly what got me into trouble in the first place."

"That's different. You weren't broken up then. And David was sleazy."

"But it's okay for me to spend time with a man who kills cute, innocent little squirrels for sport."

"I've always thought squirrels were kind of gross. They're like big rats with bushy tails."

"I don't care!"

"Carolyn, is there a problem?" My mom looked over and noticed she was not at work. "I hate to be a nag, but there's so much to do, and the sooner we get those salads done the sooner we can move on to other stuff."

My mom is usually laid back, except when it's a major holiday or the weekend of the stuffing convention. I had warned Carolyn of this, and she had agreed to humor her. But Carolyn also is capable of losing her temper, especially when matters of the heart are at stake.

"Kay. Relax. I'm on the salad, all right? Give me one more second." My mom's face registered her surprise at the tone, but she said nothing in response. "Look. I need you to do this for me, Faith." Carolyn was now whispering in my ear. "I am weak. But I'm telling you, under no circumstances are you to let me go fishing with Harry."

I whispered back. "If you can't control yourself, maybe you shouldn't be getting back together with Charles."

"Excuse Me!?" Carolyn growled, causing my mother to look up from her work. She resumed whispering. "I am completely capable of fidelity, Faith. But I'm not with Charles right now, thus I haven't had sex in a very long time! My hormones are telling me one thing, and my heart is telling me another. It's up to you to make sure that my heart wins!"

She poked me in the arm for emphasis, then returned to her vegetables with a ferocity that did much to convince me of her point. That carrot she was chopping with such vigor could have been my head, after all.

My father walked into the kitchen. "Kay, is room 4 ready yet? The Gradys are here early."

"Oh my!" My mother proclaimed. "That's never happened before. They usually show up late."

"I know, which is why I'm asking you if their room is ready."

"Well, of course it is. I always have the rooms ready by 10:00am; to do otherwise would be unprofessional."

"Great. Can you go out and help them, then? I was right in the middle of showing Kyle Jordan the space for the skinning workshop."

"I'm right in the middle of something too! Can't Kyle wait a few minutes? I'm trying to get dinner prepared."

My dad shifted his weight from foot to foot, and took on his "I'm getting impatient" stance. "Kay, dinner isn't for several hours. I think what I'm doing is a little more pressing. He needs time to set up the workshop…"

"I'll do it!" I cried. The last thing I wanted was for my parents to come to blows right in front of Carolyn; she was obviously shook up enough at the moment. "But I have no idea who the Gradys are. Are they out front?"

My mom looked at me in horror. "You know who the Gradys are! The father and son, they've come every year for the last few years."

"Yeah, but Mom, I haven't been up for the stuffing convention in like forever."

"Faith, they're right out at the front desk," said my father. "Just go out there and show them to room 4."

That seemed easy enough. I left my mother and Carolyn behind in the kitchen, and walked out towards the front entrance. There I found a rather slim man who looked to be in his mid-fifties, wearing a fishing vest and carrying "Sport and Game" magazine. But he became a blur as soon as I realized whom he was with. For standing by his side, looking completely at ease, but (I suspect) as surprised as I was, was Ethan.

18

W hat are you doing here?"

"Faith? I... I'm with my Dad. What are you doing here?"

"My parents own this place." I was so shocked to see him that I momentarily forgot that I didn't want to see him. But once I remembered I was angry with him I found myself acting even more defensive than I felt.

"You're kidding. My dad and I have been coming up here for years. I don't remember seeing you here before."

"What, you think I'm lying?"

"No, of course not..."

"Come on. I'll show you to your room." Trying to ignore my pounding heart and the heat that was coursing through my body, I grabbed the key to room 4 and led them upstairs.

"I can't believe we didn't figure this out before. I should have said something when you told me that you're from here..."

"I can't see what difference it makes!" I snapped. There was an uncomfortable silence as I unlocked their room and led them in. His father broke it.

"Ethan, this is a friend of yours?"

"Uh, yeah. Sorry Dad. This is Faith. Faith, this is my Dad, Keith."

"Hi, it's nice to meet you." I shook his hand.

"Nice to meet you too. How do you two know each other?"

There was another uncomfortable silence. "Well, sir, your son flirted with me while he was servicing my car, took me out once, then never called. However, his supposed ex-girlfriend sabotaged me, but his aunt, your sister, offered me a job, primarily because he gave me a good reference. But we haven't been in communication lately, not since I left a drunken message accusing him of being a stalker."

Thank God I was merely thinking that rather than saying it out loud. Ethan came up with a simpler summation. "I fixed her car a few weeks ago, and we sort of kept in touch after."

"I see. Well, it's nice to meet you, Faith."

"Likewise. And I hope that you'll be comfortable in this room. Please let my parents or me know if there's anything you need." I said this all without looking at Ethan, and I rushed out as soon as I was done. Just standing next to him caused me to turn into a completely flustered idiot. I was losing my head quickly, and I had to get away.

But my efforts were to no avail. He followed me out into the hall, and grabbed me by the arm, turning me around to face him. His touch sent a simultaneous shiver and lightening rod through my entire body, and I could still feel his hand on my arm even after he had pulled away. I stood there facing him, but he said nothing. He looked at me with that intense gaze, the one that had caused me to fall for him in the first place. But I had enough of uncomfortable silences for one day.

"What?" I demanded, after a couple of seconds of him not saying anything.

"I forgot what I was going to say." He looked down, and scratched his leg absently. All of a sudden I must have felt bad, because the words just spilled out of my mouth.

"Look, I'm sorry about that message. If you hadn't already figured it out, I was drunk. I was sort of upset about a lot of things, you see, because somebody has been leaving me all these weird messages and notes and stuff, and after Glenn tripped me I thought, well I didn't think...my roommate convinced me that it was you, but I know that it wasn't, so I'm sorry. Oh, and thanks for recommending me to your aunt, she offered me the job. Did she say anything to you?"

Ethan remained focused on the itch on his leg throughout my entire speech. It wasn't until a couple of seconds after I was done when his eyes met mine. When he spoke, his voice sounded cold.

"You mean that weird message from a few days ago? The one that was left at my shop?"

Oh no. What had I done, and how could I take it all back? My mind drew a blank. "Yeah."

"That was you?"

"Yeah."

"You thought I was stalking you?"

"Um... Well as I just explained...."

"You know, that message was so garbled, I had no idea it was you until now. I erased it and forgot about it."

"Oh." Shit. Stupid, stupid me.

"So you called on the night after Glenn accidentally tripped you. Was the message meant to be a threat or something?"

"No! Wait a second. Glenn tripped me on purpose! And she caused me to bruise my tailbone really bad. It's only now that I can sit down without my donut pillow..."

"What's a donut pillow?"

"You know, a donut pillow?" I drew the shape of it in the air with my hands. Ethan shook his head in confusion. "Look, never mind. I was drunk and I was in pain, and I was angry with Glenn for tripping me. But I didn't mean what I said."

"Glenn tripping you was an accident. She felt terrible about it."

"Hah! Yeah, right. Do you know your girlfriend at all?"

"She's not my girlfriend. But yeah, I know her. And I know she wouldn't do something like that."

"Please! She threatened me, then she tripped me. For some reason she felt so threatened by me that ..."

"Threatened by you? Glenn doesn't feel threatened by anyone, so she certainly doesn't feel threatened by you."

The implied insult infuriated me. "Meaning what? Am I so low on the food chain?"

He hesitated. "Look, no offense. But you work at her mom's coffee shop. And Glenn, well she's in P.R. Image is everything to her. You're not the sort of person she would feel intimidated by."

"So I don't have an image? All I am is some lackey who works in her mother's coffee shop? Is that how you see me?"

"What I'm saying is that's how Glenn sees you." It wouldn't have mattered if he had said, "You are a goddess, please marry me and bear my children." I could hear nothing but disdain in his voice.

"Well thanks a lot! But for your information, she felt threatened because she could tell there was something between you and me, and for some insane reason, she wants to hold onto you. Although after what you did to her, I can't imagine why."

"What I did to her?"

"And you're the last person to talk down to me. At least for me, working in the service profession is temporary."

He laughed. Not a "ha, ha, that was so funny" laugh, it was more like a "you stupid, ignorant child," sort of laugh. "Excuse me. I need you to repeat that. Because it sounds like you were equating pouring coffee to fixing engines. So let's be clear. What you meant to say is anyone can do my job? That I am as much of a quote, lackey, as you are?"

"I won't be pouring coffee for much longer. I just meant I have a job now."

"Yeah, because of me."

I wanted to punch his smug little face in. "Fine! Be that way! Call your aunt, tell her I'm a nutcase, make her renege on the job offer. I don't care."

"Don't think I won't!"

"Fine!"

"Fine!"

We stormed off in separate directions, he into his room, me back down to the kitchen. When I got down Carolyn was finishing up the salads. I went straight to my fish station and started back to work. My mom was bent over in the refrigerator, grabbing more ingredients for the evening meal. But she had heard me come in, so she spoke without looking at me.

"Are the Gradys all settled in their room?"

"Yeah Mom, they're fine." She closed the fridge, and caught sight of me while walking back to the counter.

"Why is your face all red?" My hand flew up to my face, leaving some remains of the milky bread mixture I was using on my cheek.

"I don't know. Maybe it's hot in here or something."

Carolyn looked over at me. "Wow, your face is really red. It's not that hot in here."

"I'm fine. Drop it, okay?"

"Well, now you sound angry," said my mom.

"I'm not angry!"

"You certainly sound angry," Carolyn interjected.

"I'm not! I'm a little flustered; that's all."

They both looked as if they were expecting me to say more, and it was obvious they would not let the matter drop until I did. I took a deep breath. "Ethan is here."

Carolyn nearly dropped her vegetable knife. "What? He's here?"

"Yeah."

"You know Ethan Grady?" My mom wanted to know.

"So he is the one who is stalking you!"

"No, Carolyn, you've got the wrong idea."

"Somebody is stalking you?"

"Mom, I can explain."

"Please do. Tell me, how do you know Ethan, and why is he stalking you?"

"He isn't stalking me! I only thought he was because I was drunk."

"Oh Faith. Haven't I warned you about drinking in excess? Honey, you need to be more careful."

"Mom, it was one time. And that's not what this is about."

"Well, what is this about?"

"This is about..." God. I didn't know. Explaining this to my mom was going to be as hard as explaining would have been to Ethan's dad. But it turned out I didn't have to. For at that moment, Ethan walked in. All eyes turned to him.

"Excuse me," he said. "I'm sorry to barge in."

"That's okay, Ethan,' said my mother. "How are you?"

"I'm good Kay, it's nice to see you again."

"Likewise."

He turned towards me. "Actually, I was looking for you. I didn't mean to lose my temper—just wanted you to know. So, uh, no hard feelings." He walked towards me, his arm extended in an effort to shake hands. I found this gesture, which was obligatory and suggested indifference, more offensive than all the things he said.

"What, did your dad overhear us? Did he tell you to come down and apologize?"

Ethan's hand dropped to his side, and his voice regained the icy quality it had earlier. "I wanted to bury the hatchet."

"You know what? We can bury the hatchet when you recognize the evil thing your girlfriend did by tripping me and causing me to fall on my tailbone. Or when you apologize for leading me on, then never calling."

"I can explain why I didn't call," he said, but I cut him off.

"Don't bother! I don't want your explanations, because I know all about you."

"Know what? You keep saying stuff like that, but I don't know what the hell you mean!" He yelled this, so I guess we both forgot we weren't alone. I blabbered on, aware of nothing but my anger towards him.

"If you don't know what I mean, than that makes it all the worse."

"That old line? You don't even know what you're saying."

"Sally told me! She told me all about you and Glenn, how you got her pregnant then abandoned her! How could you be so low?"

Ethan's face turned white, and all expression drained from his face. Very quietly he replied. "I see. Well that explains everything. Never mind about asking for my side of the story." He turned to go, and I wanted to puke all over the raw fish below me. I instantly regretted my words until he turned back around and calmly laid into me. "Do you even know what friendship is? Are you capable of keeping an open mind, of forgiving anyone but yourself? We're all human, Faith. So get over it. Life goes on."

He stormed out, leaving me as torn as an old bank statement put through the paper shredder. Half of me was furious for how he had spoken; the other half wanted to run after him and make everything okay. So I compromised, and stood there, frozen in my thoughts. My mother's words woke me up.

"Well, that was dramatic. You two must genuinely like each other."

"Very funny, Mom."

"I'm serious. We don't bother to get angry with the people we don't care about, now do we?"

"You could be right. But what does it matter? Maybe he liked me at one time, but he seems to have gotten over it."

My mother put down the loaf of bread she was holding and walked across our large kitchen to stand next to me. She put her hand on my shoulder as she spoke. "I doubt his feelings have changed so quickly. My guess is he's like you; he has some baggage to work through before he can figure things out."

I looked over at Carolyn, who shrugged her shoulders and nodded her head at the same time. I turned back to my mom.

"So what do I do?"

"Isn't it obvious? Work through your own baggage first. It's the only way you'll know if the anger you're feeling should truly be directed at him."

❋   ❋   ❋

A few Sundays ago I read in *The New York Times* style section that I am a part of a whole generation of prolonged adolescents. As someone who's made a career out of teaching adolescents, this is not good news. I see the way they act: their self-absorption, their superior attitude combined with immaturity and a still developing brain. It troubles me to think I am functioning at the same level as they are. Yet, I can't deny it. As long as I am living only for myself and my primary concern is dissecting my personal life, I am no better than a teenager.

So what did I do? Something purely selfish – naturally. I abandoned my parents and Carolyn, and drove straight down to Duluth. I promised to be back soon.

19

I was on my way out." Lacey squirmed in her living room, where she remained standing. "I wish you had called first. This is not the best time."

"I'm sorry," I replied. "But I need to know something. It's kind of urgent."

"Okay..." Lacey said. "This is weird, Faith. You show up out of the blue, when I thought you were never speaking to me again."

"I know, but if we could sit down, then I'll explain."

"I don't have the time. I am supposed to meet Peter in twenty minutes."

"Okay, fine." During my drive down I envisioned Lacey as being happy and relieved to see me, but uncomfortable and impatient was more like it. I pushed on anyway. "Here's what I need to know; does Peter actually make you happy?"

"What?"

"Does he actually make you happy? Do you feel like he's 'the one'? And if so, have you always felt that way, like, since you first met him? And does he treat you well? Is he there for you? Has he helped you deal with your dad?"

"That's way more than one question. You should have called."

"I know. But given the circumstances, I think I deserve forgiveness."

Lacey put her hands on her hips. "Meaning?"

"Meaning you stole my boyfriend! How about cutting me some

slack? Instead you accuse me of being self-involved every time I express my anger."

"I didn't do that, and I didn't steal him. He came willingly. Look, I truly am sorry about everything, but what do you want me to do?"

"I want you to explain how you could throw away our friendship."

Lacey rolled her eyes and took an indignant breath.

"What?" I said in response to her nonverbal answer.

"I love him, and I need him. And our friendship... well, don't you think we were both outgrowing it a little, anyway?"

Her words were a slap in the face. She continued. "I mean, what do we have in common anymore? We don't even know how to talk to each other."

"You're saying that because of your dad," I replied. Lacey shook her head.

"No."

"Look, I'm sorry. I never knew how to be a friend to you after he died. But you could have given me a clue."

"Or," Lacey said tersely, "You could have simply figured it out. Peter was able to."

"So that's what this is about?"

Lacey collapsed onto the couch, and buried her head in her hands.

"Okay, then answer this, does he make you happy? Yes, or no?"

"Of course he makes me happy! Do you think I would be marrying him if he didn't?"

"I don't know, because as you just implied, I don't know you anymore. But I've been trying to forgive you anyway, and I figured something out. If I truly thought this was for the best, if I could believe he gave you something no one else could, something I failed to give you after your dad died, than maybe I could forgive you. But as little as I know you, I still feel like I really know Peter. And it's hard to believe he's giving you all that."

Lacey got up to angrily fluff pillows and arrange things that weren't out of order in the first place. "You have no right to come here and say these things to me! He's my boyfriend now! I'm sorry if you don't like it, but that's how it is."

"Were you even listening to me?!"

"Yeah, I was listening, and you can drop the guilt trip."

"It wasn't a guilt trip!"

"What do you want from me, Faith?"

"Honesty! And perhaps a little compassion! I want you to listen to me, and answer me, and give me half a chance at becoming your friend again! Why is that so difficult? Did our friendship mean so little that you can dismiss it so easily?"

"God! You don't get it, do you?" Lacey yelled at me. Her face was red and her eyes were squinting.

"Obviously I don't. You were my oldest friend! We shared everything, and I don't know how to throw that away like you do. I need to know what happened." Lacey didn't say anything as she sat back on the couch, resigned to the conversation. "I mean, was I that awful a friend? Was I honestly that self-involved? Because if I was, if I wasn't there for you when you needed me, then I am sorry. Really."

She sighed. "I can't believe you're apologizing to me."

Lacey's anger was gone, and I saw the beginning of tears form in her eyes. It was one more thing I couldn't understand. "What do you mean?"

"Come on! I stole your boyfriend! I should be apologizing to you. God! This is just so typical of you."

In my confused desperation I began to stutter. "B-but, you said that he c-came willingly, and that I was self-involved."

"I never said you were self-involved."

"Yes you did! You said not everything is about me, which is the same thing."

"No it isn't! But you do make things about yourself; you do it all the time. You're doing it right now."

"I am? I'm not trying to."

"You're trying to prove you're a better person than I am. You're trying to make me feel bad about what I did to you."

"No, I'm not! I wanted to see if there was a chance we could be friends again."

Lacey shot up from the couch. "I'm late! Okay? I've got to go. You... you should have called." She walked towards the door and opened it, cueing me to leave. I was out of things to say, so that's what I did.

"Faith," she said, right as I got to the door, "the thing is, and I don't mean to sound harsh, but I had to choose between the two of you. And I chose Peter. Maybe you can forgive me for that. But I don't think I can forgive myself."

"So that's it? We'll never be friends again?"

"I don't see how we can."

✳ ✳ ✳

I drove back up to Two Harbors, but I didn't turn in when I got to my parent's place. I just had too much thinking to do, and needed some alone time. I wanted to run away.

After several hours I reached the Canadian border, and I realized I had already started a new life when I moved to Minneapolis. So, I decided I probably ought to deal with the hand I had been playing before I ran away again. I drove back down. After all, I had to keep Carolyn from going fishing.

When I got inside, the place was quiet. I looked at my watch; it was nearly 11:00 p.m.! I sure had lost track of time. And I hadn't even eaten dinner. I went to the kitchen to remedy that, and I found that my mother and Carolyn had left me the dinner dishes to do. So I made myself some peanut butter toast, then set to work.

The place was still, since most everyone staying there would be getting up at around 5:00 a.m. to fish. I found washing the dishes to be almost meditative, so when I was done I decided to go ahead and scrub the kitchen floor. I wasn't sleepy at all, and the cleaning was focusing my thoughts. I felt so strong and independent that when I was done I went on to clean the oven. Missy would have been amazed and jealous that I hadn't ever done the same to our apartment.

I was reorganizing the pantry when I heard a rustling from the other room. The clock said it was close to two. I walked out of the kitchen, and found myself face to face with Ethan.

"Oh! It's you. Um, did you need something?" I stammered this, as I tugged on my flannel shirt and khaki shorts, and smoothed my hair. I knew I was a mess.

"I couldn't sleep. I was going to go for a drive."

"Oh. Well, would you like some warm milk, or something?"

He shrugged his shoulders. "Warm milk?"

"Yeah. Isn't that what people drink when they can't sleep?"

"I don't know. Have you ever had warm milk?"

"Sure. In hot chocolate, or in a latte. Haven't you?"

"I meant warm milk on its own."

"Oh. No. Have you?"

"No, but it sounds disgusting," he said, smiling ever so slightly.

"Right. So that would be a no, then. Okay, well if you don't need anything, I'm going to get back to the pantry." I started back.

"Hey Faith!" I stopped and turned back around. "What's with you?"

"What do you mean?"

"I'm nice to you and you're cold as ice. Then I yell at you, and a few hours later you're offering me warm milk. Why?"

"Because. You were right. I hold grudges. And I'm self-involved. But believe it or not, I'm still a nice person. And that," I turned to leave, "is what's with me." I said that last part with my face towards the door so he wouldn't see I was upset. No such luck.

"Hey wait, are you okay?" He lightly tapped my shoulder, and I stopped.

"Not really," I replied. "Do you ever go through phases where it feels like no one is on your side? Like you don't know how to truly explain what you're feeling, so everybody misunderstands and assumes the worst about you?"

Ethan nodded his head. "Sure. Actually, you made me feel that way."

I looked down at my feet, studying my worn fake Birkenstocks.

"Sorry," I murmured.

"It's okay. I can't blame you. I said I'd call, and the next time you see me I'm with Glenn. But I can explain about that..."

"You don't have to," I said. "I'm sure you have a lot going on right now."

"I... didn't you have a good time when we out?"

I looked back up at him, and my attempt at playing it cool melted away. His glasses were crooked, his hair was sticking up in chunks, and I found him completely irresistible. But those who've been burned are prone to fear fire, and I was no exception.

"Sure, but this whole thing between us, it's too confusing. Maybe it shouldn't be so much work."

Ethan shrugged his shoulders and took a step away from me. "Okay. But about before, you made me angry, that stuff you said about Glenn. And you've got it all wrong."

"Ethan, I don't need to hear about you and Glenn. You and I are just going to be friends, so it doesn't matter."

Ethan crossed his arms over his chest. "Then let's move on."

"Okay."

"I'm sorry," he said. He held out his hand and I shook it.

"I'm sorry too." I breathed deeply, relaxing into the situation. When I looked up at him I noticed a half smile on his face before he continued speaking. "I can't believe your parents own this place." He was still holding onto my hand.

"I can't believe that you stuff dead animals." I made a gesture with my free hand towards all the mounts that had been set up in the room. "Are any of these yours?"

He pointed over to the biggest one, a deer that was standing on all fours, its head gracefully turned over its shoulder. It was like someone had stuffed Bambi's mother. "Just this one," he said.

I tried to be polite. "Wow. That's cool."

He laughed. "I'm kidding. None of these are mine. My dad is the one who is into this stuff. I come up here because it's a chance to spend time with him when he's relaxed and happy."

"Oh. Male bonding, I see."

"Something like that." He was looking at me again, his eyes concentrated, full of an emotion I couldn't identify. Then he tightened his grip on my hand and pulled me towards him. We were so close I could feel his breath on my face, and I had lost my own ability to breathe, to think, to move. In the space of an instant, his arms were around me, and his lips were on mine. Our tongues and our lips struggled with each other for a moment before we found the perfect rhythm, and I lost myself to passion and sensation. I don't remember having any conscious thoughts during that moment, but if I did, I'm sure I was thinking nothing ever felt so good.

"Maybe we should rethink this 'just friends' thing," he whispered into my ear.

"Mmmhmm..." I replied. I was going to say more, but he cut me off with another kiss. After a long time we pulled away from each other.

"I wasn't expecting that," I said.

Ethan smiled and stroked my cheek. "I don't believe you."

"I honestly wasn't."

"Then you're dense. I've liked you since the first time I laid eyes on you. The entire time, all I've wanted is this." And with that, he grabbed me and started kissing me again. Now, if I was smart, I would have stopped and let him explain about Glenn and why he never called. But I didn't stop.

Instead I let him lead me over to the couch, where he laid down on top of me. I arched back as his hips, his chest, his everything met my own. Soon I was so lost in the feel of him that I didn't realize the moan I heard was coming from my own lips. I forgot I was on my parent's couch, in the front room of their bed and breakfast, surrounded by dead animals. I was aware only of the baby kisses he planted up and down my neck, which I returned by kissing him, hard, the way I had wanted to for so long. And I didn't stop to contemplate anything as our bodies merged together as one. But as soon as it was over, I thought to myself, "God, I'm easy!"

Later we were still sitting on the couch, both of us sloppily redressed and dazed. Ethan was running his fingers through my hair, and the only noise in the room was the sound of our breathing. Neither of us knew what to say, so we sat there, afraid to break the spell that had been cast between us. But nothing lasts forever, and it was inevitable that one of us would start thinking about reality. Of course, that person was Ethan.

"Do you know what time it is?" he asked. I looked at my watch, which had miraculously remained on my wrist.

"It's close to three."

"I should probably get upstairs. My dad and I are going fishing in a couple of hours."

"So you do fish, huh? Do you hunt as well?"

"Yeah. My dad and I usually go at least once a season."

"Do you kill animals when you hunt?"

"Um, isn't that the definition of hunting?"

"You said it was your dad who was into this stuff. I meant do you, personally, kill animals?"

Ethan yawned. "If I say yes, will you still like me?"

"I'm just curious."

He laughed softly. "No, you're just strange. Your parents run a taxidermy convention, and you have some moral grudge against hunting."

"I never said that. Actually, it's Carolyn who... Oh, crap!"

"What?"

"Carolyn! I forgot. I promised her I wouldn't let her go fishing."

"Huh?"

It was then that I realized my dream had, in fact, come true. I felt great, better than I had in a long time, and I knew that I had to get to Carolyn – immediately. "I'll explain later. Look, I have to go." I shot up, arranging my clothes so I was presentable enough to travel upstairs. Ethan stood as well.

"Okay. I need to get upstairs too." He didn't seem as concerned about his appearance as I was about mine. He fastened his pants, grabbed his shirt, and started walking. No "talk you later," no kiss on the cheek. I walked to keep up with him, hoping he would offer me some sort of reassurance before he disappeared behind door number 4. But all I got was another yawn, and "Man, I'm tired. Maybe I can nap for a couple of hours before it's time to get up again." And with that, he was gone.

I went to the room I was sharing with Carolyn. She was sound asleep, stretched diagonally across the bed that was barely big enough for the two of us. So, true to my word, I grabbed a pillow, and curled up on the floor. A couple of hours later I awoke to knocking at our door. Carolyn is a much deeper sleeper than I am, and didn't even budge. So I got up. I was fully expecting to find Harry on the other side of the door, ready to take Carolyn out on the open lake. So imagine my surprise when I opened the door to find Charles. He looked like he hadn't slept for days, and that breathing itself had become a major chore. In other words, he looked as bad as I knew Carolyn felt.

"Hey," he said. "Sorry to wake you. I ran into your dad downstairs. He said she was in her room. Can I come in?"

"Charles, how did you even know to come here?"

"She called me a few hours ago and we talked. I guess we're both miserable."

He pushed past me and entered our room. I almost started to cry as he approached the bed. He lay down and kissed the top of her head as if she were the most beautiful and precious person in the universe. I think he was completely unaware I was watching him. We were both caught up in a reverie, which is why the knocking on the door that followed startled us both.

He looked up. "Aren't you going to answer that?" he said, after a few seconds had gone by and the person on the other side of the door felt it necessary to knock again.

"Um. Yeah." I opened the door, and my worst fears were confirmed, Harry was standing there, fishing rod in hand.

"Hi. Is she ready to go?" Charles' head shot up, and I had to do something fast to save the situation. Luckily, I had not changed out of my clothes from yesterday, so the solution I came up with was almost feasible.

"Harry! I sure am ready! I can't wait."

"Well, but what about…"

"This is so exciting! But we had better get going. We don't want to miss the good catch!" Before he could reply, I pushed his chest with two hands out the door, and closed it behind us. He was looking at me like I was a lunatic, which I suppose was understandable.

"What about Carolyn?" he said, thankfully out of Charles's earshot.

"She can't go. Her boyfriend is here."

He pondered this as if it was a profound philosophical riddle. His brow furrowed, he studied me with a quizzical look. But soon enough he came up with a solution, and his brow and his manner relaxed back to their normal state.

"Okay. Well, you'll do. Come on, let's go." He started down the hallway. For a moment I considered not following him. But then again, if I didn't, how soon would it be before he noticed my absence and began knocking on the door to Carolyn's and my room? So I did follow him, but only so I could catch up with him and explain why neither Carolyn nor I could go. Unfortunately, when I made it to the front entrance there were a bunch of men gathered all prepared to go catch some fish. Among them were Ethan and his father.

"Are you coming?" Harry shouted over to me. It was then that Ethan noticed my presence. And in order to get over to Harry, I had to walk past him and all the other men, all of whom seemed to have nothing better to do than stare at me. So what if my hair was mussed, my clothes crumpled, and I stank of sex? It was none of their business. Okay, maybe it was sort of Ethan's business. But that's it.

I made it over to Harry. In a low voice I tried to explain. "Look. I don't think I should go after all. My mom needs me to help her this morning, and I don't want to cramp your style."

"What do you mean?" Harry bellowed. "Two minutes ago you said you could hardly wait."

"I know." The room was silent, save for Harry's and my conversation. Staring at me wasn't enough; everyone wanted to hear what I was saying as well. "But I changed my mind. I need to stay."

"Look," he replied. Why did he have to speak so loudly? "I didn't even invite you. But there you were, begging me to take you fishing. So let's go fishing. I'll get you back in a couple of hours. You'll have plenty of time to help your mom."

I was so tired I couldn't even think. All I knew was I wanted this humiliation to end. So I took the path of least resistance. "Fine." I said. "But I do need to be back in no more than two hours."

On our way out the door I looked over my shoulder, and saw Ethan still looking at me. I gave him a feeble wave along with a tentative smile, but he made no response. My stomach lurched, sick at the idea of hurting him. It was then that I finally admitted to myself he had truly captured my heart. Was it such a short time ago that I believed I could never love again?

However, while it may be that the heart needs no redemption, the same is not true for the whole of a human being. My journey had only just begun.

20

an you imagine what Dad would have done if he caught the two of you? You wouldn't have to worry about whether or not Ethan is going to call, because he'd be dead."

I had gotten back from the stuffing convention and was in the middle of telling Margaret the whole story.

"You're the one who told me to follow my instincts. That's all I was doing."

"But I didn't tell you to be reckless. Did he at least use protection?"

"Yeah. He had his wallet with him, since he had been planning on going for a drive. Is there some rule that all guys have to carry condoms in their wallets?"

Margaret didn't answer, but she shook her head at me like I was playing with matches and lighter fluid. I answered her silent recrimination.

"You said I should let go a little!"

"Yeah, I said let go a little. Sorry I didn't explain the concept of a little to you."

"Well if you had I probably wouldn't be in this situation."

"So it's my fault? How was I supposed to know you'd suddenly be reckless or even follow my advice in the first place? You never have before."

"Well this time I did. You always seem so happy with yourself. I thought if I acted more like you maybe I could adopt that attitude."

"Faith, if I'm happier with myself than you are, it's because I don't think everything to death, and I don't beat myself up about every single little mistake I make. It's not because I'm reckless."

"Thanks. That helps." Unexpressed anger was gurgling inside me even though none of this was her fault. I settled for speaking in a sarcastic tone.

"You're welcome." She replied cheerily. Sarcasm is usually lost on Margaret. "So you never even talked to Ethan after that morning?"

"I never got the chance! He wasn't around after that. And once Carolyn left with Charles I had so much work to do for Mom and Dad that I didn't have time to go and look for him."

"But Carolyn and Charles got back together?"

"I don't know. They looked pretty happy as they were leaving. They said they were driving north to explore the area while they talk things out."

"Well, that's good anyway."

"Yeah. I know." I was happy for Carolyn, but jealous there wasn't a happy ending in sight for my love life as well. "So, how are you and Missy? Any developments on that front?"

"We're just hanging out, Faith."

"Are you ever naked when you're hanging out?"

"I'm not having this conversation with you."

Margaret got up and walked into the kitchen. The cats' food bowls needed to be filled, so she went about completing that task. I stood and watched.

"Why won't you talk about it? I thought you were Miss Loose and Free."

"We need more cat food."

"Tell Missy."

"Why, don't you ever buy any?"

"They're Missy's cats."

"Yeah, but you pet them. You get enjoyment out of them."

"So do you."

"Fine. I'll go buy some cat food right now." Margaret walked out of the kitchen and went to grab her purse.

"Are you that desperate to avoid the conversation that you have to leave?"

"How can I avoid a conversation that I've already told you I'm not having? There is no conversation to avoid." She walked towards the front door and opened it. Before she had taken her first step out, we both noticed what had been left outside. Margaret reached down to pick up two small and flimsy nightgowns, one pink and one blue. There was (of course) a note attached.

One for you and one for her. Maybe this time you'll be able to figure out who wears the pants in the relationship. In my book, you both ought to be.

"Huh. Don't these look like they're from K-Mart? They remind me of something Grandma Florence would wear, only more skimpy." Margaret waved the nightgowns back and forth, as if to assess their quality. "But at least we can use these. I don't know when any of us will ever use that witch's hat, except maybe at Halloween."

"Margaret, did Missy go to the police the last time this happened?"

"No. I think she thought you were."

"But I said she should go. Remember, last time we decided that all of this is about her."

"I don't think she thinks that."

"Well, she ought to. Don't you think this note makes it sort of obvious?"

Margaret looked at me blankly with her head cocked. "The note, Margaret. It is obviously referring to your and Missy's relationship."

"Faith, how many times do I have to say it? I'm not going to talk about Missy and me." Margaret stepped past me and left to go buy cat food. I couldn't figure out why she was so uptight, but I wasn't going to harp on it. I went to the desk in the living room where I had left all of the previous notes. I grabbed them and headed out to the police.

In the parking lot I saw Bill walking back from somewhere, his laptop in hand. I waved, and he came over.

A huge smile spread across his face as he spoke. "Hey there! I haven't seen you around lately."

"Yeah, I was up north at my parents' place."

Bill raised an eyebrow. "Oh. That's nice. So you got a break from the city."

"Yeah, the way things are going, I wish I was still up there."

Bill moved in closer and leaned up against my car. "Why? What's wrong?"

"Some freak has been leaving Missy all these phone messages and notes outside of our door, and she refuses to do anything about it."

"You mean like that one when I returned your purse?"

"Yeah, only there have been more of them. You haven't noticed anything since then, have you?"

"No. Nothing." He paused, scratching his forehead and wrinkling his brow. "You're sure they're all meant for Missy?"

"Yeah, why do you ask?"

"Well, did they have her name on them?"

"No. But there's no reason that they would be for me. Whereas Missy... well, I'm assuming it's one of her customers. She does phone sex."

Bill laughed. "Lucky you, getting to be her roommate. I don't know what a nice girl like you is doing, living with her." He shifted again, than leaned in even closer. "I don't want to shock you or anything, but I hear Missy goes both ways."

It was my turn to laugh. "Believe me; it's way too late for me to be shocked."

Bill raised an eyebrow. "Oh yeah?"

"You bet. I'm not as nice or as innocent as I may appear. And Missy... well, she's been getting some lately. So nothing you could say is going to shock me." Bill's face grew pale. "Are you okay?" I asked him.

He straightened up and stepped away from the car. "Yeah, but I should go. See you later."

He began to walk away. I didn't answer him, but wordlessly got into my car. What was up with him?

* * *

"So has your home been broken into?"

"No."

"Have you been threatened physically or attacked?"

"Well, no. But the notes and the messages definitely imply a threat." I had waited for over two hours to speak with an officer. Once I finally got my chance, I told him the whole story: of the messages, the notes, and how this person mysteriously seems to know about Margaret and Missy's involvement. I told him Missy is in the sex business, indicating there could be any number of her customers as suspects. But I also mentioned Max. I didn't mention Ethan, for I was convinced he had nothing to do with it. The officer listened to me patiently, recording everything I said on some police department stationary. But once he started asking me questions, I knew what his answer would be.

"Ma'am, I will keep these notes and your testimony in a file, but for the moment, that's all I can do."

What could I say? I'd seen enough suspense movies to know this is the drill, and besides, there were people in the city who had much bigger problems. I couldn't expect police protection simply because some weirdo had been calling and leaving notes and gifts outside our door. I thanked him and got up to go.

I didn't feel like going home. Margaret was probably back by now, and if Missy wasn't home, she would be soon. I didn't think I was up to facing either of them, nor did I want to talk about this whole stalker mess. They were so oblivious, and if I had to try and explain the seriousness of the situation one more time, I was sure I would lose it.

But if I wasn't going home, I didn't know where I was going. Carolyn was still out of town with Charles. I could go to the coffee shop, but if I did, I ran the risk or running into Glenn, and perhaps Ethan, and I didn't feel up to that either. All at once I felt more alone than I ever imagined I would. There was no one to offer me safety while I was scared. I sat in my car and stared at the cracked pavement outside my window. I wracked my brain to come up with options. Where could I go? Who could I turn to? I made a mental checklist of every friendship I ever had. What had gone so wrong that I had no one to go to now?

In the midst of overwhelming self-pity, I was startled by some noise. A woman, drunk out of her mind, was being led by a police-man into the station. With worn clothes and ratty hair she displayed that classic homeless look.

"Get your hands off of me! I need to find Marcus! Let me find Marcus, he'll take care of this. Are you listening to me? I need to find Marcus!"

She screamed as she was being led in, her voice pure desperation. Had there ever been a time in her life when she was happy, when she was taken care of, provided for? And who was Marcus? Boyfriend? Hus-band? Son? Dealer? Did he truly have the power to make everything okay? Or perhaps she was doing what so many of us do – endowing him with an omnipotent authority because she wanted to believe one person's love could make all the difference. And although I was lucky enough to be safe inside my car while she had the misfortune of her own situation, I felt a connection with her nonetheless.

I shook my head to discard the trance I was in. I turned the key in the ignition and pulled out of the parking lot. I wasn't sure where I was headed, but I knew one thing without a doubt: It was time to move on.

❋ ❋ ❋

I ended up going to the Mall of America, where Max had taken me on our first date. Usually it wouldn't have appealed to me, but today I liked moving amongst the crowds of people shopping so I could lose myself, and after a while, I did. I cleared my mind, and began to have fun. Fact was, I needed new clothes for my new job.

I bought a charcoal A-line wool skirt at the Banana Republic, along with a cream-colored, button-down blouse with over-sized cuffs and collar, and a hand-knit cotton cardigan sweater with wooden buttons. It was all very teacher-like, but stylish at the same time. And to be kicky, I added in a pair of knee length suede boots to complete the ensemble.

I imagined myself teaching in this outfit, feeling purposeful. I also imagined going out in this outfit after school one day for drinks, with my new teacher friends, friends I was sure to make. Both scenarios fit, and I was so encouraged that I continued shopping. I bought a lot of basics, long sleeved t-shirts at the Gap, comfortable khaki pants just formal enough to work in, socks and underwear. I threw in a light blue silk scarf, long enough to wrap around my neck a couple of times, with fringe on either end. I also bought expensive lipstick and perfumed lotion. I figured, why not? Maybe I didn't have the life for these things right now, but that didn't mean I never would. I had to start with my attitude.

After treating myself to dinner at the crepe stand, and to a movie and a box of Junior Mints, I was finally ready to go. I wound up putting close to a thousand bucks on my credit card, but I justified it as more effective than therapy, plus I actually had some material things to show for it. I drove home in an excellent mood.

When I got to my apartment building I pulled up to the curb and parked. I was fishing my packages out of the back when another car pulled up behind me, and stopped. I didn't turn to see who it was until I heard the voice behind me.

"Faith?"

Then I didn't have to turn around, for I would recognize that voice anywhere.

21

I should have known. Isn't it a law of nature: as soon as you are over an ex; the ex shows up? There's only one catch—for it to work you have to be so truly over your ex, that it would never occur to you that he might come around. Thus, you're not thinking about him. At all.

Peter and I were sitting at Perkins, which was not too far from my apartment building. He said he only wanted a cheap cup of coffee, so I took him there. Yes, I could have asked him in, and in retrospect, I wish I had. But at the time I wasn't ready to let him into my living space, and I wanted to talk to him without having Missy and Margaret around.

He looked terrible. His eyes were bloodshot, his hair hung in greasy clumps as if it hadn't been washed in days, and his beard was growing out in a scruffy fuzz. His hand shook as he raised his coffee cup to his lips. He was like some bad cliché of a broken down man from a 1930s film noir. Or maybe that was the image he was trying to portray. I don't know. With Peter, image and reality tend to merge.

"So, what's up?" I asked. He hadn't yet told me why he was here. Instead we made small talk, as if him driving down on a surprise visit months after our breakup was a completely natural occurrence. He took a sip of coffee, then set down his cup and gave me a defeated smile.

"You look great, Faith. It's really... it's so good to see you."

"Uh huh. Why are you here?" I was determined to get to the

bottom of this, and to not let him get to me in the process. Already my insides felt like a jellyfish. There were too many memories attached to Peter for me to be impervious to his charm.

"I wanted to see you. To talk to you. I heard you came to see Lacey. That was when I started wondering."

"Wondering what?"

"How you are."

"You couldn't have called? You had to come all the way down to find out?"

"It's easy to hide on the phone. I wanted to see for myself how you actually are doing."

"What makes you think I have anything to hide?"

Peter rattled his empty cup, and reached for the coffee pot to refill it. He didn't look at me as he replied. "That's not what I meant."

"And why is it so important to you anyway, to see how I'm doing?"

"Jesus, Faith, what's with the interrogation? You told Lacey you still wanted to be friends. I thought you might feel the same way about me. Is that so wrong?"

"It's not wrong, it's just inaccurate."

"I see." He kept his focus down, as if he was examining his fingers, checking they were still the same fingers that he had two hours before. "That's too bad. We shared a lot. I hoped we could remain friends."

A million different replies ran through my mind. Here was my chance to tell him off. He was sitting right in front of me, vulnerable; it was the perfect opportunity to hurt him. But those words remained frozen on my lips.

"Tell me why. I need to know what about me is so expendable that neither you nor Lacey minded hurting me."

"You're still hung up on that? I've told you before, it wasn't about you. We fell in love."

"Peter, you act like what happened was nothing. I loved you. I loved Lacey. Nothing has ever hurt me more. And then the two of you act like I'm imposing on you for being upset. Do you have any idea how maddening that is?"

"I suppose I never thought about it."

"Thanks," I said sarcastically, "that helps."

"Lacey and I always knew you would analyze the situation enough for the three of us, so I suppose we felt that she and I didn't have to."

"I should throw this coffee in your face for that. Do I mean so little that you have to be insulting on top of everything else?"

Peter's shoulders sagged. "You know, you're taking the whole thing way too personally. Did it ever occur to you that we're just more selfish than you are?"

After being accused of my own selfishness time and again? I shook my head. "We weren't thinking about you. I was thinking about myself, and about Lacey."

I pondered this. Could it be that the flawed parties here were Peter and Lacey, and not myself? Interesting. But I wasn't entirely convinced. "Okay, but why Lacey, and not me?"

"Faith, what's the point of talking about this? It's water under the bridge."

"Yeah, Peter, but I'm still on that bridge, gazing at that water. I need to know."

He sat up straight, as if to brace himself with better posture. He squared his shoulders and his eyes met mine. Now was the moment. "I felt more crucial to her. With Lacey, it was like we became a part of each other, thoroughly. There was no room for surfeit baggage. Our souls, in poverty, replenished each other. Her love and craving for me was all encompassing, and there was no way I could defy it."

"Are you quoting yourself, Peter? That sounds like something you would write in your journal."

"You read my journals?"

"You read them to me! Don't you remember? You used to insist on it, always late in the evening when I had to be at school early the next day."

He looked down, and drew an imaginary circle on the plastic tablecloth. "And that's the other thing. I never understood why you stayed with me for as long as you did."

"Because I loved you. Didn't you know that?"

"I knew you loved me. But I didn't know why. With Lacey, I knew. Without question. I'm weak, Faith. I need that constant reassurance."

There was nothing I could say. I got my retribution without even asking for it, at least not directly. How fitting, given the once true nature of our dead relationship.

"I'm sorry – not for anything I did. I mean, I'm sorry how we ended." I truly was. Hours ago I wouldn't have believed it could happen.

"Me too."

We sat in silence for a moment. I gazed at him, this man who was so achingly familiar, yet so distant. He did look terrible, like something was very wrong. Then it occurred to me.

"Peter."

"Hmmm?"

"You talked about Lacey in the past tense."

"Huh?"

"You were referring to your and Lacey's relationship as if it was in the past tense."

"No I wasn't."

"Yes you were."

"Well, I didn't mean to. Don't read too much into it."

"What's the real reason you're here, Peter? Are you and Lacey having problems?"

"You tell me. You're the psychic one." Peter forced a laugh as empty as a worn wading pool collecting the rotting leaves of autumn.

"I'm starting to think I'm not all that psychic. So maybe you should tell me."

He ran his fingers through his grubby hair, and squeezed his bloodshot eyes closed for a moment.

"The other day I was on her computer. She's been kind of depressed lately, so I thought I'd surprise her with a trip. You know how she loves Chicago. I went online to make reservations at this hotel where we'd stayed before. We went for the weekend a while ago, and Lacey booked the room. So I clicked on the website history button, to see if I could find a web-address for it, and I noticed she visited several websites about prescription drugs.

"I went to them, and there was information on each site about how many sleeping pills it would take to kill you. And the only thing I could think was, 'God, that's so like Lacey. She has to do research before actually killing herself. She couldn't be messy and take the whole damn bottle.' The idea actually made me laugh, in a sick-hearted sort of way.

"I asked her about it, and she got so upset. Said she wasn't planning anything, that she wanted to know so she would never make a stupid mistake and take too many. Then she threw me out. Said our relationship was over. I didn't know what to do. So I came down here. You always knew her the best. I figured maybe you could talk to her."

I shouldn't have been surprised. All the signs of Lacey's instability had been there. But I was surprised, surprised that somehow I hadn't escaped from the bonds of friendship, even though those bonds had escaped me.

"Peter, I don't know what to tell you. Lacey won't even talk to me. I don't think I can help.

"You don't get it. A lot of what she's depressed over is you. She thinks she's a bad person because of what she did to you. Her guilt is affecting her mental stability, and in turn, our relationship. The way I see it, you're the only person who can help."

"It's not that easy."

"I don't care. Try anyway. You have to help me, Faith."

"Um no, actually, I don't. The two of you betrayed me, remember? I don't owe either of you anything."

Peter's face fell. The artificial light and stagnant air at Perkins closed in on us. Out of the corner of my eye I noticed a young couple, both with tattoos and piercings all over their bodies, attending to a baby while they ate omelets and smoked cigarettes. I hoped the child was not their own, that perhaps they were babysitting.

Peter turned to see what I was looking at. He saw the same couple, but something completely different as well. "Cute baby, huh? And well behaved too. I didn't even know it was behind us."

"Sure," I replied.

"They seem happy."

They did? "How can you tell, just by looking at them?"

Peter poured some sugar into his coffee and stirred it in. "I can't tell. I was saying what they seem like."

"Right. Look Peter, I should be getting back. It's late, and I work tomorrow morning."

"Do you ever want to have kids, Faith?"

"Yeah, I suppose I do, but I don't feel like talking about that right now."

"I never knew I wanted to have kids until I fell in love with Lacey. But with her, somehow, everything dropped into place. And you're right, you don't owe either of us anything. So I suppose it's a lot to ask. But I was hoping you would say yes anyway."

"I wouldn't even know what to say to her. The last time I tried to talk to her I said all the wrong things. She threw me out too."

"So, you try again. Besides, there's no one else I can ask."

"What about her mother?"

"No. She's as screwed up as Lacey is, if not more."

Peter was right on that count. I sighed, resigned to finish the conversation. "I'm not surprised. They don't talk about things in that family. If you ask me, Lacey needs to be in therapy. I don't know who her physician is, but his license ought to be taken away, giving her all of those drugs without making her be in therapy."

Slowly a tear trickled down Peter's face. He wiped it away, and buried his face in his hands. In a muffled voice he said, "I'm very worried about her."

I can't tell you how many times I had wished for this, wished to see Peter in the same kind of pain I had been in. True, I wasn't the cause of his pain, but that only angered me, which increased my desire to see him cry.

I picked up my purse, found my wallet, and left a five on the table. Finally, I had the chance to orate the speech I prepared in my mind about a million times since being dumped.

"Peter, I loved you once. But I don't anymore. I don't feel anything for you, and that includes friendship. I accommodated to you way too often when we were together, so I'm going to break that pattern now that we're not. Goodbye."

I left Peter at the restaurant. He would have to walk back to my building to get his car. It was only a couple of miles, so he'd be fine. I drove home, and walked into my building and headed towards my apartment. I thought I should feel something powerful, but all I felt was tired. Suddenly I could think of nothing other than sleep.

As soon as I opened my door I was aware only of the hands that grabbed me, smothering me, forcing me towards a chair, and a place at the table which was already set for me.

22

To see what is in front of one's nose is a constant struggle." That's the quote Ethan was trying to remember that day in the garage. George Orwell said it; I know only because I looked it up later. For some reason I couldn't stop thinking about it. Perhaps I wanted to comfort myself over missing so many clues. I don't know why it hadn't occurred to me that it had been him behind all of the notes and messages. After all, the whole thing had started on the night I was doing laundry. How could I have been so blind?

"I found the aloe," Bill sighed, as he walked towards Margaret and me, tied securely to our respective chairs. He had burned himself in the process of cooking dinner. "When's Missy getting home? Our date can't officially begin until she's here too."

"I think she's working until close tonight," said Margaret, "so she won't be home until well after one."

He looked over at the clock. It was only a little after 10. "Well, we'll wait for her. Not to eat, of course. But for what is coming after." He went back into the kitchen, and I wondered, what is coming after?

Around half an hour had passed since I'd walked into the apartment. I learned that approximately an hour before Bill had let himself in using a copy of my key, which he made after finding my purse. Margaret was home, but since she was napping in the bedroom she did not notice his presence until she heard him making noise in the kitchen. Assuming it was me she emerged, which was when he whacked her and tied her up.

How did I learn all this information? Well, it seems Bill is a very chatty abductor, and insistent on following at least some rules of decorum—a habit which he feels a woeful few of us observe.

"Wait!" I yelled. He returned to face us. "Um, I just remembered something. Missy's going out tonight."

"She is?" asked Margaret. I shut her up with a dirty look and continued.

"With some guy she met on the internet. I don't think she'll be coming home tonight, and if she is, it will be with a man."

He laughed, a deep chuckle that lasted for a long time. "Really? With a man, huh? I suppose it figures. Is there anyone that slut won't sleep with?"

"Missy is not a slut!" cried Margaret.

He turned to her, suddenly angry. "What do you know?" he yelled as he leaned into her. "You don't know anything about me."

His anger bounced off her like sunlight off a mirror. With a smile she said, "I don't claim to know anything about you. I wasn't even talking about you."

He took a step back. "If you were talking about Missy, then you were talking about me." With calm patience he explained, "We're all connected here, can't you see that? You can't isolate people; we're not plants in little clay pots. We're trees, and our roots reach out and tangle with each other, until soon it's impossible to tell where one tree's roots end and the others leave off."

"Yeah, I can see what you mean," I lied. "But, um, anyway, seeing as how Missy won't be showing up, and seeing how you burned yourself, maybe it's best to postpone for another night. Like later this week. Margaret, you're free on Thursday, aren't you?"

She looked at me like I was the insane one, but went along with it. "Sure. Thursday's good."

He scratched his forehead and his eyes narrowed. "But the food is almost done. Plus, Thursday is my night to stay in. Good television watching night."

"Yeah, but the whole thing is incomplete without Missy. And you don't want her to miss it." He eyed the chairs, and our hands and feet, which were tied to them. I was telepathically willing him to come over and untie us, and it almost felt like it was working, when the door opened, and in walked Missy, alone.

"Missy, go! Get help!" I yelled to her, but it was too late. She was already in the apartment.

"What the...." She exclaimed before his hand covered her mouth. He grabbed her in the same way he had grabbed me. She put up a fight, but he was big and strong enough to still win easily. Then she was tied up too, and the trio was complete. I cursed the day I ever picked Missy as a roommate, along with an apartment with unusually thick and soundproof walls.

"Why?" Missy asked, once she was securely trapped to her chair.

"If you don't know," Bill answered, "then I'm certainly not going to tell you."

Missy simultaneously let out a huff and thrust out her chest. "That old line? Come on Bill, certainly we can solve this like reasonable adults."

"You betrayed me," he yelled, directing his rage equally towards the three of us. "So now we're going to do things my way!" I hate to admit it, but he was reminding me of myself. "You all are going to take turns. When it's not your turn, you will watch. Then you will know how it feels."

"How what feels?" Margaret asked.

"How it feels to be betrayed." I answered for him. He turned to me.

"Oh, so you understand. Wonderful. You get to go first."

"I have to go the bathroom. Could you possibly untie me?" Missy squirmed in her chair for effect. Bill stood over us, a menacing presence.

"How stupid do you think I am?" Bill verbalized my thoughts, but directed them towards Missy. "I'm not untying you. Not until our date is over."

"Well, what kind of date is this, where the lady isn't even allowed to use the toilet?"

"My mother always said it was rude for a lady to use the facilities in the presence of a man." Bill replied.

"Well, she must have been better at holding it in than I am. If you don't untie me, I'm going to end up peeing on myself."

"You would do something crude like that. I can't believe I ever saw anything in you." Bill marveled.

"Then what are you doing here, you freak?" retorted Missy.

"Missy!" I broke in. "He's not a freak. He's trying to show us a good time, aren't you Bill?"

"Shut up, Faith. Bill knows he's a freak. Stroking his ego isn't going to make any difference."

"It's not my ego that needs stroking." Bill leaned behind me as he said this. "You don't fool me, Faith. You called me a freak this morning, before you knew it was me who you were talking about."

"Yeah, but..."

"And how couldn't you know it was me, after everything I did for you?"

My mind raced to find the right answer. "You mean, like when you worked for me on the day I fell?"

"I mean everything!" he yelled. "Returning your purse, returning your quarter, talking to you all the time while you're working. What does it take to get your attention?"

"I'm sorry. I've been a little preoccupied lately."

Margaret piped in. "That's true. She's had a lot going on."

Bill ignored her and continued to address me.

"Newsflash. We all have a lot going on. That doesn't excuse anything. Now, you were about to go first. How about it?"

"Um, weren't we going to eat first? And you never finished showing us your photo albums."

"I messed dinner up. There is no dinner."

"We could order pizza!" interjected Margaret. "I don't know about you guys, but I'm starving. And whatever it was that you were cooking smelled really good. It made me hungry."

"Oh yeah?" asked Bill. "Because I totally ruined the sauce for the polenta."

"No, it smelled great," said Margaret. "And I don't care so much about sauce. Why don't we eat the polenta anyway?"

"No, we can't. I also picked the wrong kind of wine. I misread the label at the store. No. The whole evening is a disaster." Bill kicked a table leg, which in turn made his photo album fall to the floor. When it landed on the ground a picture of him and Missy fell out. They were smiling towards the camera, their arms around each other, the epitome of a happy couple.

Bill saw that I saw the photo. He snatched it up, and waved it in front of me. "Yes!" he cried. "Here's the evidence. So you see what you've done!"

"I don't understand," I said. I turned to Missy. "You and Bill were a couple? Why didn't you ever say anything?"

"We were hardly even a couple," she replied. "We went out for a few months, until I realized he has no social skills. After that I blocked the whole thing from my mind and did my best to avoid him completely."

Bill's eyes continued to sear into mine. "We were happy, and you came along and ruined it! Because of you my heart was broken! So tonight you're going to pay. Tonight you're going to give me what I have coming."

I didn't know what to say. But Missy sure did. "Bill, you are such a moron! I didn't leave you for Faith. I left you for Nina, who lived here before Faith. Remember?"

Bill's face turned bright red. "I can tell the difference between Faith and Nina, Missy. But can you? Aren't all of your sexual partners interchangeable?"

"I don't know what you're talking about." Missy looked towards the floor, and squirmed in her chair once again. "Can I go to the bathroom now?"

Bill loomed over Missy. "I think you do know what I'm talking about. Somehow you find it possible to sleep with me, tell me you love me, and at the same time, betray me with your roommate." I surmised that Bill was referring to the roommate with whom Missy had, as she put it, a falling out. Or was it a breakup?

"I never told you I loved you."

"Yes you did! You've probably forgotten because obviously, those words don't mean anything to you. How long did it take for you to say them to her?" Bill pointed towards me.

"I don't love Faith!" exclaimed Missy.

"Oh, so it's just about the sex then?"

"You're being ridiculous! Faith is my roommate. That's it! We're not a couple."

"That's not what Faith said this morning," Bill replied.

"What?" I said. "I didn't say anything like that."

"Liar!" Bill yelled, with a false smile boding evil. His face had grown more red as the evening progressed, until now it was so bright it made his gray hair appear white in comparison. His voice took on a high pitch, mimicking my own. "I'm not that innocent! Nothing about Missy is going to shock me! Missy has been getting some!" He resumed his normal tone. "I know what I heard."

I tried to lean away from him. No wonder he seemed so upset earlier today—my words must have driven him to this point. "Look Bill, you've got it all wrong."

"Exactly," Missy broke in. "Whatever Faith said, you misinterpreted it. She and I aren't involved. Believe me."

"Yeah, and that's what I was supposed to believe about Nina, right Missy? It's all about sex, isn't it? Let me tell you something, sex should be about love. And love is the most important part of being alive. But you treat love like it's nothing."

Now, I may not be the world's best authority on love, but I can claim superiority on the subject over Bill, who was nutty enough to not only date Missy, but to want her back. Besides, his treatment of the three of us that evening wasn't exactly a testament to his skills at affection. However, some of what he was saying made sense. I looked over at Margaret. I don't think she had enough sense to be scared, but her face was crestfallen.

"Why didn't you tell me that you and Bill were a couple?" Margaret asked Missy, with a threat of tears in her voice.

"It wasn't important," Missy replied.

"Sure. I can see how that wasn't important enough to mention," I broke in.

Margaret spoke again. "If what Bill is saying is true, then I agree with him. You treat love and sex like they're nothing."

"You say that because you're convinced by him? You trust what he has to say? He's crazy, he doesn't know what he's talking about." Missy did her best to lean towards Margaret while she said this, but it was difficult, because she was tied up pretty tightly.

"I thought we were friends!" Margaret responded.

"We are! I don't see how this changes anything."

"You should have said something. I told you all about my past. And I was honest. But you lied."

"How did I lie?" Missy demanded. Bill and I were both silent with anticipation, waiting for Margaret's explanation.

"You told me you hadn't been involved with anyone seriously for years."

"She said that!" demanded Bill.

"Yes! And she also said that she doesn't sleep around."

"That's a laugh!" said Bill.

"Maybe I have a different definition of what sleeping around means," said Missy. "To me, if you're friends with someone first, then it doesn't count as sleeping around. The sex simply becomes an extension of your friendship, a different way of showing affection. And it's possible to love someone as a friend, and to love another person as a friend at the same time. Why is that so wrong?"

"It just is." said Bill.

Missy turned her attention toward Bill. "So you're going to get back at me by forcing me and my friends to have sex with you? Isn't that like, way too extreme? Especially considering how badly I have to go to the bathroom."

Bill considered Missy's statement while rubbing his chin and furrowing his brow. "I would say that you have a point, Missy. However..." he began to pace around the room, "You're not the only one here who betrayed me."

"Who else?" demanded Missy.

"Faith did! I admit, at first, I was going after her to get to you. But then I actually started to develop feelings, and she completely ignored my attempts to let her know."

"I wasn't ignoring you! I didn't know you felt that way. You could have been more clear; why didn't you just ask me out?"

"Why didn't you? You answer your door with your boobs hanging out, you flirt with other men in front of me, and you tell me you're not so nice and innocent. If that's not an indirect come on, I don't know what is."

And then I said the number one most insincere line in the human language, the one I'd heard from Peter, the one I swore I'd never condescend to say to someone else. "I'm sorry. But can't we be friends?"

"No," replied Bill. "I don't want to be friends. I want you all to hurt as badly as I did."

Peter's crying face popped into my mind. I realized in an instant that seeing him hurt brought me no satisfaction. If only I was a more forgiving person maybe I wouldn't be in this mess.

"You just think that's what you want," I said.

"No, I actually do want it." Bill went towards my chair, and started to untie me. "Let's get going here. You were going to be first."

"Stop!" cried Margaret. "You're making a mistake. Missy wasn't lying. She and Faith have never been a couple. If first and foremost you want to hurt Missy, you should choose me. I'm the one she was with."

Bill stopped untying me and stood up and went towards Margaret. The ropes were just loose enough that I could begin to squeeze my hands out of them.

"You honestly expect me to believe that Missy didn't make time with her? I thought we had already established that she'll sleep with whoever's willing."

"Yeah, but Faith wasn't willing. I'm the one who was willing."

"I wouldn't have slept with Faith even if she had wanted to. She's too uptight." said Missy.

I started to protest, but bit my tongue and let out a loud breath through my nose instead.

"It's true," replied Margaret, "she is uptight. But I'm not. Which is why Missy fell in love with me, not with Faith."

Bill's back was to me as he faced Margaret. I was trying to make eye contact with her over his shoulder, but I couldn't, he was too tall. So I didn't know if Margaret was simply trying to distract him, or if she was being selfless, sacrificing herself for my good. It didn't matter; I managed to get my hands completely loose as Bill went to untie Margaret.

"Okay," he said. "If you insist. We'll start with you."

"No!" I yelled, my hands still behind my back as if they were tied. "Do me first. Margaret's lying. I'm the one who Missy loves."

For once Missy and I were thinking along the same lines. She witnessed me freeing my hands from the ropes, so she knew enough to stay silent. Bill turned back to me.

"If you think that Missy actually loves anyone, then you're delusional. But your sister's right. You do seem uptight. So we'll get you out of the way first. Sort of like a warm-up for coming attractions."

Sick fear gripped my stomach. This was actually happening. I knew I had only one chance to save myself, Missy and Margaret, so my mind raced back to the self-defense class I took years ago. As Bill leaned down to continue untying me, my hand shot up, and I punched him, my fist starting underneath his nose and shooting upwards.

My instructor warned us that a punch like that could actually kill, because in essence, you're shoving a person's nose into their brain. However, my punch wasn't quite that powerful. Bill was very much alive, but he was now sprawled out on our floor, blood spurting out of his nostrils.

"You bitch!" he groaned. He was probably in shock, but he seemed to have given up on the idea of "our date." Looking at him bleeding on the floor, I deduced he was no longer in the mood.

"Faith! Come grab my cell phone from my pocket!" Missy insisted. So that was why she had wanted to go to the bathroom. I scooted my chair over a few feet and reached in. As soon as I was done calling 911, I untied Missy's arms, Margaret's arms, and my feet. By the time the police came, took Bill away, and took our statements it was after 5:00 a.m.

❋　❋　❋

I had to be at work in less than an hour, so instead of going to sleep I took a quick shower, then went outside to watch the sunrise. It was a particularly beautiful one that morning, turning the scattered clouds a bright pink and shedding warm light on the brownstones along my block. It was a new day, and amazingly, I felt an overwhelming sense of hope.

23

At work my mind began to drift. I probably should have called in, but I promised Sally I would work extra shifts after the stuffing convention. I would have felt guilty not coming in, especially since I was the one who was opening.

Lucky for me it was a slow morning. Sinister clouds moved in, causing a summer storm to begin at around 6:45, and by 8:30 it still had not let up. Probably the unnaturally dark sky caused people to get up later, and they didn't have time to stop for coffee—or they didn't want to get soaking wet on their way to work, running from their cars to the coffee shop.

So at 8:30 I was doing nothing but standing at the counter, day-dreaming. I was playing and replaying the previous evening in my mind, trying to find rhyme or reason to the whole ordeal. The weight of the events from last night sat in my stomach like an anvil I had been forced fed. And its weight was forcing me to admit to myself some painful truths: I wasn't psychic, and my self absorption went beyond being a mere inconvenience for myself and those around me.

Then my mind forced me back to another time when I simply didn't get it.

❄ ❄ ❄

It's an afternoon in late winter. The sky and the ground offer varying shades of gray, white and brown. This makes for little contrast with the navy blues and blacks most people are wearing on this most somber of occasions. What can anyone say about a fifty year old man with a wife and daughter, an upstanding member of the community?

"Are we going soon?"

He's standing before you, a cup of coffee in his hand. He's wearing his usual suit, but the red socks have been replaced with white ones, and his fedora is absent. He looks almost dignified.

"I thought we would stay until it's over. That's the nice thing to do."

The funeral reception has been going on for a couple of hours. It is in the living room of the house she grew up in, a house where you spent hundreds of hours as well.

"Yeah, but you're not even talking to her." He gestures toward your best friend, sitting alone in an armchair by the window. The sun has peaked through a cloud and is shining down on her, making her beautiful in her silent misery. "And the weather is getting bad."

"So what are you saying, that we should abandon her?"

"No. But if we're going to stay, we ought to make it worth her while. Go talk to her."

"I don't know what to say."

He sets down his coffee on a nearby table and takes your hand. "Come on, I'll help." He leads you over to where she is sitting.

"Hey, how are you holding up?"

She looks up at you as if it is the first time she has seen you in months, her eyes registering surprise at your very presence. "This is so stupid," she says. "Everyone here is pretending. People who barely knew him are pretending to be sad, and the ones who did love him are pretending to be fine."

You think back to earlier that day, when she snapped at you for crying during the service.

"What can we do?" asks your boyfriend.

"You can get me out of here," she replies.

The three of you go to the nearest bar, where he orders you all shots of Tequila. Your best friend tells him she has never done Tequila shots before, so he is obliged to show her the process of sucking the lime and licking the salt. Watching her knock back the shots is the first time you have seen her smile in weeks, so you let her have your shot as well. (You've actually never liked tequila, at least not in shot form.) After about half an hour they're both plastered, so you remain as the sober designated driver.

"What did you think of the service?" she asks, directing the question only towards him. "Did you like the part where my dad's boss talked about his years of service in the mining industry? What a joke! Like all those years in the mines didn't contribute to his cancer!"

"He didn't have lung cancer though. Maybe the mines had nothing to do with it," you say.

"Yeah, right." She croaks, with a dismissive wave of her hand. "It's what everybody is saying though. Nobody wants to believe that a middle aged man could die so quickly when he didn't do anything wrong. Let's blame it on the mines!" She yells this last part, waving her arms in the air, attracting attention from the rest of the bar.

He gently takes one of her hands, and lowers it to the table, where he continues to hold onto it. For a moment you think he's going to reach down and kiss her hand as well, but he doesn't. He just looks like he wants to. "When my dad died it was the same," he says.

"Your dad died?" she asks. "When did he die?"

"When I was seventeen."

"How?"

"He choked to death on a carrot. He was watching television while he was eating, and was alone in the house. The doctors said we found him probably fifteen minutes after it happened."

"That's awful." She replies. You agree but say nothing. You've been in this relationship for two years, yet he's never told you how his dad died; it was one of the few subjects he wouldn't discuss. But now he's telling the story to her, and you realize your presence at this occasion is completely irrelevant.

"Yeah. And after it happened people asked the most inane questions. Did he have a history of bad teeth or indigestion? What kind of carrots was he eating? What had been on the tv? Nobody wanted to believe that the exact same thing could happen to them at any moment."

His words make her laugh, softly at first, but progressively harder. You squirm in your seat and reach to rub his shoulder – a gesture he seems not to notice.

"What's so funny?" he asks.

She speaks through her giggles. "They asked what he had been watching? What did they think, that he was watching a cop show or something? Like he had witnessed some violent crime and that's what caused him to choke?"

He shrugs his shoulders. "Actually, he was watching football. Some important game between the Vikings and the Packers. The Packers won."

At this she laughs even harder, collapsing against him. He is joining in, laughing as well. "I suppose that explains why I never have liked sports..." he says, as their laughing increases in pitch and volume, "or carrots."

You sit at the bar, torn between jealousy and relief. At least someone has gotten past the wall your friend has erected, even if that someone wasn't you. And you finally know about his father's death. All he ever told you was it had been sudden and awful, but due to people's reactions, he didn't want to talk about it. But he could tell her, and what's more, they could laugh about it.

❋　❋　❋

How did I miss their connection for so long? I shook my head as if to rid it of all the unwanted thoughts, and began to wipe the already clean counter. I looked up as the door opened. In walked Glenn.

My stomach tightened and my shoulders stiffened. I told myself that after what I'd been through the night before I had no reason to be scared of Glenn. But I wasn't entirely convinced. I heard once that if you can't be brave, then the bravest thing you can do is pretend to be. I decided to make a valid try.

"Hey, Glenn," I said, concentrating on keeping my voice low instead of high and squeaky. "Did you want a latte'?" It was the first time I saw her since she tripped me, and though it was inevitable we would face each other again, knowing this did not make the encounter any easier—especially since I slept with her boyfriend in the meantime. I wondered if she knew.

"Sure. Thanks." Amazed there was no snide comment attached, I turned to make her drink. Despite my fatigue, I achieved the perfect amount of foam. I tried not to let my face betray my pride as I set her drink down in front of her, but it didn't matter. She wasn't paying the least bit of attention to me or to the drink. Then I noticed she was crying.

"Is everything okay, Glenn?"

She was looking off into the distance, but with my question her head snapped around, and her sad expression turned into a malicious one.

"Like you don't know," she said.

I am such an idiot. Given how much Glenn hates me, I should never have acknowledged her having a weak moment. But it was too late, and I had to ask.

"What don't I know?"

"Ethan."

My face grew red at the mere mention of his name. "I... I, um, sorry Glenn, but, um, what about Ethan?" I stuttered my question, my face growing hotter by the second. She must have noticed my cheeks were now the color of a lobster, because her eyes narrowed into her slits as she raised one eyebrow. (It was actually sort of a cool trick, an expression I tried to mimic later on in the mirror. But I looked like a drunk stroke victim, instead of off-putting and detatched like Glenn did.)

"He told me last night. Apparently he's 'content but not satisfied,' and he's taking your advice to sell his shop and travel the world."

"What? My advice?"

"He told me all about your date several weeks ago. That you encouraged him to take a step back from life in order to gain perspective, or some crap like that. I don't know. But he's leaving. That much is clear."

"Oh." I didn't know what to say. I barely remembered saying

those words to Ethan.

"Tell me something, Faith. How is it that you managed to ruin my life so completely is such a short amount of time? I'd like to know."

"I ruined your life? Glenn, believe me, even if I wanted to ruin your life, which I don't, but even if I did, I'm not nearly that powerful."

"You turned Ethan against me. You turned my mother against me."

"What? No." Is that really what she thought?

"Everything was fine until you came along."

"Glenn, forgive me, but I don't think so."

"Yes, it was."

"But your mom told me about, you know…" I spoke without thinking. My exhaustion made me reckless. What was the difference anyway? "…about you and Ethan. How he treated you so terribly. And I can kind of understand still liking him, I mean, there is definitely something about him. But I don't think you can blame the downfall of your relationship on me."

"What exactly did my mom tell you?" Her voice was softer than I ever heard it. It almost made me trust her for a moment.

Delicately, I asked her. "Are you sure you want me to say?"

Her voice returned to its normal, harsh tone. "Oh, you're gonna say. Tell me what she told you."

I took a deep breath. "You know, about how he wanted you to have an abortion, and left you when you wouldn't."

Then she laughed. "If you believe that, then you are as naive as my mother is."

"Why? What do you mean?" I asked, but she laughed again and shook her head. I threw down my sponge, not caring if my words made her angry or not. "I'm naive and I'm your enemy? Those are two rather large yet contradictory accusations for one morning."

She continued laughing. "I didn't say you're my enemy. I said you've ruined my life. What makes it even worse is that it was unintentional. If you actually had a mean bone in your body, well, at least I could respect you. But you don't. So I figure my best revenge is to make you feel guilty."

I grew indignant. "Guilty? Why would I feel guilty? I don't even like you."

"I'm heartbroken." She took another swig of her coffee. This time there was no foam to wipe away. "But you will feel guilty. I know, because I used to be like you. I used to internalize everything. Then I grew up, and I decided to make other people pay, rather than paying myself." She got off her stool and wiped invisible dust particles off her sleek black outfit. "Which is why I will always be one step ahead of you. You may have unintentionally ruined my life, but at least I don't leave myself open. I'll rebound quick, and you'll still be obsessing, still wondering what you did wrong. That is, until the next Ethan comes along, uses you, and leaves."

And with that, she made her exit. She was right. Never in a million years could I pull off a speech like that, which was testament to every point she had been making. But somehow, I was too tired to care. I was sure I'd start internalizing tomorrow, but for right then, I continued to wipe microscopic crumbs off the counter and stare at the clock. All I wanted was to go home.

The minutes crept by. A few customers came in, and I served them coffee and pastries. I went through the motions of being a coffee shop worker, anonymous, without a history or a life that extends beyond the counter I was standing behind. Maybe if I truly believed that, it would come true, just like in a Disney movie. Sort of. Only without the prince and the happy ending.

Finally my shift ended and I could go home. By this time my eyes were clouded over, and I was not watching where I was going as I made the short trek back to my apartment. So I didn't notice the abandoned skateboard resting on the sidewalk before I tripped over it. This time I didn't fall backwards, but forwards. The wheels on the board gave my fall an added momentum, which is why when my head hit the ground, everything went black.

24

Being in a life-threatening situation is not all it's cracked up to be. I dare say I've seen too many movies that glamorize being at death's door and have built up some sort of expectation as to what it should be like. You know, all of the people who hurt me come running frantically to my bedside, desperately praying that I pull through so they can right all of the wrongs they have done to me. It would have been quite a crowd at my bedside: definitely Peter and Lacey, as well as Margaret, Missy, and even Glenn, for good measure. And of course, Ethan would be there as well.

But unfortunately, none of them were by my side because none of them even knew about my horrific head injury. Margaret and Missy turned the ringer off on the phone and the volume down on the answering machine so they could get some sleep after the night before. Caroline, my emergency-contact, was still on vacation with Charles. Peter was on his way back to Duluth to tend to Lacey. And Ethan was getting ready to travel the world.

And how did I know all of this, as I lay unconscious in my hospital bed? Well, if ever there has been doubt about my psychic abilities, this certainly clears things up. Being on the brink of death brought my abilities to a new level. The knock on my head corrected whatever problem there had been and my powers were back. I became downright omniscient! But was it worth it? My head hurt like a cow in labor, and I was very frustrated that while I finally could see things clearly, I couldn't do anything about them. I saw everyone in my mind's eye, all of these people who had composed my world in the last few months or years, and suddenly I knew what I wanted to tell them.

Carolyn was walking the streets of Winnepeg with Charles, laughing at a joke he just told, although he was still uncertain about whether or not he could trust her. But she took his arm and pressed herself against him, trying to diffuse all his doubts with her touch. And I wanted to thank her for teaching me that love doesn't have to be perfect to be worthwhile.

Margaret and Missy were lying together in the same bed, although they were not touching. Margaret woke up, raised her head, and looked at Missy. She saw her for everything she is, flaws included. And although she was not clear on how to define their relationship, she was not afraid of Missy's loneliness. She could see the good in her too, and was brave enough to remain open to all the possibilities. And I hoped she knew how much I respected her at that moment.

Glenn was working out at the gym. With every move, every breath, she grew stronger. She wasn't exaggerating when she said she would move on quickly, she was already beginning to leave thoughts of Ethan, and me, behind. And even though I didn't like her, I began to admire her.

Peter was in his car, driving away from me, back to Lacey. It was her he was thinking of, her he has chosen, and it is the right choice. I guess I'd known that for a long time, yet I was unwilling to accept it. But now, somehow, it didn't hurt anymore—perhaps the agony caused by my head injury was so bad it blocked out all other forms of pain. But when I looked at Peter, I felt something that resembled forgiveness.

If love is blind, then friendship has vision. Perhaps there are exceptions to this rule, but Peter and I are not one of them. I knew nothing when I fell in love with Peter, but now my eyes are open. If only I could find a way to garner my newfound wisdom, maybe I'd be ready for a healthy relationship. Why is it that we experience clarity when it is too late?

"Okay, Faith, the x-rays do not indicate any internal bleeding, so we believe you are good to go. Is there anyone who can come take you home?"

The doctor at the emergency room declared my healthy state of being as I sat on the examining table, pondering over whom I could possibly call. So, maybe I was being a little melodramatic and misleading when I indicated my situation was life-threatening. But you see, when I fell, I did actually pass out. Somebody on the street did actually find me and call an ambulance. I was then rushed to the hospital, where they did x-rays on my head to make sure I didn't have a concussion, or some such injury.

Luckily though, it seemed my passing out was due to fatigue as much as anything else. But I did have a terrible headache, and the whole life/death trauma thing really did bring me clarity, so I wasn't exaggerating too much.

"Faith?" The doctor implored, demanding my attention. "We can't let you go unless there is someone who can come and get you. For the next twenty-four hours you need rest, and supervision. That way if you start to feel worse, you can be brought back in."

"Okay."

"I understand there has been no answer at your home phone or from your emergency contact. Why don't you have a seat in the waiting room, where you can keep trying those numbers, or different ones. Let us know when someone has arrived to take you home, and I will sign your release papers." With that, the doctor ushered me out into the waiting room.

I was beyond caring about anyone or anything. And, despite the aforementioned clarity of which I spoke, I couldn't help but be pissed off at Margaret and Missy for not answering the phone. I couldn't think of anyone else to call. My parents were hours away, and there was no point in freaking them out by calling them from the hospital. But I didn't even have anyone else's phone number memorized. If I could've simply taken a taxi home, then I would have, even though I would be leaving against the hospital's advice. But the staff certainly wasn't going to call one for me, and I had forgotten to charge my cell. Besides, all I had in my purse were my keys and a five dollar bill—definitely not enough to pay for a cab.

"Can I get you anything while you wait?" A young woman in a candy striper uniform approached me.

"Something to eat?" I realized I hadn't eaten for hours and was suddenly very hungry.

"Oh. We don't have any food to give out, but there is a cafeteria downstairs. Or vending machines. But I don't recommend either."

"Yeah, well seeing as how I'm stuck here, my options are somewhat limited."

"Don't you have anyone you can call? A boyfriend or something?"

I heard the pity in her voice, and my eyes took this girl in for the first time. She was blond, tan, and doll-like: the sort of girl who in high school always had a boyfriend, and laughed at the other girls who didn't.

"He's busy," I lied. "In the middle of some very important meetings. So it's going to be a while before he gets here."

Her blue eyes widened to the size of saucers, and her mouth pursed slightly before she spoke. "Wow. They must be important meetings if he can't even get away to pick up his girlfriend from the hospital."

The words flew from my lips. "Yeah. He has one of those financial management jobs where millions of dollars can be made or lost in a single afternoon, like Richard Gere in *Pretty Woman*? It's tough sometimes, loving someone so busy and powerful, but it's worth the sacrifice."

"Really?" The candy-striper crossed her arms and shifted her weight.

"Oh sure. I mean, in every other way, he's perfect. He's got the most caring, sweet nature. And he's smart, and funny, he's incredibly good looking, and he loves me. How can I complain?"

"Because you're stuck at the hospital! I'd complain if my boyfriend made me wait like this."

"Yeah, but..." I struggled to continue the lie. I could see the disdain in this young Paris Hilton look-alike's eyes, which also happened to be large, blue, and perfect. They fit with everything else about her perfect appearance, and I hated her.

"I haven't even called him!" I declared. "I don't want to bother him, that's all."

"Oh, I see. That's how it is." She smiled a smug little smile, and walked away. Exactly what did she see, what did she mean, 'that's how it is'? I considered calling out to her, but I didn't have the energy to make a scene. But when I saw her talking to another volunteer, looking my way, and laughing, I decided enough is enough.

So I strode over to the pay phone and called the person who was my last resort. Miraculously, his business card was the one other thing in my purse.

25

onest Abe's Garage, Ethan speaking." I resisted the urge to hang up as soon as I heard Ethan's voice, and forced myself to speak.

"Hi Ethan. It's Faith."

"Oh. Hi." His voice sounded flat, but I didn't let it bother me.

"How are you?" I asked.

"Fine." Great. He was supposed to ask me how I was, and that was going to be my lead-in. But he didn't, and nothing but silence passed over the telephone line. Then my words came out in a nervous rush.

"Um, look. I know you probably don't need this right now, but I have a huge favor to ask. I hit my head this morning, hard, and I need someone to pick me up at the emergency room. I called my sister, but there's no answer. You see, we were up all night because our neighbor took us hostage, so she's sleeping off the trauma. And my other friend is away. So can you come get me?"

"Faith, I don't have time for games. Tell me what you want."

"Ethan, I'm serious!"

"You really are at the emergency room, and you were really held hostage?"

"Yes, I swear!"

He sighed. "So what is it that you want me to do? Come get you?"

"If you don't mind. I would appreciate it!"

* * *

He agreed to come. When he arrived he was wearing an old pair of Levis, and a pale soft cotton shirt without any grease stains. Even though his hair was combed and his glasses were on, he did not look as if he came from an important business meeting. I told myself that it was no matter. He's a guy, he's cute, and he was here to pick me up. That was enough to prove something to that candy-striper. We were at the desk getting me released from the hospital. The nurse on duty was going through all of the instructions with us, and the candy-striper was unfortunately listening in.

"If you experience any nausea, sudden blindness, vision problems, or dizziness, come in at once. Do not sleep for more than two hours at a time for the next twenty-four hours." She spoke to Ethan. "And you need to watch her for that amount of time. Please leave a number where you can be reached so that we can call to check in."

"What?" Ethan turned to me. "I have to watch you for the next twenty-four hours? Why didn't you say that when you called?"

"I forgot?"

"You forgot? It slipped your mind to mention that? Great. Thanks Faith. Thanks a hell of a lot!"

I wanted to die of embarrassment. So I channeled my emotions, telepathically willing that nosy little blond thing go away. But unfortunately she had a mind of her own.

"Oh my God!" she exclaimed. "What sort of a man are you? This is her time of need!"

Ethan regarded the candy-striper. "Excuse me?" His mouth opened to say something more, but his shock at being berated was evident.

"Never mind." I said. "It's fine. If you can't watch me, take me home. Margaret is probably there, she's just not answering the phone."

"I can't release you unless he promises to supervise you. It's a legal matter," said the nurse.

"Fine!" I exclaimed. "Can I talk to you for a second, over there?"

I asked Ethan this as I tugged him away from the desk. Once we were out of earshot, I continued on. "Look, I'm sorry. But nobody was answering their phone, they wouldn't let me take a taxi, and I want to go home. I feel okay, so just drop me off and go back to work. Okay?"

Ethan's cheeks were flushed pink and his eyes were gleaming with irritation. He looked even more worked up than he had during our argument at my parents'. "I can't drop you off! What if you go into a coma or something? Then I would be responsible. The last thing I need is your blood on my hands."

"Okay. If I die, I promise I won't blame you."

"It's not you I'm worried about."

"What, is it the hospital? My family? Are you worried about getting sued?"

Ethan said nothing, instead he nodded his head in an upward motion, like he was acknowledging what I said, but wasn't necessarily confirming it.

"Look," I told him. "I will write a note, dated and signed, that says I refused your help, and you had no part in my death, were it to occur. All right?"

"Sure! Great! Everything is just perfect, Faith! Thanks so much!"

"Oh my God!" The voice of the candy-striper startled us both, not having been aware of her approach. "I don't know why you stay with this bastard," she exclaimed to me.

"Who the hell are you?" Ethan asked. His voice sounded like it'd been swallowed by death.

The Paris wannabe started waving her fingers and circling her head, imposing upon Ethan's space. "My father runs this hospital! And he would not be happy, knowing that one of his patients is being dissed so bad by her own boyfriend!"

Ethan took a step back, stunned for a moment, the pale pink of his cheeks turning to a deeper red. "You make no sense!" he yelled at her, then grabbed my arm and dragged me up to the desk. "Give me the papers, I'll sign them!" The nurse, intimidated by his intensity, silently pushed the papers towards him. With his right hand still tightly clutching my arm, Ethan signed the papers with his left. With his hand still grasping my arm, we left the waiting room.

On the way to his car he still had not let go of me, but I didn't exactly mind. "So, are you left handed?" I asked.

"What?"

"I noticed you signed with your left hand. Are you a leftie?"

Ethan looked at me as if I had escaped from a mental hospital, rather than a regular one. "Yeah."

"That's so cool! I've heard that left-handed people tend to be more creative and intelligent, on the whole, then right-handed people."

"Yeah, it's really cool. Do you know how hard it is to find left-handed tools for cars?"

"You need special tools?"

He didn't answer, but simply rolled his eyes and shook his head. "Oh,' I replied. "I guess that makes sense. I remember how in grade school there were those special scissors for the left-handed kids. The handles were always coated with plastic, and I thought they looked more like adult scissors, so I was always jealous of the kids who got to use them. I even tried once, to cut with my left-hand, just so I could use the left-handed scissors, but that, obviously, was a disaster. I suppose we have to play with the 'hand' that we were dealt, huh?"

We arrived at Ethan's car, and he opened the door for me to get in. I climbed into the passenger seat, then leaned over to unlock his side. He got in without a word, and started the car.

To prevent an awkward silence, I continued talking. "I suppose that's how it always goes. The grass is always greener, right? The right-ies want to be special, like the lefties. And the lefties want to be like everyone else. It's too bad. If we could all be satisfied with ourselves, I suppose the world would be a better place. Don't you think?"

Silence. Ethan turned left at the stop-light. "Um, Ethan? If you want to get to my apartment then you needed to turn right. Sorry I didn't say before, but I thought you knew."

"We're not going to your place. We're going to mine."

"Huh?"

"If I have to supervise you, then I want to do it at my place."

"Yeah, but you don't have to! Margaret can…"

"Margaret didn't sign the papers. I did. So I'm going to supervise you. Besides, I put down my number for where they should call."

"You didn't have to do that."

"Yeah, I did. It's what good boyfriends do, right?" His voice was tight, as he stared intently ahead at the road.

"I'm sorry about that. I didn't mean to make that girl think you were my boyfriend. I just…"

"You just wanted her to think I'm a bastard, right? Because that's what you think of me."

"I never said that!"

"You've hinted at it enough! All your jibes about how I treated Glenn…"

"It was none of my business. I'm sorry."

"And you certainly didn't wait long to criticize me about hunting."

"All I did was ask if you kill animals."

"That's not all you did. You're afraid to say what you think, so you ask these questions as a form of indirect criticism."

"You're being way too sensitive."

"Oh. Am I being too sensitive about seeing you go off with another guy two hours after we got together?"

"I can explain that…"

"Then you avoided me for the rest of the time you were up there…"

"I wasn't avoiding you!"

"And you left without saying goodbye. Now the next time I hear from you, you tell me some story about being held hostage, and demand that I pick you up at the emergency room, where some insane candy-striper yells at me for being a bastard boyfriend. And I'm being too sensitive?"

"Yes! You have got it all wrong. And if you would let me explain, then you would know that."

Ethan abruptly pulled the car to the side of the road. He turned the ignition off, and faced me. Suddenly the space between us felt very close. "Okay," he said. "Explain."

"Well..." How do I begin? "Okay, keep in mind, I know this sounds far-fetched, but I swear, it's all true. First of all, that guy I went fishing with, I did that because my friend Carolyn's estranged boyfriend Charles showed up." Ethan's face registered confusion, so I explain further. "Carolyn had made a date to go fishing with this guy, but regretted it later. But before she could break the date, her boyfriend, whom she wanted to get back with, showed up. So to cover for her, I pretended like it was me who had made the date with this guy. Then I couldn't get out of it, as you overheard."

"Okay," Ethan said. "But you could have told me that once you got back."

"I did look for you, but you never seemed to be around. Plus, I had a lot of work to do for my folks. I already flaked off the night before and that morning, so I needed to make it up to them. Besides, you were sort of distant right after, you know..."

I stammered, but Ethan knew what I meant. "I didn't mean to be distant. I suppose my etiquette for after-sudden-intimate-encounters needs work."

"Do you have them a lot? Sudden intimate encounters?"

"Not a lot," he said. "Why do you think my etiquette is so bad?"

"Well," I replied, "I don't have them a lot either."

Ethan's reached out and brushed his finger briefly over my hand. "I'm sorry," he whispered.

"For what?"

"For... for it being so sudden. It probably would have been better to wait."

I straightened up. Did that mean he regretted sleeping with me, or that he merely regretted doing it so soon? I couldn't tell, but I decided to continue on rather than ask. "Anyway, after I got back to Minneapolis, things got crazy. First my ex-boyfriend showed up, telling me my best friend, who he left me for, is suicidal, and it's up to me to do something about it. Then, later that evening, I'm taken hostage by this neighbor of mine, who wants to molest me, my sister, and my roommate."

"What! You were serious about that?"

"Yes! He had been stalking us for weeks; that's why I left you that crazy message. I didn't know who was behind it all. But it was this guy who lives down the hall, and he used to date my roommate, until she left him for another woman, and he's been insanely jealous ever since. So it was his form of revenge."

Ethan rubbed his eyes, and I couldn't tell if he believed me, or if I was even making sense. But I kept talking.

"But I managed to free my arm, and I shoved his nose into his brain. It was enough to knock him out long enough to call the police."

"And this happened last night?"

"Yeah. But I went to work anyway, I don't know why. Then on my way home, I stepped on this skateboard, fell, and hit my head.

"So I was knocked out for a while, and I assume someone called an ambulance. But I'm fine. Just tired, and frustrated that I had nobody to call. Then that mean candy-striper was making these condescending comments to me, and I sort of lost my ability to reason. So I told her that I had a boyfriend, but she didn't believe me, so I called you." I stopped, and took a deep breath. "And that's the story."

Cars were whizzing by us, but other than their noise, it was silent. I couldn't read Ethan's face, but for once, I was going to wait for his reaction rather than say something. It felt like an eternity, but finally he responded.

"Are you okay?" He asked me this gently, and clasped his entire hand over mine. I nodded my head.

"Did you use your right hand to punch him?" I nodded again, and he lifted my right hand and kissed it. Then with tender fingertips he touched the spot on my forehead where the bruise was forming. "And this is where you fell?" I nodded again, and he leaned in and kissed my forehead. "And who all should we put on the list?" he asked.

"What list?" I replied.

"The list of people who need their asses kicked." I laughed but said nothing. He continued on. "Let's see, we'll start with your ex-boyfriend. He'll be first. Then there's your neighbor. His ass-kicking will be the worst. I suppose I should include whomever left out the skateboard you tripped on. But we'll definitely end with the candy-striper." He smiled, and I smiled back.

"Who's going to do these ass kickings?" I asked.

"Whom do you think?" he said. "If I'm going to be your boyfriend, then I'll have to do it. But I might need your help. It sounds like you're a lot tougher than I am."

"Ethan, the whole boyfriend thing… you don't have to feel obligated."

"And you don't have to tell me how to feel."

"I'm not. I…" He leaned in to kiss me. I wrapped my arms around him, and took in his feel, his smell, and the taste of him. His kiss was so sweet and warm that for a moment all my fears and concerns melted away. But only for a moment. He pulled away, and put his seat belt back on.

"We should probably get you home. Or to my home, anyway."

I leaned my head back against the seat and closed my eyes. As far as I was concerned, I already was home.

26

Ethan's apartment was neater than I would have expected, but it was very bare. He had hardly any furniture, just a couch, some book-shelves, and a quite nice dining room table set, which he told me he inherited from his grandmother. His television was in his bedroom, which was small enough to be taken up almost completely by his bed.

We ordered a pizza and lounged in his bed all afternoon. We alternated between making-out, which we did until my head hurt enough that we had to stop, and watching television. I was not supposed to sleep for more than two hours at a time, but I found it hard not to drift off during the Maury Povich show. Ethan turned out to be a good supervisor, because two hours later he woke me, and handed me a cup of coffee. After a lot of gentle probing, I sat up and took a sip.

"How are you feeling?" he asked.

"Okay." My fatigue was hanging on me like a wet towel; by all rights I ought to have been able to sleep for hours on end.

"Do you want to take a walk? Some fresh air would wake you up."

"Do we have to?" I whined. "I'd rather stay here."

"If we stay here, you'll fall asleep again."

"No. I won't. I promise." But even as I said this, my eyes were flickering shut.

"Faith! Come on, you can't fall asleep again."

"Hasn't it been twenty-fours yet?"

"No."

"But I'm fine."

Ethan ran his hands through his hair, a gesture that was starting to become endearingly familiar. He tugged at my foot and shook it, as if that alone would stir me into a more alert state.

"Hey, maybe what you should do is call some people, then we could go for a walk."

"Call some people?"

"Yeah, like your sister. Don't you think she might be worried?"

"I don't know. If she is, it serves her right for turning off the machine." I realized how petty that sounded even as I said it, so I added on, "but I'll call her."

"What about your friend?"

"My friend?"

"You know, the suicidal one?"

"There's nothing I can do for her."

"You're sure about that?"

"Ethan, this is a very long story, and a very complicated one. Believe me, I've tried. I honestly have. The last time we spoke she told me we would never be friends again. If she's not going to let me help her, then there's nothing I can do for her."

"Yeah, but your ex-boyfriend thinks differently."

"That's irrelevant."

"Okay. Well, then never mind." He walked into the living room and grabbed the cordless phone, walked back into the bedroom, and handed it to me. "Here," he said, "call your sister."

I dialed my home number with Ethan standing at the foot of the bed. The answering machine picked up yet again, so I left a message.

"Hey Margaret. It's me. I got into a small accident after work, nothing serious, just fell and hit my head. But I can't be unsupervised for several more hours, so I'm at Ethan's. He came and picked me up since I couldn't get a hold of you. I'll talk to you later. Bye."

I hung up and handed the phone back to him. I could sense his disapproval. "Okay," I said. "You're right. We should go for a walk."

We put our shoes on, and walked out into the warm dusky air. Ethan walked at a brisk pace, and I was so tired that I had trouble keeping up. He was nothing like Peter, who always walked slowly enough to drive me crazy. Peter was always so lost in thought that everything he did was lackadaisical. But Ethan walked with a purpose, taking in his surroundings in an almost aggressive manner.

But he wasn't paying much attention to me. I told myself it was probably nothing, but I decided to keep my bases covered.

"Hey, we never finished our conversation from before, in the car." I said this and slowed down at the same time, in an effort to make our walk a little more leisurely.

He kept walking at the same pace though, so I sped up. "What do you mean?" he asked.

"Well, I know I don't need to tell you how to feel, but I want to reiterate something. I mean, I'm not assuming anything, okay? This is all happening sort of fast, and I do like you, but maybe we shouldn't be rushing into anything, you know?"

"Sure. I understand."

"You do?"

"Yeah," he turned to me and smiled. "We'll be super-casual, if that's what you want."

"Um..."

"Do you want to walk down to Lake of the Isles?"

"Uh, sure. But can we slow down a little? I mean, literally slow down? I'm still sort of tired."

"Sure. Sorry. People always tell me I walk fast." He smiled again and took my hand. This was the sort of walk I imagined us going on, hand in hand, unhurried as we walked around the lake on a calm late-summer evening. But all was not right. And I knew I shouldn't say anything, but I couldn't let it be.

"Um, so what do you mean by super-casual?"

"You know. Casual. In a super sort of way."

"Thanks. That clears things up."

"Faith, do we have to figure it all out right this minute? Can't we enjoy our walk?"

"Yeah, of course. I just have to ask...."

"Yes." He said, in a decisive tone.

"What?"

"Whatever your question is, the answer is yes. Can we enjoy our walk now?" He squeezed my hand and kissed me on the cheek. So I nodded and shut up. But inside my injured head thoughts were screaming to be heard. Did super-casual mean he could date other people, like, say Glenn? Did he even want to date me at all? He seemed so relieved when I told him we didn't have to rush into anything. Was he now regretting what he said in the car? And what about selling his shop and traveling around the world? I decided to broach the subject in a different way.

"Glenn stopped in the coffee shop this morning. We talked for a while."

Ethan stared straight ahead. "Oh yeah? Do you think she's the one who planted that foul skate-board on the sidewalk?"

"Very funny. But I wouldn't put it past her. She did trip me before, you know. I wasn't making that up."

Ethan steered me towards the lake path. "I believe you. It's just hard not to defend her."

"Why? Because you're still in love?"

"Because she's so vulnerable."

I struggled not to laugh. "Glenn's vulnerable?"

"I know, it's tough to believe if you don't know her, but it's true. She's a needy person. At first I liked that, because she needed me, you know?"

"Hmm. That sounds familiar."

Ethan let go of my hand to scratch his head. He then slipped his hands into his jean pockets, and sped up a little. "What do you mean?" he asked.

"Peter, my ex. He said the same thing to me last night when he was explaining why he chose Lacey, my best friend from childhood, over me. He said he felt more necessary with her."

"And Lacey is the suicidal one?"

"According to Peter."

"Lacey and Glenn must be a lot alike."

"Why? Glenn isn't suicidal, is she?"

"No. Not exactly suicidal." Ethan strolled off the path to stand at the edge of the lake. A mother duck and her adolescent ducklings were swimming by, looking for food. Ethan said, "I love coming down here at the beginning of the summer, when the ducklings are little. They're so cute when they're small."

I leaned against a tree. "Yeah. But once they become teenagers they're not nearly as endearing, are they? No wonder the dad isn't around." I said this as a joke, but Ethan didn't laugh. He turned to face me.

"That's pretty cynical. How do you know he isn't around? Maybe he's off, hunting for worms or something."

"Yeah. You're probably right. He's off hunting for worms." I tried to make my voice sound genuine, but I failed miserably.

"Not all men are jerks."

"Ethan, we were talking about ducks."

"Never mind. Let's turn back, okay?"

"No! We hardly have walked at all. And it's nice out."

"Fine." He walked away from the lake at his same old fast pace. For a moment I considered not trying to catch up with him. Should it be so difficult this early on? But I did catch up with him. Maybe I'm a fool, and maybe I will manage to mess up every relationship or potential relationship that I will ever have, but enough was enough.

"Ethan, tell me what's on your mind. Something is obviously bothering you."

"Yeah, but it's only sort of about you."

"It's sort of me?"

"Your life sounds complicated. And so is mine. I wonder if this is actually a good idea."

"Because you're going to sell your shop and travel the world?"

The shock spread across his face. "Glenn was chatty this morning, wasn't she?" I nodded my head. "What else did she tell you?"

I took a deep breath, knowing it was time to finally confront the elephant in the living room. "She told me I was naive if I believed what her mother told me, about you wanting her to have an abortion."

"Is that it?"

"More or less." Ethan sighed, and strolled over to the bench on the side of the walkway. He sat there, deflated, and I joined him.

"When I broke up with her, I didn't know she was pregnant."

"You broke up with her?"

"Yeah, in June. Then she called me with this story about how she'd been pregnant, but was too scared to tell me. So she had an abortion she regretted. She was sobbing and threatening to kill herself. So I took care of her and promised to be her friend and all, but she kept trying to get back together. She wouldn't accept that I didn't want to."

"That sounds awful."

"It was. It still is. And at the same time that all of this was going on, I met you. Even though I wanted to, I couldn't start dating you, because I was too freaked out about Glenn."

I traced an invisible line on his hand, and silently composed what I wanted to say before I uttered anything. "I understand. I felt the same way, sort of. It's hard to let go of one relationship while starting another at the same time."

"Yeah." He nodded his head, then stared out at the lake. "I had no idea that your life is as screwed as mine is."

A gentle breeze stirred the air and, oddly, it gave me strength. I pushed past my fatigue and headache to explain what I needed Ethan to know. "My life used to be screwed up, but I think I'm beginning to figure things out. For a while I was so hurt I didn't know if I could ever let anyone else in. Now I'm finally starting to see outside of myself enough to realize that everything happens for a reason." I chuckled softly, realizing I was quoting Lacey.

"It sounds almost like you've forgiven them."

"Almost," I said. "I suppose I still have some work to do, otherwise, I'd be contacting Lacey and making sure that she's okay."

Ethan smiled. "You're awfully hard on yourself."

"How can you say that? You're the one who was chastising me earlier for not calling her."

"I wasn't chastising you. I just know from experience what an awful thing guilt can be. But she'll be okay. She has Peter, and if she was really intent on killing herself, I doubt she'd be leaving a bunch of warning signs."

"I hope you're right."

"Even if I'm not, you've been through a lot in the last twenty-four hours. I think you need to make sure that you're okay first, before you start worrying about other people."

I didn't know what to say, so I scooted in close and leaned my head against his shoulder. "Tired?" he asked.

"Exhausted." I answered.

"You want me to carry you back?"

I laughed and responded gently. "You like being needed, don't you?"

He ran his hands through my hair, and despite myself, I felt turned on again. He kissed the top of my head and spoke at the same time. "I don't mind being needed. But I think Glenn cured me of it being a requirement. Besides, if I needed to be needed, I wouldn't want to be with someone as self-sufficient as you."

"I'm not self-sufficient. I'm self-involved."

"Hmmm. Perhaps. Or maybe you need to be a little of one to be a lot of the other."

My eyes teared up. "Do you mean that?"

"Sure," he answered, looking at me directly. "Anyway, you don't seem that self-involved. I think you're actually very perceptive."

I laughed, unwilling to let Ethan in on the joke. Instead I leaned forward and kissed him, hard on the mouth. After I pulled away I simply said, "You have no idea."

27

Ethan and I agreed to just be friends. Once we got back to his place I slept most of the night and into the morning, although he still woke me up every two hours. But I could only stay awake for around thirty minutes or so, and we would play cards or watch whatever we could find on television. We didn't talk much, except for this brief conversation during a hand of gin rummy.

"So, do you want to travel the world with me?" he asked as he discarded the queen of diamonds.

"Maybe someday," I replied. I picked up his queen, and discarded the four of spades. Ethan drew from the deck, and discarded the queen of clubs without a thought.

"I'm leaving next month. I already have someone who is interested in the shop. I've actually been planning this for a while."

"I can't go in a month," I said as I picked up the queen and discarded the eight of hearts.

"I don't know when I'll be back. Or if I'll be back. Or what I'm going to do once my money runs out. But I need to get away and figure things out. It makes me wish I hadn't met you yet. I guess timing is everything." Ethan grabbed my eight and discarded the six of spades. I drew from the deck, and lo and behold, I drew another queen. That's all I needed.

"Gin!" I cried as I spread out all of my cards.

"Congratulations," he said, smiling.

"I can't believe you got rid of both those queens."

"Tell me about it. So what do you want to do?"

I gathered up the cards, thinking. When I looked up at him, he was still smiling. His glasses were on crooked, one lock of hair was standing straight up, and he was badly in need of a shave. I asked myself what I saw in this drifting, moody guy. On paper he would appear to be a very bad choice, yet when I'm with him it feels like margaritas and moonlit walks on the beach.

I said, "Well, we have a month, right?"

"Yeah. But do we want to complicate things by growing even more attached to each other?"

"From the way you asked that question, I'm guessing no."

"I like you Faith. You're strong, you know what you want. And you seem to want to be with me, which is totally new. I'm only used to being needed in a blind-leading-the-blind sort of deal."

"I know I don't want that."

"Me neither," he said.

"So we'll get to know each other. We'll keep in touch. We'll figure out what our faults are, and if the timing is ever right, and we're still interested, then, who knows?"

Ethan reached over his fancy dining-room table and grabbed my arm. He pulled on it gently and I got up as he guided me into his lap.

"I love your dining room table," I whispered into his ear.

"Oh yeah?" he whispered back. "Then why don't you keep it for me while I'm away."

"Really?"

"Sure. It wouldn't travel well. But I'm going to want it someday. So if nothing else, I'll see you again if only to get my table back."

"Okay." We hugged, and he picked me up and carried me to bed. And then, well, maybe we are a little more than friends. But I'm trying hard not to define it, and I'm certainly not going to predict what will happen.

However, Ethan kept his word, and I now have his dining room table. Actually, I now have his entire place. He sublet it to me for eight months, the amount of time he expects to be away. During that time we agreed we are both free to see other people, but he said this way, he'd know where to find me once he comes back. I get postcards, e-mails, and phone-calls from him every so often. Whenever it happens it always makes my day.

Margaret moved into my old room, and she is now pursuing her master's degree in Environmental Science at the University of Minnesota. She says she and Missy are just good friends, which I sort of believe; but she is also sort of seeing some guy with dread-locks whom she met at a rally on the steps of the state capitol.

Carolyn and Charles are planning their wedding. I hear Charles is doing most of the work, since Carolyn is in New York right now, shooting a film. She says they will stay rooted in Minneapolis for as long as possible, but there will be months at a time when she is away. Charles said he was okay with that; relationships are all about compromise. I'm keeping my fingers crossed for both of them.

Now it's a beautiful autumn Sunday, made especially nice because tomorrow is Columbus Day, and I don't have to work. Don't get me wrong; I love my new job. But it's nice to have some time to myself. Actually, I decided to drive up to Duluth today to see Lacey. After everything that happened, I realized how easily love can make us sour, bitter people. That is, if we don't forgive ourselves, and each other for all our many shortcomings. I know I don't want to end up like Bill, and I certainly don't want Lacey to end up like Glenn. And maybe I can't control everything, but I can at least give it my best shot.

This time I called first to let her know I was coming. I told her on the phone about Peter's visit, and I think it was his concern that convinced her to see me. We decided to meet for coffee, and as I walk into the coffee shop where I first met Peter, I see her sitting at a table, alone. I walk over, resist giving her a hug, and sit across from her.

"Hi." I say. I see she's already ordered. She has a cup of coffee, and a more than half-eaten sandwich on the plate in front of her.

"Hi. I hope you don't mind that I started eating without you. I'm starving." She takes a huge bite of her sandwich, and nearly finishes it.

"I don't mind. How are you?"

"I'm good. Well, I'm better anyway. How are you?"

As we sit there, discussing our lives and the people in them, the first stitches towards the mending of our friendship are sewn. And the itching in my toes tells me this is just the beginning.

Following My Toes
A Reader's Guide

Reading Group Questions

for Reflection and Discussion:

1. One of the major themes in *Following My Toes* is forgiveness. Which characters deserve to be forgiven, and why? Can anyone truly earn forgiveness, or is it something that needs to happen organically by the person who is bestowing it? When has forgiveness been a major theme in your own life?

2. Is Faith self-involved, or are the important people in her life merely projecting their own flaws onto her?

3. How does setting play a part in this story? Do the various settings: Duluth, Minneapolis, and Two Harbors, alter in any way Faith's mindset? How much do our surroundings affect our mental health?

4. Given the context of the story, how is friendship defined? Of Faith, Lacey, Carolyn, Margaret, and Missy, whom would you label as a "good friend"? Why?

5. Which one of the love relationships in the story do you think is the healthiest: Charles and Carolyn, Ethan and Faith, or Lacey and Peter? Were you disappointed that Ethan and Faith didn't end up "together," or did the ending seem appropriate?

6. How does Faith's outlook on love and friendship change over the course of the story? How does her self-image evolve?

7. Although Faith is the older sibling, she ends up taking the advice of Margaret and follows her instincts. Was this the right thing to do? Is Margaret wise in how she chooses to live her life, or is she careless and lazy? Which sister has the more mature life outlook? Which one is the wiser?

8. Where do you see the major characters of *Following My Toes* ten years after the novel finishes? Which characters will still be in contact, and who will be considered a success?

9. All of the flashback scenes were written in the second person, which is an unusual choice for popular fiction today. Why do you suppose the author chose this technique, and was it effective?

10. Consider the scene where Peter confides to Lacey the details of his father's death. Is the established connection between the two of them enough to justify their unapologetic betrayal towards Faith?

11. *Chick lit* is an increasingly popular genre of fiction. How does *Following My Toes* compare to other books of that genre? (Examples could include *Good in Bed* by Jennifer Weiner, the *Shopoholic* series by Sophie Kinsella, and *Something Borrowed* by Emily Giffin.) Consider similarities and differences in plot, theme, character, and tone.

12. If Following My Toes was being made into a film, whom would you cast in all the major roles?

Acknowledgements:

Many of my friends and family read a draft or two of this book while it was being written and revised, and to all of you I say; thanks!

In addition, several people gave me extra support and encouragement, and deserve a special mention. They include my mom Lynn and stepfather Allan, my good friends Shauna and Megan, my wonderful writing buddies Matt, Brett, and Mary, and my husband Rich (whom I love very much!)

Finally thanks to PMI Books. Your vision and support means more than I'll ever be able write about!

To learn more about Laurel Osterkamp

visit her website:

LaurelOsterkamp.com

PMI Books
Boulder, CO
pmibooks.com